Threads and Tethers

A Novel

Mira Martinovic

Seattle, Washington, 2025

THREADS AND TETHERS

For information about permission to reproduce excerpts from this book, write to miramartinovic@miramartinovic.com.

MIRAMARTINOVIC.COM

Developmental edits by Rachel Weaver and Scott Driscoll
Copyedits by Jin Zeng
Cover design by Milica Golic, using photograph by Aleksandar Juric

ISBN 979-8-9941763-0-6

To my husband and our children.

To my sister and our parents.

To all our extended family—those who are dead, still living, and yet unborn.

CONTENTS

Prologue

Dear Someone,

Ever since Grandma told me that people really die only when you forget them, all I've ever wanted was to keep them alive. But then, the new boys in the village shouted, *You'll be no more*, and life took off as it did. And here I am, far from home with all my dead within me.

However, Will came into my life. And then we had our girls. So, there must be hope—despite it all, there must be hope. For the future, if not for the past.

I devote my story to the people of my ex-Yugoslavia, and to all the people of the Troubles in Northern Ireland, the north of Ireland, the Six Counties, Ulster—or however else it is that you call these ancestral lands, Will's and your own.

And, of course, to Dad. I will never stop missing him. And Grandma, and Grandpa, and all my twelve generations all the way to the first Popovics. The entire three hundred years of our stories etched in the stones of our bereft home.

Your narrator,

Marica (Popovic) Ford

Midnight, May 12th to 13th, 2018
Seattle, Washington

Today: Seattle

The Letter

Emma sits on my lap, wrapped in my arms, and we gently rock. We're both light, but the wicker deck chair underneath us squeals in protest of our swaying. I'm aware there's a chance it could collapse under us, but the comfort I find in its methodically predictable sounds eclipses the warning of a fall. I breathe in time with the chair's steady creaks, hoping the rhythm will pulse calm through my body.

"I tried to be care-ful…" A sob intercepts Emma's claim. "I really, really tried, Mama."

The four of us were about to begin dismantling Ugly, a previous owner's decrepit shed in our backyard, when Emma raced to get her rosemary sprig from the table, ran into the edge of the deck, and scraped her knee.

Our little girl is turning nine years old today! I'm bracing myself for that moment when I'll be left behind as the primary source of relief for all her scrapes, bruises, hurts. I know it'll come soon enough, I know it from Mariah. At eleven years of age, Mariah mends her wounds mostly on her own, quietly. If she tells me about an ache, it's only in passing, when she's already tended to it. I take a big breath, thread my fingers through Emma's silky hair, and pull every beat of my thoughts toward willing time to slow down, however little.

"I know you tried, *Liubav*," I whisper to her. "I know you did."

In moments such as this one, there's nothing else. No past, neither Will's nor mine. No memories. No regrets. Not even the dread of "healing" that Will started ramming into me ever since the Belfast suitcase arrived two months ago. In moments such as this one, it's just the four of us—Mariah, Emma, Will, and I—in our beautiful present.

That's how it always is in moments such as this one. Always—except for this morning and his letter-snatching.

I lean my head against Emma's and take a sideways look at Will. He and Mariah are standing side-by-side about ten feet from the deck where Emma and I are sitting. They face the shed with their backs to us, quietly considering where to begin cutting into the metal.

No, there's nothing unusual about him today. I've watched him like a hawk all morning and I've seen nothing unusual. Nothing—after the letter.

It was so unlike Will, I could almost believe I invented it. When he grabbed the letter from my hand and sent the other mail I was holding to fly across the carpet, for a moment there I thought he was being playful. Will is playful, he's always been playful. Like last night, when the kids went to bed. He started throwing handfuls of soil at me and then looped his teasing ambush into a long beguiling night. When he snatched that letter from my hand, that's what I thought, that he was playing around.

But he'd only said, *That's for me*, and stashed the letter into his front jeans pocket, crackling and wrinkling the paper. He turned around and went back to the garage, leaving me to collect the other mail from the floor. So *very* unlike my Will.

Now, he and Mariah stand in the exact same pose facing the shed. Their feet are shoulder-width apart, and they're leaning ever so slightly toward Ugly, as if straining to hear something that the soon-to-be-demolished shed is whispering to them.

I've long been convinced that Will and Mariah have a language of their own, that they can read each other's minds. In their only audible exchange since Emma fell—Mariah's *That's it for Ugly, huh*, and Will's *Aye*—they seemed to pack a whole life's worth of understanding, comprehensible only to the two of them.

Like Dad and I, a lifetime ago.

Emma nestles her face into my neck again, masking my struggle for a breath. Her movement sets off a light breeze that cools her warm tears on my skin, triggering goose bumps. I feel an urge to shrug my shoulder and rub it against my cheek to calm the goose bumps. But I don't. I let them be. I just rock Emma, feeling her soft palms under my shirtsleeves like warm poultices, absorbing her into me, as if we were one body again, as if I could protect her from everything.

No, there's no trace of the letter in Will's pocket now.

The moment before he snatched it from my hand, I saw the Queen's image on the stamp. The return address said *Belfast, Northern Ireland*. That much I saw, clearly. Northern Ireland, not United Kingdom. The suitcase from two months ago had *United Kingdom* inscribed in block letters, bigger than everything else, bigger than even our Seattle address, as if proclaiming everything and everyone insignificant in comparison to the United Kingdom.

But also, the letter this morning was written in fine cursive. A woman's hand. Not his father's hand. I'd recognize his father's handwriting in a heartbeat. The curving script in this letter was nothing like the serrated words on the pages that his father had sent with the Belfast suitcase. Impossible to imagine inside it the likes of *For God and Ulster!* Or the dedication *To my son William, named after the Great William of Orange*. The letter this morning was written in a gentle woman's hand.

As if he knows I'm staring at him, Will turns around and looks into me, as only my Will knows how to. He's reading what's in my expression, love and concern in his eyes. But then he moves his gaze from me a little too quickly. His hand attempts to touch his front jeans pocket, but his fingers stop a few inches away and spread wide as if flexing.

He nods toward Emma. I lift my eyebrows and lightly shrug my shoulders to say I can't tell how much longer she'll need. He nods and beckons Mariah to the side of the shed to look at the wall seams we'll need to cut.

When the Belfast suitcase arrived and we read his father's letter, Will said, *He's dying,* which made Will the last of them living. But the letter this morning came from Belfast, too.

I regret… No! I repent staying in the room with Will when he opened the Belfast suitcase. That's *his* matter! The past, his or mine, is a cross we each carry on our own, imperceptible to the other person. That's how it's always been between us—how we've made our happiness possible for two decades. There's no way for the likes of Will and me to be a family like any other, except to have our pasts inaudible and invisible. Especially since we've had our girls! How would they ever grow up as joyful as they are if they sensed that their mother was younger than they are now when she knew what a human face broken into Picasso's *Weeping Woman* looked like? No, it cannot be. Whatever either Will or I hold onto from the time before we met, whether deliberately or as nightmares, must stay within, unspoken. It's the only way for us to live a beautiful present.

But then the Belfast suitcase arrived, and "healing" invaded our family. Had I not stayed to witness the suitcase contents, Will would not have shifted on me with that "healing" of his. I'm sure of that.

In my defense, when the postman rang that Saturday morning, the kids were at their swimming lesson, and my guard was down after the rare morning we had alone. We were both at the door when the postman had chimed his jolly *Hey Fords, you get a foreign treat today.* He extended his arm toward us, holding a small, old-fashioned fabric suitcase. *It's from Britain, look.* I almost took it, but Will shoved his arm in front of me to stop me. The postman raised his eyebrows in surprise, then he frowned at the sight of Will's face with no blood left in it; he looked at the suitcase hanging in the air between us and himself, then slowly laid it on our doormat as if expecting something to be ticking inside. He mumbled about having to go, then rushed down the path to the street.

Will and I stood staring at the suitcase. After a moment, I picked it up, closed the door and put it in the living room. Will followed the suitcase and me. *It's John's.* His voice came like a yelp without a breath, like his first nightmare sounds I'd heard two decades ago. *He was supposed to take it to America.*

I would've gone from the room, I really would have, but for his pleading eyes to not leave him alone with the suitcase.

This morning, however, there was no hesitation, no pleas to stay with him. He'd simply grabbed the letter from my hand, like he couldn't wait to read it. Alone.

*

I hug Emma harder and remind myself to breathe with each slow creak of the wicker chair. I look around and see that Will and Mariah have lined up all our gloves and goggles on the toolbox. Metal clippers and shears are next to them, gleaming in the sun. I'm grateful that Will doesn't allow a single speck of rust on the tools.

"Did Deka also carry a Band-Aid in his back pocket?"

Emma asks this as I'm taking a deep breath, and she must repeat her question before I catch it. When she asks the second time, she straightens up on my lap and takes my cheeks into her hands, forcing me to look at her.

"Mama!" No more whimpers. She's just looking at me as if she lost me somewhere and is using all her might to snatch me back. "Are you listening to me?"

Both Emma and Mariah sometimes look at me this way. I've strained to figure out where that fear stems from. We've never been apart a night in our lives, except for when they've chosen to go to their friends' sleepovers. I'm always around and always interested in everything and anything that they do, say, or think. I don't understand how, looking at me, their eyes could ever read distress.

"Are you listening, Mama?"

I smile and nod, sharpening my mind to attend to Emma's words fully.

She speaks again without dropping her gaze from mine. Her words are slowed down, emphasizing each phrase. "When you were little and hurt yourself, did Deka have a Band-Aid in his back pocket like Pa always does?"

"No, he'd pluck a broadleaf plantain to heal it," I say with a smile, every bit of me fixated on dispersing concentration in her eyes.

She instantly opens her eyes wide, back to her normal, astonished little self, and for a moment there, I'm happy to have interrupted her intensity. But then, Will and Mariah step back from the side of the shed and set their eyes on me. And I know why.

I palm the back of Emma's head again, hoping that we'll continue swaying in the squeaking wicker chair, avoiding all that might come next.

But Emma will not let us return to the peace of a moment ago. She first stares at me, her body stiff and straight, and then she adds on a string of sentences, clutching a trapped opportunity. "He did? Deka did? What was he like? Do you have his picture? Was he tall, like Pa? Was he nice like Pa? Did he play with you and Aunty Katya?"

Then Mariah's voice intercepts, calm and curious. "What's a broadleaf plantain, Mama?" I know she's calculating the way to open a dialogue. "Is it that long banana that Diego's mom baked for my class last year?"

I shift my gaze from Emma to Mariah, speed-thinking and keeping the same smile on my face. "No, it's a different kind of plantain plant." My voice is as carefree as I can make it. Slow. "It's just a leaf bunch, it grows everywhere, Liubav." I point at a small green tuft between the deck and the shed. "Look, it's there in our backyard."

I see the kids' eyes follow my hand.

"I heard from Baka that's what Deka would do when either Aunt Katya or I hurt ourselves." My throat is closing on me, but I force myself to breathe. I figure damage control as I speak. "He'd go to a park in Belgrade and pluck a broadleaf plantain to wrap our wounds."

I continue smiling, looking intermittently between Mariah and Emma. I don't look at Will, though I know his gaze is grinding into me. I hope I won't choke on my words and go red-faced. I hope all the years that I spent learning the tricks of public speaking, without ever intending to speak in public, will help me now.

"Remember the park where Baka, Pa, and I would take you two to play in Belgrade, the one behind Baka's apartment building?"

Mariah and Emma don't blink. They just stare at me. I hope with my whole being that I sound like my usual self. I control the pauses between words, so that I keep my breath steady.

"That's where he'd go to pluck a broadleaf plantain and put it where we hurt." Then I speed up a little, looking only at Emma, "I can't remember him, you know that, but that's what I heard from Baka. I was too little to remember him, you know that, he died when I was too little to remember him."

I sneak a peek at Mariah, just enough to catch her blinking in the way she does when she's unsure about what she hears. Her eyes are on me as she blinks, and I know what she's doing. She's considering whether Emma would remember the four of us, now that she's nine years old—the same age I was when Dad died.

But Emma's strong hug gives me a reprieve, and Mariah doesn't add anything. I seize the moment and cup the back of Emma's head again. Her chin digging into my shoulder sends new waves of goose bumps to my skin and I lean my head against hers. I'm too hasty as I resume swaying, and the sharp squealing of the wicker chair brings a heightened threat to send us sprawling onto the deck.

"When we go to Belgrade this summer, I'll show it to you," I add in conclusion.

I look at Mariah again, and her eyes are on me for a moment longer before she turns back to the shed. I look down, keeping the smile on my face and using all my powers to appear calm. I hope Emma won't sense my heartbeat zooming inside me.

I don't look at Will. Not for a moment through all of this do I look at him. My throat continues to tighten. I keep my head stiffly nestled alongside Emma's. Her hair clings to my face, and I close my eyes, doing my utmost to let her little being overwhelm my senses.

But the only thing I feel is Will's eyes on me. They're pained, I know, with that message in his eyes: *We need to heal*, and I feel a storm forming inside me. What is it that he can possibly see in me that needs patching up? In all our years together, I've been like everyone else—ordinary. The only pain that he knows from my past is from the time we met in San Francisco—Yugoslavia in a violent civil war, falling apart, with Mom, Katarina, and all my living family there in Belgrade. That's all he knows. Then there was the NATO bombing that followed with all of them still there, of course. But carrying that pain is no different than for any other Serb anywhere.

As for the rest, he'll never know. It taught me well, that one time I confided in someone. When people know your pain, they see you as broken. Irreparably broken. In their eyes, you're never again like everyone else, ordinary, normal.

It was back in Belgrade, with my soft-spoken and mellifluous word-threading high school boyfriend, the son of a psychiatrist. I learned my lesson with him. For weeks and weeks, he pleaded with me to tell him all about myself, and when I finally did, he could barely muster a response. He would not look me in the eyes. He only said that I needed to forget, that I had to "heal." We broke up soon afterward, unable to return to the joy we had before I told him.

I lift my eyes to Will now, controlling my fury. What, should I describe to our eleven-year-old Mariah and nine-year-old Emma what it was like to be in California, unable to reach anyone in Belgrade? To wonder, with each NATO bomb, where Mom was likely to be at that time of day—and

Katarina, Simonida, Uncle Sima, Aunt Vera? To wonder for days on end if anyone survived, and if they did, how? Is that what I should tell our little kids?

Or better yet, Will could show them John's bloody shirt and describe his brother's body parts as they were assembled for the funeral? Is that what this "healing" is? Because surely the kids will ask for details. If I say anything—if *we* say anything—they'll only want to know more.

This "healing" would destroy who we are, who we've always been together: a happy family, a family with peace within.

Will isn't looking at me. He's turned back to the shed, but I see his hand slide up and down his front jeans pocket. I don't know if I imagine it, but I hear paper crackling.

Today: Seattle
We Got This

Birds are chirping, whooshing above our heads as they play their courting games. I listen for the spotted woodpecker with a red moustache and a smiling black bib, but I don't hear him around. I watched him drum rat-a-tat-tat-tats on our gutter for days on end. He must've found his life mate and gone with her. I find comfort in the idea that he's accomplished his most important mission, and is now with his love, building their nest.

Will and I, we can deal with whatever is in the letter he snatched from me this morning. We've been building our life together for twenty years. Whatever comes at us, we can manage it together. I'll just remind him that we need to think primarily of the kids. If they ever sense we're withholding anything from them, they pay extra attention to everything and never stop asking questions. Will is a father like no other, like Dad used to be, protective and loving. He'll be careful.

And fine, I'll meet him halfway. It'll be a shift from what we've always been, but a controlled shift. Whatever he needs to process from his past, I'll be there to listen. This "healing" the Belfast suitcase brought on— it's what *he* needs. Not something he wants from *me*. There's nothing he knows about my past before the two of us, so it must be his own "healing" he's seeking. And I'll be there for him. Today is too hectic to talk about it, but tomorrow, after we return from church and the girls are resting, we'll talk, and he'll understand. I know my Will. He'll probably show me the letter then.

With that plan, I'm calm again.

Emma is lightly fidgeting in my lap, and I can tell that in a few minutes she'll be ready to be her typical happy little self again. The tools that Will and Mariah lined up in front of the shed are waiting for us. They've just stepped into the house, and I look at my watch. It's past eleven already. We must begin demolition soon, if we're to have it all cleaned up before Emma's friends come for her birthday sleepover party at four o'clock.

I take another mental walk through the steps: Dismantle the shed, pack it in the pickup truck, pick the area clean of sheet metal, wood scraps, and nails (I do not let the word *nails* linger and form an image of a blackened foot in my mind). Take it to the dump (Will), finish the final preparations for the party (the kids and I), get some rest (the kids). *There's still time*, I comfort myself.

When Will and I bought the house twelve years ago, we intended on removing the shed right away. It was old even then, an unseemly structure leaving behind only an idea of its once-golden exterior and oiled door tracks. In our Eden-like backyard, the shed has always looked like an attempt to disrupt the harmony of our Lilliputian Chalet—the name Will gave to our house. But before we could arrange to remove it, it turned out that we needed to set up a nursery. And so the shed remained, until Emma asked that we *fi-na-lly* take it down today as one of her birthday gifts.

It's thoroughly unreasonable to be dismantling the shed today, when Emma's sixteen friends are coming in just a few hours. But we're honoring Emma's birthday wish. We must. You never know when things might change, and you won't be able to honor anything anymore. Besides, Will convinced me: *It'll be simple, two hours max, easy to clean spotless.* So I surrendered.

Emma straightens up on my lap and touches the Band-Aid covering her scraped knee. Then she starts whimpering again and looks at me with a pout on her face.

"Will my friends see I cried?" She leans her head close to my face, believing that it will help me see her better.

"No Liubav, they won't." I wipe the tears from her face with my palm as the breeze cools them on my skin. "It's only eleven in the morning. Your friends are coming at four this afternoon. They won't see that you cried."

"But will they see the wound?" Emma straightens her spindly leg and points at the Band-Aid on her knee, afraid to touch it directly.

I hold Emma's leg, which is splotched all over in shades of red, blue, and green. She loves pointing at each bruise and narrating the exact moment and place she got it. *This is from yesterday, or was it the day before, I don't know… anyway, it's from the recess when Yitzen and I were telling Mr. Francesco that Kami was still eating her lunch and I tripped and fell and hurt my shin on the playground-barrier thing, the one Mr. Aaron put in and it still smells yucky… you know?* And she'd touch the bruise and squeeze her face, as if in pain but determined to take it bravely.

I kiss the hand she's pointing with. "I think they'll see your Band-Aid, but I don't think it'll be bleeding when they come."

I still cringe inwardly at the sight of a skin rupture, no matter how slight, and my legs go wobbly. The time for Tetanus vaccines is never far from my mind. Mariah got her Tdap last January, but instead of obsessing over thinking that Emma has two more years to wait, I make the wicker chair squeal again as I bend over Emma's legs to check the buckles on her Mary Jane shoes. I buckled them tight when she came out to the deck half an hour ago, but I make sure of it again. It helps. Just like it helps to check all their shoes every night—for flailing laces, broken or loose buckles, worn straps, sole holes. No soft-sole shoes in our household. No flip-flops, slippers, or any loose-fitting footwear. Especially no bare feet! Safety is the one thing that brings my voice into high decibels. I don't raise my voice for anything else.

When I confirm Emma's shoes are secure, I'm ready to go back to her knee. She looks on intently while I peel off a small area of the Band-Aid under the gauze. Her face is equally prepared to cry as it is to squeal with joy. We're both relieved by what we see.

"Oh!" Her eyes widen and she smiles at the few faint pink scrapes, healed nearly invisible. "It's nothing." She waves her hand, dismissing it, and squeezes her arms around my neck in a hug, as if I made it all miraculously disappear. Emma's hug lasts only a moment before she turns toward Mariah and Will coming out of the house, causing another protesting squeal from the chair.

"Masha! Look! Gone!" Emma points at her leg as proof, seeking her older sister's confirmation.

She has always sought Mariah's approval. Even when she argues back with her older sister, in the end, when Mariah says something's fine, then it's fine. The way our girls are with each other reminds me of how I was with my Katarina, and I love it.

Emma feels my instinctive sigh. "It's nothing, Mama, don't worry. It doesn't even hurt." She squeezes me back, and the soothing warmth of her body runs through me.

Mariah and Will are looking at Emma with identical full-face smiles.

"That's super, Emmie," Mariah says. "No one will see it."

Will snatches a look at me for a split second, not enough time for me to process its meaning, then, the smile not leaving his face, steps toward us. He takes a Band-Aid from his back pocket, bends down, and offers it to Emma. As he bends down, I listen for the paper crackling in his front pocket. But Emma swings her legs at the same time causing the chair to groan and I don't hear the crackle.

"Another, for my wounded Wem?"

Will's *wee Em* evolved into *Wem* almost right after Emma was born. I call both our girls Liubav—Love.

As Will offers Emma a new Band-Aid, I get a glimpse of the leftover, mischievous traces of soil underneath his nails. I look up at him, he catches my eye. His eyelids drop as he's looking at me, and I know he remembers last night. I feel the night stirring inside of me.

Emma doesn't notice the exchange between the two of us. She responds to Will's offer of a new Band-Aid. "No, Pa, no need." Emma's all grace, waving her head and letting her hair fly around it like a halo that captures the sun, the ends grazing my face. "It's just a scratch." She completely peels off one side of her Band-Aid to show him the barely visible blotch. "See, all better."

"My brave lassie." Will strokes her head, a smile still sweeping over his entire face, flashing a reminder of why I fell in love with him years ago. His cheeks push his lower eyelids up, his eyes squinting almost shut, and his head leans back a bit, making him look like a little boy without a worry in the world. I love seeing the same smile on Mariah.

His look glides from Emma's face to mine for another eyeblink, and last night is alive inside of me again.

Emma jumps off of my lap, touching the ground only for a moment before launching herself into his open arms, the free end of her Band-Aid flapping against her knee. Will catches her, lifts her up, and kisses her on the cheek as her bony arms try to reach around his wide, square shoulders. He closes his eyes and imbibes the scent of her silky hair, the way I did a moment ago.

"You're a grand *craic*, my Wemmie."

I stopped noticing Will's controversial Belfast expressions years ago. No matter how much he tries, they inevitably slip out of him. I still remember seven years ago when Mariah's preschool head-teacher, the terror-instilling Mrs. Basel, summoned us for a "serious talk" when Mariah said she had *craic* at a friend's birthday party. "Crack, Mr. and Mrs. Ford? *C-rack*?" I still cringe at the memory.

I get Will, though. You can't simply unlearn something you've known all your life, just because you become a parent. But our girls are sure to remind us of the slip-up.

"Pa!" Mariah is the first to notice, as usual. "We can't say that word."

Will turns around to face her, grimacing an apology. Emma glances at Mariah, remembers what *that word* is, then wags her index finger in front of Will's nose, still in his arms.

"Yes, Pa, no more craic!"

"Sorry my loves, you're right." Will tries hard to look serious. "No-more-craic!" He proclaims.

Will's response launches our well-practiced Serbian-Belfast-American ripple repartee.

"*Malo sutra*," says Mariah, cocking her head to the left and raising her eyebrow.

"I will, yeah," giggles Emma.

"Yah, sure, aha," I add.

We all find our joke extremely funny, and I feel confident that "healing" is what Will is seeking for himself. That the letter is nothing serious. That all will be kept under control with a little talk tomorrow.

Will, still holding Emma, steps off the deck onto the lawn towards Mariah. He beckons to me, opens one arm for Mariah, with Emma still sitting on his other arm, and the three of them wait for me to walk into the hug. The kids are entwined between Will and me, and Will's arms are reaching all the way around us.

I want to hold onto this moment. I want to stay in it, not let it go. I know how quickly it can all disappear. The new boys. A nail. Six suitcases. Four one-way train tickets. A death. That's all it can take for the life you know to be no more.

Today: Seattle
The New Boys' Kin

Emma interrupts my thoughts by pushing herself against Will to get him to let her down, and she breaks our hug. She's on a mission, filled with speed, running through her sentences as she runs with her legs. She was simply not born with the ability to take anything in life calmly. It's ingrained in her to be ecstatic about a blazing orange sunset we catch over Green Lake before the sun dodges behind the Olympic Mountains, a new scented soap bar on the bathroom sink, or a friend who writes the third *U R my BFF* note of the week—as if it's the first time she's ever received one. She slows down only when she's hurting.

Mom describes Emma as a vial bursting with energy. *If you shake it, it will explode.* I'd add to Mom's description: *a spangle-packed vial*, like a snow globe with sparkles instead of snowflakes. At least that's what every piece of clothing Emma owns looks like—shimmer erupting in a million shades. When she twirls in all that color, she reminds me of my childhood's Christmas tree ornaments reflected in the window, an infinite flicker of glowing hues. The Christmases of my childhood, from a lifetime ago—sometimes I wonder if I imagined them.

Once, Mom made a mistake and compared Emma to me in front of our all-reason-and-facts Mariah. It was three summers ago, I think, which would've made Mariah eight years old at the time.

"Emma is just like her mother used to be," Mom said, winking at Mariah.

Mariah blinked, then stood speechless for a moment, processing the information. She looked at me, at Emma, then at me again, and when her eyebrows knitted together, so much like Will's, I knew an objection to her grandmother's claim was coming. "*Baka*, that's impossible! Mama is al-ways calm!"

Mom, face long-wrinkled and back slightly stooping, sighed a thought I tried my best not to share. "She is..." Her concession came with a bone-deep regret. "You're right, Masha, your mama is always calm."

I wish that, by some magic, I took my diaries with me. That at some point, the girls could read what fun it was when I was Emma's age, before it all happened. Not about leaving, just about home as it was when we were all there. Before the new boys and their families.

*

"Mama! I forgot!" Emma rushes to say it all at once. "Remember Nora, my new friend who just came to my class yesterday? I invited her to my birthday party!" She hugs me around the waist, and her thin arms feel like a soft belt around me. Then she looks up again. "I told her she can just come at four with a sleeping bag and a pillow. I wrote our address and our phone number for her mama to know where to bring her." She stands still, ready for praise.

Then she remembers something and smooshes her face into a sad expression. "She never speaks of her pa. Kami says she knows a kid who doesn't have a pa." She lets go of me and leans into Will for a hug. A moment later, she switches back to her excited self. "But her mama is really pretty." Then she stands still again, waiting for our response.

The non-negotiable Ford family rule is that everyone is always welcome. Particularly people who have no friends. Or kids who have no fathers. No kid should ever know what it was like when Fancy-Eva invited every other girl from third grade to her birthday party except for Mara Popovic—me, a friendless, fatherless nine-year-old refugee in Belgrade, just three months after the screeching one-way train ride. *I can't be expected to invite every peasant there is to my home*, Fancy-Eva had said to another girl from the grade, loud enough for me to hear. Will and the kids know nothing about Fancy-Eva, or the train, or that I come from anywhere other than Belgrade, but our Ford family rule is engraved in stone: Everyone is always welcome.

"But her mama doesn't know us, Emmie," Mariah rationalizes. "Mama and Pa would never let you go to *her* home before they met all the grown-ups and knew they have no guns."

"I know, Ma-riah!" Emma snaps at her sister. "I took care of it." Emma's hands are in fists on her hips, and her face is in a frown. She expects praise, not to have to explain anything. *It has all already been arranged, isn't that obvious,* her pursed lips seem to say. "I told Nora's mama that we have no guns, that she doesn't need to worry, we're the best family ever, and Mrs. Williams was there and she said everyone knows we invite everyone who can't be with family and friends to our humongous Fourth of July party, and everyone loves us." She nods her head, as if to say, *See?*

I catch a moment to speak when she pauses to breathe.

"It's kind of you to invite her, Liubav, and we're thrilled to have Nora over, but don't expect her to come and then be heartbroken if she doesn't."

"She will come!"

Emma is usually fixed on her beliefs, and when it's not too important, I just let it go. She'll have sixteen other friends over, so if little Nora is unable to join, Emma will still have enough kids to celebrate with.

"You did well, Em." I rub her back gently. "She's new and probably has no friends yet. It's kind of you to be her first friend."

Emma stands still, proud of herself for a moment, and then she looks at Will.

"Fair play, Wem." Will's smile is proof enough of his pride.

"I like her name," I say. "Nora."

Without ever mentioning it to Will, I did consider *Nora* for Mariah but decided against it. I always knew somehow that we would have more daughters, and since there's no match for the name *Nora* in my mind, we'd be left with a second-best name for our other girl. There's just no equal to Nora—Ibsen's Nora, who found strength within herself to overcome. *A chip off of the mountain*, as Grandpa used to say. *Mariah* and *Emma* are Will's choices, and I think they're the right names for our girls.

"Like Ibsen's Nora," I say aloud.

"What's *in bzin*?"

"Remember that play Mama took us to when Pa had to work late?" Mariah, as always, remembers everything.

"Oh, yeah, that ballerina," Emma exclaims. "I love that ballerina, she's so pretty!" Emma twirls and the spangles shimmer on her flowy dress, her earrings, and her shoes, winking and dancing in perfect accord with her little body. "When I grow up, I'll be a ballerina!"

"It wasn't ballet, Emmie. Nobody danced. It was a play. About a husband who betrayed his wife and she left him, remember?"

I'm always amazed at how Mariah can summarize anything in a single sentence. Will can do it in a single word sometimes. As can my sister Katarina.

"What's *buh-trayed*?" Emma asks.

The letter from this morning flashes in my mind. Will looks at me, and his hand reaches toward his jeans pocket.

"He was mean to his wife." Mariah answers.

Will turns around, lifts his work gloves from the toolbox, stands still for a moment as if considering something, and then lays the gloves back on the toolbox.

"Oh." Emma puts her finger to her forehead to help her think, and then, just as quickly, forgets all about it and switches to another thought.

"She was so happy when I invited her, she hugged me real hard." Emma leans her head onto Mariah's chest and wraps her arms around her older sister to mimic Nora's hug.

We don't need to wait till tomorrow. When the kids go to bed, I'll ask Will about the letter. It's simple, it'll be simple. I'll tell him he can talk to me about anything, then I'll ask him about the letter.

"I'll be happy to share a piece of *Zhito* cake with Nora's mom." My voice is solid and stable. It'll be fine. Will's no pretender. "All the parents love Zhito cake."

I make this cake for the kids' birthdays every year. I can't make myself let go of feeling Grandma's presence when I prepare it, even though I gasp when I see the kids only eating the filling and dumping the rest into the trash. I make it regardless of the waste.

Long ago, when Grandma and I had all our days for each other, and I was younger than Emma is today, Grandma taught me how to layer and bake Zhito cake. We made it together for my birthdays then, and now I make it for Emma's and Mariah's birthdays. Grandma would be happy that I welcomed Nora's mother with our cake.

*

I look at my watch. It's already eleven twenty-five, and we're running late. "Okay, Fords." I clap my hands. "Let's begin."

Emma runs back to the table on the deck for her sprig of rosemary, and she slips on the step again. My heart skips a beat, but she doesn't fall this time.

"I'm all fine, Mama," she shouts, turning back to me.

When we're all ready, we stand in a line facing the shed. Will and I flank our daughters, Emma next to me, Mariah next to Will. I take in the whole picture with one big breath: Will, the girls, our bright yellow two-bedroom house that Will christened Lilliputian Chalet, Ugly-the-Shed soon to be gone and replaced with a trampoline, three Douglas firs, and a low stone wall framing the yard. The yard is as green as the valley in springtime from way, way back. Sometimes, when I sit on the house steps overlooking the backyard, it feels like I'm back home, sitting on the steps of the old stone house where I grew up. The tall trees, the valley, the mountains guarding us—they're all alive in my mind's eye, as if they're right in front of me. Even thirty-five years removed, I could describe every detail of my home in every season.

"Okay," I say, swiping my thoughts away. "Everybody knows what needs to be done, correct?"

Will smiles, Mariah nods, and Emma shouts while performing her version of clicking her heels and saluting, "Yes, Mama! We know!"

Emma steps forward to offer the first commemoration to Ugly. We all wait, straight-backed, for Emma to begin, but right before she's to start, new excitement spurts out.

"Mama! I forgot to tell you!" She turns back around and jumps at me, almost toppling both of us over. "I forgot the best thing ever!"

Her face beams, but an unexpected chill gushes through me, making me shiver.

"Her mama is also from axe-Yugoslavia."

Both kids pronounce ex as *axe*, exalting at the power of the word, thinking that *axe*-Yugoslavia possesses magic: the power to hatchet a continental divide along the soil. They have no idea how true it is.

"Whose mama, Liubav?" I'm careful, a warning bellows within me.

"Nora's mama!" Emma's voice is rushed, impatient.

Will stares at me, concerned.

"But she's not from Serbia," Emma continues. "She's from, she's from...
oh, she's from Kosova, Mama! She's from Kosova!" She stands tall, her
hands on her hips, one hand still squeezing her rosemary sprig. Her back
is straight, and she's proud of herself for having remembered it all.

Time slows down, like in a dream, right before you realize you're stepping into an abyss. You could still turn around, but you know you won't.

Emma senses my struggle to understand her words.

"She's from axe-Yugoslavia, Mama, but not from Serbia," she says.
"She's from Kosova!"

Then comes that moment. That unaccounted, dreaded moment when the
tether holding me together, me as my present self, a wife, a mom, an
American-with-Serbian-origins, me as Marica Ford, is all torn apart, and
I am again a little girl without Dad, without home, without ground under
my feet.

The voices of the new boys in our village thunder in my mind. The
voices come from further back, way back, when we still had a home,
when we were all there in our old stone house. I hear the new boys'
shouts into our faces, my cousin Simonida's and mine. *Kosov-a, not
Serbi-a, Kosov-a, not Serbi-a.*

Will's, Mariah's, and Emma's faces come at me as if I'm looking at them
through a moving water bubble that is billowing, growing bigger and
then smaller, rhythmically coming at me and then retreating. Distorted.
Unrecognizable. I can't look at them—I must close my eyes.

When I open them again, I don't intend to shout—the voice comes out
all on its own.

"Kosov-*o*! O!"

My cry bursts the bubble, and I see Emma's curls jiggle as her head
moves back, the shout startling her.

Then everything stops. Nothing moves. The name of the home I haven't spoken out loud for decades, not since Dad died, is floating in a complete void. A surprise out of time that stops everything in its tracks. I'm in a vacuum and there's no one and nothing around me. It's as if life itself pauses, erasing the very existence. An absolute nothing.

I'm not sure how long this hollowness goes on for. When time resumes, it comes in slow motion. The name of my home starts replaying inside my ears, raising in volume with every repetition, threatening to ascend to unchecked decibel levels.

Then the stabbing pain comes. The *O*, the single syllable that reveals the side of the pain you're on, has yanked my jawbone open, triggering my joints to click. The name blasting in my ears and the pain in my jaw merge as one. My hands instinctively push my lower jaw back into place through a glitch of agonizing pain as it unlocks. But the push stops the stabbing.

"O… Kosov-o." I knead the hinges of my jaw with my fingertips, speaking through a thick fog, unsure whether the name actually comes out or if it stays within me.

Emma's and Mariah's shock is reflected in their stunned faces, but their alarm does not penetrate through me. I notice, but I don't feel. Will's frowning face flashes into my peripheral vision, and I recognize it as the same expression he kept for seventy-eight days straight, back when we lived in California and NATO was bombing my family.

I'm aware of their expressions, but I'm removed, untouched by any of them. I'm all separate, an island.

The sensation inside of me is all I feel. As if lead is slowly being poured inside a mold that's scaffolding around me. I cannot move, but I also have no will to try to break out of the lead-scaffolded mold.

"We say Kosov-o, wee love… that's the proper name." Will's even tone sounds like it's breaking through space. "Kosov-o, with an *o* at the end."

Mariah's and Emma's heads move in a synchronized motion toward me, then toward Will, then back at me.

Time in slow motion makes me notice every breath I take. Specks of dust levitate in front of my eyes. The sun's rays reflecting off of the shed's formerly golden-yellow metal frame make them spangle like pixie dust.

As I inhale the specks, they smell of bleach. It somehow doesn't surprise me that dust specks in our Seattle yard should smell of bleach, like a hospital floor. It's ordinary, as in a movie where scenes change from one to another, and the viewer accepts whatever comes next. The bleach smell blends with blaring white walls and rectangular yellow floor tiles. I don't know if I close my eyes, but I see it all play out in front of me.

I'm simultaneously in two scenes, as if caught in a movie transition that reveals one frame overlapping the other. The adult me, Marica Ford in our Seattle yard, overlays a scene of the little me, Mara Popovic in a Belgrade hospital.

At the hospital, an old nurse in a glowing white uniform with a meaty, drooping face guards the door, which I, the little Mara, want to open. The nurse's legs are spread wide apart on the brick-shaped yellow tiles. Her feet are in white twill open-toe shoes, and I see her big toes push her nylon stockings over the edge of the shoes, making her look mountain-solid.

I try to get past, but I'm too small and cannot barge through the impenetrable nurse guarding the door. I throw myself on the hospital floor, hurting my knees, screaming to go to Dad. Mom and Katarina are nowhere to be found. Years later, Mom told me she had to go fill out the forms for his funeral release. She didn't notice that only Katarina followed her down the hallway. They were both in a daze, and even as a child, I knew that.

In the scene transition, I, the adult Marica from our Seattle backyard, reach out for the little me screaming on the hospital floor. But the nurse impedes my attempt. She lifts her walkie-talkie radio and calls for assistance. Another nurse rushes in with a syringe and jabs a needle into my little thigh, right through the brand-new white stockings I wanted to show Dad. Just like Grandma used to knit them, thin snow-white braided thread.

Then nothing. Again.

I transition to a new scene that still has the adult me in our Seattle yard standing above the little me when I wake up in the hospital room. Not Dad's room. Mom and Katarina are sitting on either side of me and holding my hands. Their faces are swollen-unrecognizable. Mom gets us a taxi back to the tiny apartment, not our Kosovo home. We're in big-city-Belgrade, where we came three months ago with four one-way train tickets and six suitcases. But there are only three of us now going to the tiny big-city-Belgrade apartment.

Then the transition ends. All of me is back in our Seattle yard, just re-membering. How, the summer after Dad died, and I was still nine years old, I started anew. No longer clinging to my Kosovo accent, no more planning to go back home, no falling apart when someone asked about Dad, about home. I was all done with that.

They all cried, Mom and Katarina to no end. The uncles, the aunts, the cousins—they all cried for years after gliding along the same railway in one direction with their own six suitcases, one per child, two per adult. But I didn't. I stopped crying for home and for Dad. Just stopped.

I failed in this only once, with my Belgrade high school boyfriend.

*

Emma's arms tightening around my waist startle me out of remembering. Mariah's head and torso nestle into my back. I instinctively extend my arms over their bodies as much as I can reach. I now see Will with his frown again, looking on in quiet pain. I'm back here and now. I see and feel it all, scene transitions dissolved.

"I'll tell Nora when she comes that she calls it wrong." Emma's voice is vibrating against the side of my torso, where she burrows her head. Nothing comes out as a single word this time. She's careful saying the final vowel, her words are slow. "O, Kosov-o, not Kosov-a." She looks up at me for confirmation.

I imagine Nora's mother laughing with the new boys, shouting *Kosov-a not Serbi-a* into our faces. I have a suffocating urge to run to the attic and feel under my fingers the thread of my sunflower tablecloth. The one thing I have from home, Dad's last gift to me. To affirm that I *am*, despite the new boys' prophecy *You'll be no more.*

1982: Kosovo

Home Diary

The lyrics come to me in Mom's and Dad's barely audible voices. Their slow rhythm lulls me so that I have to fight against dozing off. I wish to hear it, I wish to sing it with them. But the fever makes it hard, so I follow the words in my head: the sunset, the mountains, the girl lying ill.

'Ayde sunce zadje, medju dve planine, nane mila
'Ayde sunce zadje, medju dve planine.

I'm eight years old and I have pneumonia. Mom's slim body cradles me on the couch, my head nestles on her chest, and my short breaths are soothed by the vibrations of her voice buzzing from her body into mine.

Dad is sitting at the bottom of the couch, my feet on his lap. They're wrapped in vinegar-soaked cloth scraps that hold potato slices against the burning soles of my feet. Mom tied plastic bags around them to keep it all in one place, *to best draw temperature out.* I know that the stink of vinegar would make me feel nauseous if I could smell it, and that's probably why Katarina said she'd do her homework in our bedroom today. But Mom and Dad don't seem to mind being so close to the smell.

When I write about pneumonia in my diary, I won't mention how Katarina didn't want to smell the vinegar. But I'll be sure to write about how awful it was to just lie there when I couldn't even sing.

I asked Mom to buy me a new notebook, because I only have two pages left in this one. It will be my seventh diary notebook, even though I only learned to write last year! My letters are getting smaller and more stable, just like Grandma said they would, so I don't need a new notebook every three months anymore. But two pages are barely enough to describe having pneumonia. And after writing about pneumonia, I'll have no space left for anything else.

It was Grandma who told me to write it all down, so that I could become the family story repository. That's what Grandma called me—*the family story repository*. She said that when we grow up and everybody forgets what Grandpa said about Sava and Milka Popovic building our home over three hundred years ago (even though I can't imagine anyone forgetting any of it since Grandpa said it so many times that even the stones in the walls of our home know this fact by heart, but anyway), or how Uncle Bekim carried Grandpa on his back all the way to the clinic after a pile of bricks fell on his leg during that work party building the post office where Mom and Uncle Sima now work, or about my pneumonia—when they forget any of it, they'll ask *me*. That's why I have it *all* written down in my diary. When I become a family story repository, *I* will be the one to remind them. Just like Grandma said—everyone will know that *I* was the one who didn't let anyone die.

And no one will treat me like a baby anymore, just because I'm the youngest child!

I'll begin my new diary with Grandma's words about *real dying*. That's how I began all the other six diaries, too. Grandma said that people really die only when we forget them. In my seventh diary, though, I'll add that I sure won't let *anyone* forget Grandma!

*

I feel the full weight of Grandma's blanket on me as I lie on the couch, leaning against Mom's chest. With the tip of my index finger, I follow the silky embroidered thread in rhythm with Mom and Dad's humming. The silky trail feels slick against the thick-woven yarn around it. It's like a glen looping through the rough mountains of yarn. Like I can feel in Grandma's blanket the foothill where our home stands here in Kosovo.

I know Grandma's blanket like I know my own freckled face reflected in the River Ibar on a summer day. The blanket was a part of Grandma's mom's dowry. I've never met my great-grandma—she died when Grandma was a little girl. But Grandma loved to talk about her, about her pale slim fingers threading through the wool. She sure wasn't letting her mom die. But I also think that Grandma missed her so much. Grandma said that just because people die, we don't stop loving them. I think I know this. I still love Grandma.

Grandma's blanket is the color of our pine trees, with a gold and maroon cross-flower-rhombus pattern repeated along it. The crosses are gold-threaded, and they shimmer like the halo around the head of our Saint Nicholas icon. The center of each cross has an eight-petal maroon peony flower, and on either side of each cross there are four golden rhombuses. Each rhombus is framed in a maroon rim.

Grandma's blanket has thirty crosses, thirty peony flowers, two-hundred-and-forty petals, and two-hundred-and-forty rhombuses embroidered on it. I've known this for longer than a year now. Grandma taught me to multiply on this blanket when I'd just started school last year. Now, fully eight years old, I can recite my multiplication tables without even looking at the blanket anymore, right in my head. Six columns by five rows, eight petals by thirty peonies, eight rhombuses by thirty crosses.

I wrote down all of that already in diary number four. I even described Grandma's blanket, though it's a little silly to describe something that we'll always have. But anyway.

Well, what I'll never-ever write down in my diary—ever!—is anything about the new boys in the village. Not-a-thing! I don't want anyone *so* not nice to be remembered.

When Grandma was lying sick and I curled up with her underneath her blanket, I told her that the new boys in the village still didn't know how to multiply. Grandma knew that they were older than my cousin Simonida and me, so I said it because I thought it would make her less worried. Grandma always told me that learning is power, and I wanted her to know that because the new boys didn't seem very interested in learning, they would never be more powerful than Simonida and me. We always completed *all* our homework.

What I didn't tell Grandma is that Simonida and I called them stupid. Of course I didn't! Even sick in her bed, she would've given me the biggest talking-to for being unkind to anyone. *Hurtful words and deeds are never welcome in our village, in our Kosmet, in our Serbia, in our Yugoslavia*, she would've said, in that order, like she always did.

Grandma called our home Kosmet, like it's written on our school maps. She called it Kosmet, because her family came from Metohija, not Kosovo. *The proper name for our home is Kosovo and Metohija, Kos-and-Met, Kosmet.* That's how she taught me to remember.

I looove Grandma's Metohija. Especially her hometown, Orahovac. We visit with family there twice a year, for Saint George's Day and Saint Demetrius' Day. I sneak more pastries when we go to my Great Aunt Sofia's than Mom and Grandma would ever allow me. She sees me but never says a thing. I looove my Great Aunt Sofia.

I didn't write about the pastries in my diary, though. That would be a terrible example for my kids one day. But I wrote *all* about Grandma's Kos-and-Met, Kosmet.

I don't know where the new boys came from, but they call our homeland Kosov-a, with an *a* at the end. That's how Uncle Bekim and Aunt Fatima call it. Kosova. Grandpa says it's all the same. *What's important is that it's home to all of us, Serbs and Albanians, to our* brotherhood and unity. *Never mind the one letter*, Grandpa says.

But these new boys don't just call it Kosova, they get very close to our faces and shout into them, *Kosov-a, Kosov-a, Albanian Kosov-a, this is not Serbi-a.*

That's what gets my cousin Simonida and me so angry. Kosovo is a part of Serbia, and Serbia is a part of Yugoslavia. It's not Albania—that's a separate country. That's what all our teachers say, that's what all our grownups say, and that's what's on all the maps on the walls in our classrooms and in our world atlases. How can Kosovo not be a part of Serbia—call it with an *a* or an *o*—when it is?

These new boys' families are like no other families in our village, Albanian or Serbian. There are eight older Albanian households in our village, but all of us kids go to school together. Our classes are separate because they learn in Albanian and we learn in Serbian, but we all play together. And we all speak both languages.

That's how it's always been in our village, Grandpa says. *The only difference between us*, Grandpa also says, *is that they go to their mosque and we go to our church.* But I also know that the Albanian families don't color eggs for Easter, and I'm really sorry they miss out on the fun of cracking eggs and winning best village egg for a whole year. I've never won it. Petar, my cousin, won it last year, but I'll try it again this year.

All our grownups say that Serbs and Albanians in our village are the same in everything other than the mosque and church thing. I believe it, of course I believe it about everyone—except for the new boys.

*

When Grandma was sick and I curled up next to her, I told her only about the multiplication, though. Nothing about *stupid*. But at the mention of their names, her face wrinkled and her soft hand tightened on my arm with the little strength she had left. I think she looked even more worried than when she'd made Simonida and me cross ourselves in front of our icon and make promises to Saint Nicholas that we would never-ever-ever go anywhere with these new boys or their brothers, that we would never-ever-ever take anything from them, even if it looked like the sweetest candy, and that we would always tell Grandma or our parents if they tried to do anything bad to us or to any other kid at school.

When we were both underneath her blanket, Grandma told me that Saint Nicholas would know if I hid anything. Before that, she always said that our Saint Nicholas loves us and protects us. I didn't like thinking that he could be angry at me for not telling Grandma about *stupid*.

I hope Saint Nicholas knows that Simonida and I didn't start the name-calling. *They* did! First, they called us *Serbian horse* for being girls and going to school and wearing knee-highs and shorts. Then we called them *stupid* for not knowing that *horse* is a singular noun, and that their five sisters—who don't go to school and are older than all of us—will never be powerful, because they don't even know how to read and write. Then they laughed at us, came really close to our faces, and called us *Serbian horse* again. Singular! Which made us really angry. Then Simonida and I shouted for the second time, *You're both stupid*, and we left. I hope Saint Nicholas saw why we were unkind.

But if Saint Nicholas also saw how sick they made Teacher Danica, he would be very angry with them. Surely they deserve his anger more than Simonida and I do. They spoke back at a teacher like no one's ever seen!

We were all in the schoolyard when Teacher Danica told them they're not allowed to use some words. Neither Simonida nor I knew what those words were, but they must have been bad because Teacher Danica told them not to say them. Instead of apologizing, the new boys shouted back at her, "We don't take orders from a Serbian hor!" Then they repeated those words that she said are not allowed in the schoolyard.

Simonida, the other kids, and I almost dropped dead right there when we heard them. We thought they were *in for a major overhaul* as Grandpa says about some really bad people. But Teacher Danica didn't say anything. She turned all pale and was shaking so hard that when she started walking back toward the school building, we were afraid she'd fall over.

Simonida and I told these new boys they're like no one'd ever seen, *really* not nice. And we told them they must learn that a singular horse is a *horse*, not a *hor*, and a plural for horse is *horses*, not *horse*. That there is no such thing as a *hor*. This really bothered us. We know their primary language is Albanian, but if they speak in Serbian, they should say it right, like we say it right in Albanian. But they just laughed at us and spelled out w-h-o-r-e. That made us even angrier, and we called them stupid again. For the third time. They don't even want to learn that *horse* is spelled h-o-r-s-e!

But we're not sorry for calling them stupid, even if Saint Nicholas is angry with us. They're *really* not nice at all.

Then Teacher Danica stayed sick for the whole following week, and for the whole week, Katarina and Petar's teacher, Teacher Borka, had to put our two Serbian classes together and teach us all, grades one-through-four.

For the whole week, all twenty-five kids in all four grades had to squeeze to use the seven double desks we have in our classroom. All with my sister Katarina and my cousin Petar. There were so many chairs in our classroom, we were stepping on each other's backpacks and jackets. All because of these new boys! I wonder that their older brothers in grades seven and eight don't tell them how to behave in front of the teachers. But I think their brothers aren't nice, either.

The new boys' teacher, Teacher Agron, gave them such stern talkings-to that whole week Teacher Danica was away. Simonida and I overheard him scolding them in the hallway. I was afraid he'd really pull out a switch and order them to show him their hands. But he didn't, and I'm glad. I don't think they were bad enough to deserve a switch. We didn't hear what he was saying exactly, but Simonida and I caught something about *hate* and *being expelled*.

Teacher Danica came back from being sick after a week, but she's not all well yet. I sometimes fear they might have poisoned her. They've told Simonida and me that they'll poison all the Serbs. *We'll stab you with poison nails and you'll all die.* They're stupid liars, and I really don't like these new boys at all. But I said none of this to Grandma when she was sick.

And I'm sure not writing *any of it* in my diary!

*

'Ayde u planine, zelena livada, nane mila
'Ayde u planine, zelena livada.

Mom adjusts Grandma's blanket on me and asks me if I'm okay and if

I'll take another spoonful of chicken soup. I straighten up a bit, Mom puts a kitchen towel under my chin, she takes the bowl from the side table next to her, and the spoon is in my mouth. I can't taste soup from water, but Mom is too worried, so when she asks if I like it, I say I do. She tells me that Grandma taught her how to stew it this way, *thick for the infirm*. But I already know.

She misses her, too. I can tell by her sigh and how she slides her hand across the blanket. I feel Dad's hand smoothing the blanket that's covering my ankles. I've never seen Dad this sad before. My sister Katarina, too. Mom has been washing and drying and ironing Grandma's cotton shirt every night when Katarina changes into her nightgown, so that it's clean and fresh for school the next day. I don't think Katarina has worn another shirt since Grandma's funeral. It looks good on her, cornflower blue rimmed with white lace. Grandma hand-sewed it herself when she was a young woman. I'm glad she left it for Katarina to be close to her, like she left my blanket for me.

The door creaks and I know it's Grandpa. He's at Uncle Bekim and Aunt Fatima's almost all the time now. When he opens the door, he stops for a moment. That's when Grandma used to say, *You and Bekim, the two of you would play chess from dusk till dawn if Fata and I said nothing about it.* But when Grandma's voice doesn't come, he looks down and walks inside.

I noticed even before now that he's a little curved, like he's trying to imitate the handle on his cane. I also noticed that he doesn't give me his sermons anymore. I know, because I don't have to make myself scarce when he's in that sermon-mood of his: what kids should and should not do, according to Grandpa. Not have any fun, if you ask him.

But he doesn't even tell our family stories for my repository anymore. I liked it so much better before, even with his sermons. I already wrote down all of Grandpa's stories in my diaries, but I still like hearing them from him again and again. *Over three hundred years ago, twelve generations of Popovics on this land...*

Last week, I started telling one myself when he walked in from Uncle

Bekim's. The one where Sava Popovic, our forefather, lugged rocks that chipped off of the mountain in his ox cart and pulled them all the way here, to our foothill, and made us a home. I began the tale, hoping that Grandpa would continue with how we are *a part of the mountain*, how *the stones that make our home chipped off of it, and because we live in a home that's a part of the mountain, we are a part of the mountain, too.* It makes me feel so strong: *a chip off of the mountain.*

But when Grandpa heard me last week, he just patted me on the head and looked like he needed to sit down.

I so wish our family stories didn't make him sad now. They used to make him so happy before! He would tell me to bring my notebook and sit down so he could dictate a story he forgot to tell me before. Like about his uncle Aleksandar, called Leca. That was such a funny story. Uncle Leca climbed an apple tree one time because he saw an apple he wanted to pick. But the problem was that he was eighty-two years old! The ladder slid from under him and left him hanging off the branch, shouting for help. After saving him, his son, Grandpa's cousin, hid the ladder from his father. That story used to make Grandpa laugh so hard, the chair underneath him would shake when he described his uncle Leca shouting for help, his cousin running up, shouting back about how senseless his father was, then holding him and swaying with him while letting him down. But Grandpa was telling all those happy family stories before the new boys and their families came to the village, and before Grandma died. Now, Grandpa's almost always sad. I worry for him a little bit.

When Grandpa walks inside now, all three of us look up at him from the couch. His eyeglasses are steamed up from the pot he's carrying, wrapped in a kitchen towel.

"What do they say at Uncle Bekim's?" Dad asks, his face all wrinkled. Mom's, too. I don't like it when their faces turn wrinkled like that. It happens so much now. Just like Grandpa's face.

But I won't write about their wrinkled faces in my diary.

1995: San Francisco
Meeting Will

Will looks at me from the other side of the conference room table, across the narrowest part of its oval surface. The shimmer of the Blazoning Inc. logo engraved along the center of the table twinkles in his pupils. His gaze is on my face for no longer than an eyeblink, but it sends a strange sensation through my whole body. As if it conceals a secret message. As if we are the only two people alive in this room.

All twelve of us at Blazoning Inc. are squeezed around the conference room table, waiting for the company meeting to begin. This is my first meeting at Blazoning, and I can't recall half the names from the handshakes on my first day here, a week and a day ago. Will's name is included in the unknowns. The names I know are Rob-the-CEO, Mark-the-HR, Dan-the-Mentor, and Lizzy and Isabella, the only other women in the company. By the end of this meeting, however, I will remember Will's name, too, as Will-to-Avoid.

When he looks at me, it's only his gaze that's lifted. Before, he was listening to Rob-the-CEO's hushed voice, their heads bent down toward the table, slanted in an inverted-V, close together. They seemed wholly absorbed by their own topic, completely oblivious to the people filing into the room. That's why, for the split second when his eyes land on me, it feels as if he looks without aim, as if I accidentally stumble into the beat of his thoughts entirely unrelated to me. But then, when his eyes stay and seek through me, I feel that electric surge.

It all lasts only a moment: He looks into me, then he lowers his gaze to the logo between us, cocks his head a bit, knits his eyebrows, and scratches his chin. He then looks into me once again, for a moment shorter than the first time, and then it's all over. He takes a breath, his head is back in an inverted-V with Rob-the-CEO's, and his eyes are once more fixed solid on the logo.

I mentally check the boxes—*yes* to 'I was quiet,' I always am; *yes* to 'he clearly knows more'; *yes* to 'the prying questions are coming'; and *yes* to 'it was the two words, *Belgrade, Yugoslavia*' when he looked up.

The colleague who sits next to me—whose name I just found out is Eric—had asked me where I come from. I'm used to the question, my accent loudly calls for it. Despite all my efforts ever since I landed on American soil three years ago, I've not been able to Americanize it. It's usually the first question I get after the name exchange.

Before I answer, I always carefully gauge what would produce the fewest follow-up questions: *Belgrade, Yugoslavia,* or *Serbia.* How serene it would be to declare the name of any—any—other country except for the one in the headline news.

The people who ask me typically fall into three broad categories: those who only vaguely recall something that passed by their observation, those who know it by *the bloodshed in Yugoslavia*, and those who know it as *Milosevic's Serbia.* I invariably hope for the first, but always judge what to say by measuring the inquisitor through the lens of the last night's news.

To Eric I say, "Belgrade, Yugoslavia," and right after, I follow with "And you? Are you from San Francisco?"

People like to talk about themselves, I've learned, they generally prefer talking to listening. Not with this Will, though, I can tell.

As Eric gives his origin story, and I focus my eyes on him, nodding and smiling, my mind prepares a response to Will's follow-ups. I inwardly replay my answer, which I perfected during my college years in Lexington: a shoulder shrug combined with a grimace-apology for my ignorance. *Yes, it's horrible, I don't know what to say. I really don't. I'm from Belgrade and my whole family is from Belgrade. No, I don't have anyone in Bosnia or Croatia. No, not there, either.* (I never repeat the name of my home when they say it. I call it *there.*) *No, I don't know anything about the camps and cleansings. I don't watch the news. I'm sure you know better than I do.*

Often that last sentence invites the examiners to take over, to tell me what they know. It prevents their fingers from scoring through the wound. But if they continue prodding, I keep shrugging my shoulders and make sure my path never crosses that of the examiner again.

My first boyfriend, back in Lexington in my sophomore year, took months to start poking around. He held back at the beginning, either out of tact, or from not catching up with the news quickly enough. His confession finally came in a barrage of repetitions—*Wouldn't it be fascinating to be a fly on the wall there, just to see how it all plays out? I mean, a war! Wow!*—all wide-eyed and spellbound, as if in disbelief that he'd discovered me, an exciting novelty he proclaimed to others as *My girlfriend, she fled a war, you know!* After this, I found the first excuse to leave. A fly-on-the-wall boyfriend, craving to watch others dress their wounds and do their best to survive. *Just to see how it all plays out*—like pain was being performed for his personal entertainment.

My second, and final, boyfriend in Lexington caught up with the news almost immediately. Starting from our first week together, he forced the subject like a substance between us. We didn't make it through the first month.

As I sit in the Blazoning Inc. conference room, I realize that Eric is describing his college years somewhere in Oregon. I nod at him and smile as his words come at me like they're pixelated, all cut up into bits. I have to restrain myself from looking in Will's direction. I can't help but wonder, *Is it human nature to want to see the hideous, to smell the reek of the infection and then pull away, repulsed?*

Like the pull I got to know when Dad died, and I was *that girl* the kids pointed their fingers at, their hands over their mouths as they whispered to each other while looking at me.

I wonder.

I knew to stop talking about home, even before Dad died. When he was at the hospital, and I was still convinced that our stay in big-city-Belgrade was only temporary—even then I knew that my home, my twelve generations, needed to stay inside of me. *At least until we return to Kosovo*, I thought then. The faces of the kids in my third grade taught me this. When I'd tell them about jumping into rainwater barrels to avoid making things for my dowry, their faces looked deformed with disgust. To the big-city kids, dowry-making was backward, rainwater dirty, and my twelve generations of peasants an embarrassment, all to be hidden.

Soon after Dad died, Mom moved me to a different grade school, following the advice of the Belgrade therapist. *The environment change would help Marica recreate a new self, help her heal, overcome the past*, she said to Mom, right in front of me, as if I couldn't understand. But her advice helped. I guess. Before the new school started, I *leaped* into adopting the Belgrade accent, manners and all, ready to be *from Belgrade*. From my fourth grade and on, no one in Belgrade ever knew that I came from anywhere else. No one, except for my high school boyfriend. A whole, intact, self-proclaimed healer of broken souls, with horror in his eyes when he heard about my past. His *You must forget, you must heal*. My one great mistake.

Here in the US, as long as Yugoslavia/Serbia is in the news, no matter how much I keep my responses under check, the inquisitors never pick up on anything good, only the wound emanating from me. This Will-to-Avoid smelled it from five feet away.

Only a year, I reassure myself, *till next March, when my green card will be all sorted out*. Blazoning Inc. sponsorship is my one chance to stay in the US. I cannot just leave this time around.

When Eric turns away to greet someone on his other side, I take a quick glance at Will. He's back to talking to Rob. He has the demeanor of a man who grew up in perfect comfort, at home, with an intact family. His shiny chestnut hair is cropped so short that not a single strand falls out of place. It shouts *distinguished*, contrasted against Rob's long and lenient curls. Like he's someone whose commands are obeyed, whose examinations will be hard to avoid.

You need this job, Marica, I repeat to myself. *You cannot leave now.*

*

Right at the hour, Rob straightens up and announces the beginning of the meeting. Eric immediately straightens up himself, stops his sentence midway, turns to me, and puts his finger on his lips as if to let me know that we should listen now.

I have difficulty following all the discussions—about our bank client, projected deadlines, amendments to the statement of work, etc. At one point, Rob asks Will to give a status on the software development, and that's when I get his name. It surprises me that he doesn't sound American. I don't know where his accent is from—England, Australia, New Zealand maybe, but surely not from a place in the headline news.

His accent somehow comforts me, and I don't know why. Examining him as he addresses everyone, I notice something incompatible between his eyes and his mouth. Like they belong to two different faces. His thick eyebrows weigh on his eyelids, making his eyes look solemn, but his half-smile is at the ready to spread and hijack his whole face. Combined, they make him look like joy and sorrow inhabit the same space.

Something about this reminds me of our long oak dining room table, back home, where we held festivities with the whole family, all seventy-five of us from the Popovic line, with our own village and several neighboring ones. Where I rolled the dough with Grandma, when we had all our time for each other. Where Grandma's and Grandpa's bodies lay for their wakes. Our immovable, strong, old oak table, where happiness and grief spilled into each other, as if they came as one and the same.

Like the face of this Will, with his incompatible eyes and mouth. Perhaps his intact family is not quite so.

I'm so lost in thoughts that I almost miss Rob-the-CEO's invitation to officially introduce myself at the end of the meeting. I feel myself blush, as I always do when speaking to a group, but I don't stumble on my well-practiced speech.

"My name is Marica." I pronounce it clearly, *Ma-ritza*, though I expect some people to remember it by the English spelling pinned to my cubicle: *Mari-ka*. I don't want to have to insist on it, but my name is the one thing that the new boys in the village could not deem *no more*, and so I do insist. "I just moved from Lexington, Kentucky ten days ago, where I earned my bachelor's degree in marketing." I don't mention that I was on a full undergraduate scholarship, a jackpot even for an American, let alone a foreigner. I guess being a high schooler from a country starting to violently fall apart might help you get the scholarship. *If only I could've found work in Lexington and stayed there* flashes through my mind. "I'm very happy to be working with all of you and learning from all of you. Thank you for being so welcoming."

I glue my gaze to the bridge of Rob's nose. Just as I'm done presenting myself, and everyone says a chorus *Welcome* as I nod my thanks, Mark-the-HR jumps in.

"Oh, that reminds me." He wags his index finger at me, the movement following the rhythm of his words. "Jessie will call you today." He pauses, as I wonder what that means. "Jessie Aldridge, our lawyer," he explains. "I filled out everything from our side, but she says she needs some documentation from you." Mark waves his hand. "I don't know how the whole green card thing works, but let me know if you need help."

And the meeting is adjourned.

I need this job to stay in the US, to not have to go back to Belgrade, I remind myself. But my legs wobble and I can't wait to scurry back between the walls of my cubicle. All twelve chairs scrape the carpet at the same time, and I don't look at anyone, but I feel Will's gaze burning through me. *Marica with an open wound and a temporary status,* he probably sees. My future at Blazoning's mercy.

I find refuge in my cubicle, where I breathe in, hold, breathe out, hold again, for four cycles. I brace myself for the coming onslaught. For the rest of the day, I sit fastened to my chair, avoiding all other office areas except for Dan-the-Mentor's cubicle to the right of my own.

Dan, I feel, especially today, is my haven. His bald head, combined with the walls plastered with his wife and boys' pictures, feels like home. He just listens, he calls me *Ma-ritza* from the start, and he doesn't wonder aloud how it is that I worked only with the Mosaic browser in college and have no experience with Navigator. And he drops everything on a dime to answer what I ask, even when it's the twenty-fifth question of the day.

It won't be until October, when Dan's family comes to the office to trick-or-treat, that I'll see his younger boy, five years old and dressed as Superman, speak only in ASL. The four of them, his wife and their two boys, communicating soundlessly with each other, love bubbling around them. I pray from that day onward that they will always have one another.

*

Today, after the meeting, I expect Will to intercept my steps to the restroom or the kitchen, so I continue limiting my movement around the office until the end of the week. Instead of coffee, I pop ibuprofen to avoid a headache. I reason that if I drink coffee, I'll need to use the restroom. The big continental breakfast at my extended-stay hotel in Walnut Creek is all I need until I'm done with my workday.

By the end of the week, however, as the questions don't come, I think that maybe I invented the whole *we're the only two people alive in the room* thing at the company meeting. It never happened, I think, and I'm relieved. At some other moments, however, I'm convinced I invented nothing, and that he'd looked at me as a colonial master eyeing a wounded savage, with nothing but momentary curiosity. And then I get gushing-angry. I wish to shout at him that no people have a claim on violence, that it can happen anywhere—anywhere! In his refined world just as easily. *See what happens when your people miss three meals in a row, Master William.*

Eric, on the other hand, comes to my cubicle several times a day. He's about my age, with freckles covering his bony face, which looks like his see-through flesh has been stretched thin over his narrow nose and cheekbones. It reminds me of the bed sheets Mom fastened on tenterhooks long ago, where Simonida and I played *shadows and face masks* before Grandma and Mom threatened to make the two of us do the washing if we dirtied the sheets.

Every time Eric steps into my cubicle, he's excited, and insists that I come see what he's been working on. "Cool stuff you've never seen, Marica." I'm a *Mari-ka* with a *k* for him. He's the last remaining colleague who still calls me that way.

"It's Ma-ritza," I interject.

Eric's response to my correction is almost like a daily game of who'll blink first. He calls me *Mari-ka*, I respond with *It's Ma-ritza*, and he leans over outside to stare at the nametag pinned to my cubicle, as if reading each letter separately. Then he wrinkles his face and pulls his head back to create a slight double chin, says *Ah*, then looks at me, a crease between his eyebrows. As the final step in the game, he straightens up, grins, and continues as if starting over, resolved to avoid unnecessary conflict.

"I'm trying to convince Will to let me fix something up and develop a new language for the bank client software."

I don't understand much of what he says, and I just smile at him.

Eric is nice to me, he's well-meaning, and I urge myself to ignore the nervous chortles that never seem to leave him. Or his game-playing with my name. *Who knows what's behind these ticks?* I reason. He continually invites me to see the *cool stuff* on his desktop, and it's becoming difficult for me to claim busyness. His cubicle, he tells me, is right around the corner from me, in the opposite direction from the restroom and the kitchen. *In front of the offices*, he says. I know that Rob, Will, and Mark have the offices.

*

On Friday, I see Will for the first time after the company meeting. I stand up to ask Dan a question, and as my head rises above my cubicle wall, I notice Will looking toward me. He's standing with Eric on the narrow pathway two cubicles away from me. They were either on their way to the restroom and the kitchen, or back to the offices. His glance is short, but I feel it. Again.

When Eric sees me, he shouts in my direction that he'll come to me in a moment. "I watched a show about your country, Mari-ka." He gives me a preview. "It's sooo sad."

I stare at him, frozen and unprepared for this. When I say "It's Ma-ritza" this time, I'm not convinced it comes out. Will's eyebrows knit together like the day of the meeting. He doesn't say anything, but I can't look away.

"I should go there this summer. Prague is so beautiful," Eric's shout concludes.

Will's eyelids drop first, then his head turns to the side away from Eric, and he looks behind toward the wall. I imagine if I were closer, I'd hear him exhale. Again, it's as if we are the only two people alive. I sit down, forgetting why I got up.

When Eric comes to my cubicle, he describes what he saw of Prague. I just listen and don't explain that Czechoslovakia and Yugoslavia are not the same country. I'm relieved he's not talking about the news.

Isabella and Lizzy invite me for lunch when Eric leaves, but I need to finish work earlier today so I can go check out an apartment.

*

The next week is really busy. I move from the extended-stay hotel to a city studio, which claims $800 of the last $950 I managed to save in Lexington. Mark-the-HR's proof of employment letter and a personal connection helped me get a studio on the third floor of California and Fillmore. The lobby ceiling in the building is carved in white stone lace, like the stitching on Grandma's blouses. Something about that stone relief above the stairwell makes me feel like I'm here to stay.

I even meet my first neighbor, Sharina. She's two years older than me, like Katarina, and she insists that we get to know each other better. She is what I heard people in Belgrade describe as a typical American—your instant best friend. I don't know what a typical American, or typical anyone, could possibly be, but I love spending time with Sharina. We go grocery shopping together, we have coffee on the weekends, and we'll go to a movie theatre at some point when her boyfriend Jake is out of town.

All of this gives me a kind of stamp of belonging, which spills into my time at the office. I start using the restroom and filling my coffee mug again. Time at the office builds into a predictable rhythm, and I get a sense that the year will pass and I'll be okay. After that, come what may. One step at a time, like the therapist used to say when Dad died. *Little by little, you will be as you were before.*

I ask Dan-the-Mentor fewer questions as I'm getting a grasp on the web design for the Blazoning page. Sometimes I walk around the Financial District during lunch hour with Lizzy and Isabella. I enjoy them both very much.

Isabella has such grace in her moves that every man we pass by looks at her. I don't think she's very interested in men, though, but she doesn't say anything about it. Her razor-sharp mind would be my first stop with any personal dilemma, if only we didn't work together.

Lizzy is so petite, I'm sure she buys her clothes and shoes in the kids' department. She's as gentle as a child, too. Even with her Stanford electrical engineering degree, Lizzy shrugs her shoulders and smiles when giving technical explanations, as if apologizing for her knowledge.

The two of them asked me only once when it was that I came from Yugoslavia, said they were glad I was in the US, and that was all. They call me *Ma-ritza,* pronouncing it so melodiously, as if it's an American name. When I'm with them, I feel like I almost belong here.

I wish very much that we didn't work together, that we could become true friends. But things are as they are and no different. I can't let something slip that could accidentally reach Rob—or Will!—that he might misunderstand, or that makes him wonder whether I'm focused enough on work. It costs Blazoning a lot to sponsor me. If I lost this job, there'd be no time left in the year I have to complete my immigration petition with another company. I *cannot* risk it.

Last week, Eric stopped coming to my cubicle. He'd been bitterly whispering to me about how Will wouldn't trust him with some code or something. *It's expensive and unreliable*, he said, when he came to tell me about it, imitating Will's accent. *I know how to configure the code to integrate software into the Blazoning system. Duh!* He slapped his forehead with the bottom of his palm, and his knobby hand flew like a boomerang away from his face. *The bank gave us the money, and I know how to configure the option to work for us. I've done it a million times.*

I couldn't imagine Eric having done anything a million times, being only a few months out of college himself, but I think I understood his sense of injustice. Still, I couldn't let him believe that I have personal opinions at work. So, I listened to him without responding and hoped that he'd leave before anyone heard him complaining to me. I guess my silence offended him.

Then another week passes, four weeks since I started working at Blazoning Inc. Eleven months to go until my Americanization. If only time would go faster.

*

At the end of the day, the third Friday since the company meeting, Eric bursts into my cubicle, with his jacket already on.

"Barsync, Mari-ka?"

"Excuse me? And again, it's Ma-ritza." Lizzy and Isabella mentioned a bar-sink on one of our walks, but I didn't understand what it is. I thought it was a part of their work on some Fridays.

"It's *Barsync Friday*." Eric raises his nearly invisible eyebrows for effect and slows his words, as if explaining an equation to a child. "We-are-going to-a-bar, bar-sync. Coming?" He avoids responding to my name correction this time.

I turn to the right and peek over Dan's wall to check if he's coming.

He stands up from his desk to face both of us. "Unfortunately, I cannot join you. I have family plans."

Eric grins and shakes his hand in dismissal. "You, old fogy, you! Always with family. Never having fun."

I don't enjoy Eric's laughter, it's a bit loud and forced, but Dan doesn't seem to mind. He smiles back, acknowledging the words.

"I did hear it's very nice for young people," he adds, looking at me with encouragement.

"Are Lizzy and Isabella going?" I ask Eric.

"Oh, yeah," Eric rolls his eyes. "Lizzy's coming with her dude and Isabella solo." There seems to be some hidden meaning there, but I can't figure it out. I noticed that whatever Eric says, he always seems to imply something between the lines. "It's Rob and his wife Stacy, Lizzy and her dude, Isabella, Harry, you, and me." He counts on his fingers as he speaks. "Eight of us."

Will-to-Avoid is not listed. Good.

"Thanks for inviting me, Eric. I'd love to go." I'm glad Eric isn't upset with me any longer, though I'm aware I must be careful to escape any more clandestine talks.

"Great!" He points his index finger at me, the thumb up in the air, the other three fingers curled, and winks, jerking his index finger up and clicking to mimic a revolver. "Ready in five, we're leaving."

I sit back down with a feeling of dread churning inside of me. *Why?* I try to reason it through. Normally, I'd listen to this feeling and avoid whatever it's warning me about, but it's too late now to say that I can't go. I pack up for the day and get ready. When Eric calls out "Mari-ka," I follow without correcting him this time.

Just as I step in line behind the rest, Will and Rob round the corner toward us. Their long legs catch up with us in time for Will to get the door as I exit. I turn around, smile, and thank them both. Will looks at me with that smile ready to hijack his face. I didn't realize before how tall he is, and how much I need to lift my head up to look at him. We walk down the stairs, and Eric waits for the others to pass by, stepping next to me. The fresh air hits my face, opening up my lungs as we walk outside.

The city still awes me, even after a month of being in it. Market Street, where we walk now, is so wide with such grandiose buildings, I described it to Katarina and Mom as what one would imagine Paris boulevards to be like. Wherever you look on Market, everything is beautiful. Even its endless red brick sidewalk, perfectly flat for the feet, the brick laid out in an L-design with flawlessly filled cement in between the bricks. Dad's mechanical engineering eye would've admired such precise masonry. And the buildings—each one built as if to compete at an architectural pageant. Their vaulted windows, braided columns, names spelled in stone mosaics, curves, and carvings.

The people who built this city must have loved it very much. It reminds me of Grandpa's words about the work parties when we still had Yugo-slav brotherhood and unity. *Brick by brick laid with our own hands, our own money and time, made to last forever. For you, your kids, and their grandkids.* San Francisco must have been built like that, with as much love and hope.

We pass Geary, and Will doesn't split from us. Rob's wife, Stacy, meets us on the corner of Market and Kearny. She says "Hi" to everyone, kisses

Rob, hugs Will, and waves at Harry. We cross the street and head down Third toward Mission.

Eric walks next to me the whole time. I do try to hear his tale about how he came to San Francisco, but I must keep track of the street names to make sure I can retrace my way back to Market. It's getting dark, and I've never been below Market before, not even during daytime. I need to pay attention.

At once Eric stops talking to me, turns around, and looks at Will. "I didn't know you were coming?"

"Aye, coming." Will answers, without any color to his voice. As if it's plain fact.

"He's comin', lad." Harry, who does I have no idea what at Blazoning, but who seems to be entrenched in the company, turns around and with a wide grin, responds to Eric, imitating Will's accent. "So, we can't go to Murphey's, those dirty Papists, because he's comin'." He winks at Will.

I slowed down when Eric turned to Will, and now Will is next to me. I see his eyelids drop. "Aye…" He lets the word levitate around his breath.

"Or is it those damned English colonialists, I forget," Harry continues. "Tell me my lord, I prithee."

Rob and Stacy have been walking a few steps ahead of us, talking quietly to each other. Rob's arm was around Stacy's shoulders, pulling her closer to him, and her hand around his waist, her head leaning into his shoulder, like she was hooking onto the relief he offers. But when Harry bellows these words, they immediately turn back toward us.

"How about you mind your own business, Harry!" Rob stares at Harry and speaks quietly in a way I'd never heard him speak. "For once in your life." His voice lacerates the air like he's known Harry for a very long time, and that knowledge doesn't involve a hope of redemption. "Just mind your own business, Harry, okay?" I'll find out later on that Harry's sister is married to Rob's brother.

Stacy, Rob's wife, frowns and shakes her head at Harry, slowly, like she's not surprised, but disappointed. I like the way she does it, like this is no joke. Harry swings around and continues walking like nothing happened.

Will unexpectedly looks at me, and there, again, there's that sense of the two of us and a private message.

All at once, the image of Bobby Sands stuns my mind stiff. He's on a black-and-white TV screen, propped on a metal-framed bed, wrapped in a rough prison blanket. Emaciated, long-haired and bearded, unnatural, with his young eyes ossified before he's dead. Just like Dad's eyes a few years later. Mom complained when Dad insisted that Katarina and I watch the hunger strikers as they were dying. She said we were too little for such nightmares, but Dad wanted us to know what a *brother-killing-brother war*, as he called it, looked like. How it maimed everybody. The whole country. In 1981, Northern Ireland felt to all of us a world apart from our Yugoslav brotherhood and unity. Who could've predicted the years to come.

We continue walking, and Eric is telling me something I can't follow at all. I regret not listening to the feeling of warning before I left my cubicle. I wish I could be alone in my airy, white-painted apartment. I wish I could find a set of railroad tracks and cry out for Dad, for home, for Will and his people, as a train passes by. Cry out for the young Belfast woman I saw on the news when I was seven years old, in 1981, when I had a home, and Bobby Sands lay dying for sixty-six days. Katarina, who was nine at the time, looked so horrified as we listened to the news from Northern Ireland, I was more afraid for my sister than for all the people in the news. Even more than for the young woman who described the first thing she had to do every morning when she opened the clothing store, her first job out of high school. She had to overturn each item and look for a bomb. With her bare hands. I wish I knew if she made it.

I look at my Blazoning Inc. colleagues. I see Harry and Eric and Stacy and Rob and Lizzy and Isabella. I see each with two living parents. With homes. No poisons, no cancers, no gaping wounds. Do they even understand how lucky they are?

Will, I feel, he's more like me. Not intact.

I just want to leave, go back to my apartment, be on my own. But before I can claim a headache, we arrive at a bar and walk inside. Rob points at the big table, and we move to it to take our seats. Lizzy tells us her boyfriend will come in a little bit. I follow Isabella, and as I pull out a chair next to hers, my inner clock starts ticking down the fifteen minutes that is the minimum-acceptable amount of time I can stay. Dad called this respect: *You give everyone at least fifteen minutes of yourself.*

I take my seat and see Will pulling out a chair to my other side. It's spring in San Francisco, the day is warm, and there's no wind at all. It's warmer still inside the bar. Before he takes his seat, Will takes off his leather jacket. As he takes it off, his plain, indigo-colored T-shirt rides up just a few inches, exposing his belly. His bare skin is right at my eye level, only for a moment, until the shirt slides back down, but long enough for me to notice dark curls against light skin.

Will catches me staring, and I quickly turn to Isabella, my face instantly burning. But Isabella is facing away from me, toward Stacy, and I don't know where to look.

Today: Seattle

A Home?

I flex my legs, expecting the hurt in my kneecaps from the yellow tiles of the hospital floor. But the pain's not there. There's no soreness in my throat from screaming in front of Dad's room, either. I'm fully back in the present, in Seattle, in our backyard with Will and the kids, standing in front of the shed.

You're a mother, a wife, a Marica-the-American with Serbian origins, I tell myself. *You're not a refugee girl in Belgrade without Dad and without home.* This reassures me. I am only what I am today.

The urge to escape to the attic, to hide, to feel the sunflower tablecloth threads under my fingers, subsides. Mariah's and Emma's hugs help. Emma's arms are tight around my waist. I feel the slanted edge of her sprig of rosemary rubbing my belly through the shirt. Mariah's head and torso are nestled against my back, her arms looped across my chest. My hands are patting their backs, as well as I can reach them.

Will's still standing in front of the shed, where he was before Emma told us about Nora's mother. He's quiet, pained by my pain, which I see in his face. The same pain from years ago, during the NATO bombing of my family. He knows nothing about Nora's mother's kin, I remind myself—nothing about *Kosov-a not Serbi-a*, nor about *You'll be no more.* His lack of this knowledge reassures me. I'm like everyone else, ordinary, normal. In Will's eyes, also.

I force myself to think clearly, to make a plan. Plans comfort me.

For now, I decide, I'll act as if nothing happened. Then I'll figure out what exactly came out of my mouth when I lost all restraint. Emma will tell me what I need to know on her own, I can count on that. She always says what troubles her. Then I'll figure out what to do, what damage control is needed. What to deny and what to explain.

This is a good plan, I feel. It confirms that I'll be okay, that all will be okay.

Will's going to be there for me. I see this in the pain in his eyes. He knows that Kosovo is to me as it is to every other Serb—the soul of who we are. He'll help me explain it to the kids. He'll say it clinically, all stripped of emotion: *Kosovo is a part of Serbia.* He'll open our world atlas and point at the right place. *See here, Kosovo and Metohija, they are the southern part of the Republic of Serbia. Calling it anything else is incorrect.* I could imagine Will saying it, and Mariah understanding it. That also helps.

The one thing I must do now is prepare myself for *her.* For Nora's mother. The rest can wait. But just the thought of her makes me feel like I'm breathing through a tightly-woven sieve. The new boys' kin I must welcome into my home.

The word comes into my mind so naturally, it takes me a moment to replay it and grasp it.

Welcome Nora's mother into my *home. Home?*

As I breathe in, straightening up to get as much air as I can, Emma and Mariah turn around to face me. Their arms are tight around me, their whole bodies pressed along my front. Will also steps toward us, gazing at me from under those heavy eyelids. His arms wind around the three of us, his front against the kids' backs, his lips warm on my temple.

The four of us, with the love I could not have imagined existed for me before Will and I met. Like Mom, Dad, Katarina, and me.

Home?

We stand, layered like an onion: Emma is hugging me, Mariah is hugging Emma and me, I'm hugging the kids, and Will is hugging the kids and me. We both shield the heart-layer, and he's shielding me.

It's always been like that, I realize. He's always shielded me.

And this talk of "healing" is Will's way of coping with all that came in the Belfast suitcase. His father's last letter—the final bid of a dying man for his only living son to not abandon the cause. The blame. John's bloody shirt. Their family photos. This "healing" is Will facing up to his past, now that he's the only one still alive. Not a call to my own past. That's all clear to me now. And whatever's inside the letter this morning, we can deal with it together.

The sense of relief taking over me as I stand inside our onion-layered hug is like the relief from the moment I held my green card for the first time. It's a confirmation that I'm here to stay, that it'll all work out.

As I process this, I feel how my body releases itself to Will's warmth in a way it hasn't for the last few months. Not since the suitcase arrived.

Home. I still don't know if it's a revelation or a simple misspoken thought, but the injection of euphoria has already reached my veins. The feeling of Emma's, Mariah's, and Will's bodies so close to me are interweaving with this thought. *Our home.*

A picture sparks in my mind of the old tapestry in Grandma's workroom, back in our old stone home in Kosovo. Our family tree. The twelve generations of Popovics, from Sava and Milka Popovic all the way to Katarina and me. Maybe that's how homes are braced: with stories, with symbols, with traditions. With a stitch between the past and the future, with a tapestry of the family tree. With Will and me creating the first Ford stitch, loop, and tie. The starting point back in California—where Will and I took the first steps together into our beautiful future.

I hug the kids as tightly as I can and lean my head into Will's neck, passing the feeling of *home* from my body into theirs. I fear the idea's too tentative, too unprotected, that it could disperse in a moment. *Latch on to it*, I want to tell them, *make it take root*. Enough to stitch our four names, to name Will and me as great-grandparents many times over to all our descendants and all the Fords that come after us. Just like Milka and Sava Popovic.

The sensation that builds inside of me is something I'd known long ago, something I used to feel way back and never since. But my body remembers it well. The ecstasy flooding through me when I was younger than Emma, like when my cousin Simonida and I ran through the cornfield at night as a dare from our boy cousins and friends. They said we were girls and girls wouldn't dare. Well, they saw us do it, despite our hearts threatening to burst, they saw us running right through the field and coming right back through it, just to show all the boys who's scared of rats and garden snakes in tall cornfields at night. That's the kind of ecstasy rushing through me now.

Our home.

I find it impossible to stand still with this thought inside of me, to stay quiet. I have to focus my breathing and calm myself. Will's lips must feel my temple vein pulsing. I have to do something, start a task immediately. Now that I know a *home* might be.

I tap the kids on their backs to signal a reminder that we have work to do. Neither of them moves, so I wiggle out of the hug and clap my hands hard, burning my palms.

"Okay." My voice is too loud. "Okay Fords, let's start. We have a birthday to celebrate today, and it's past eleven-thirty. Come, make haste, let's take Ugly down." My index finger taps at my watch. I'm too excited, I know, and they can see that, but I cannot stop it.

The thought of Nora's mother, the new boys' kin, still scrapes at me. I have to be ready for her. But I shove the thought away. I don't want her inside of me—not at this moment. I only want this possibility, this *Lilliputian Chalet home*. I want to give it a chance to take root.

Will looks at me like only he knows how to look at me, but not for long. I have no idea how I must appear to him at this moment. Then he returns to his former place. Before turning to the shed, he gives me another quick glance. *He's there for me. Always. We'll deal with the letter.* Mariah stands next to him, then Emma, and finally it's my place.

*

When we're lined up in front of the shed, Mariah prompts her sister to begin. "Emma." Her voice is composed, as usual, but not peaceful. I don't like the way it sounds, but she'll be okay.

Emma clears her throat as if she is going to start, then she turns around unexpectedly again. Her arm spins like a merry-go-round when her torso twists, and she bumps into my side, almost snapping the sprig of rosemary in her hand.

"Oh, sorry Mama." She lays her other palm over where her fingers grazed me, then confirms her rosemary is still in one piece. "Mama, is it okay if I save one cornflower pot and give it to Nora's mama?" She's running through her sentences again, my typical excited Emma. "She has no friends in Seattle because they just moved here two days ago, and the cornflowers are so pretty and they'll make her happy, and you always say to be kind to everyone and think of others, and I'm thinking of Nora's mama and how happy the cornflowers will make her."

"Love." Will's even tone indicates *no* as an answer before I even understand what Emma's saying.

She's asking about the cornflowers that Will and I potted last night. These cornflowers grew around the shed, and Mariah and Emma dug them out yesterday to protect them from the demolition. It was the kids' bedtime before they got around to potting the first bunch, so Will and I finished the process.

"Wem," Will restarts, after a pause, without once looking at me, as if his refusal had no relation to me. "We don't know who's allergic to what, and we can't just assume we know who likes cornflowers."

I look at his nails again, and at once I see it all clearly. For Will, this has always been our home. All the love he has been putting into creating our yard, building the bookshelves, setting the floors, redoing the kitchen, and reinforcing the walls, the structure, the kids' playhouses. Even the name he gave it, *Lilliputian Chalet*—it's all been for making it into our home that can last forever, as forever as humans can imagine. These cornflowers are a part of all that, part of us and our home. I see it now clearly.

Will's *no* is also protective of the way we are with each other. Of our night after the kids went to bed yesterday. What he calls *soil-balling*: throwing soil handfuls at each other as if they are snow. I'd told him we must hurry up, finish potting the cornflowers, and go to bed early to be rested for the full day today. But Will, like a rebellious child, had patted a clod of dirt with that errant look of his, the squinting eyes and cocked head. And I knew, I just knew what that face of his meant, right before he released the first soil missile into my chest. My Will wages wars like a little boy. But I'm no meek adversary, as he knows full well. In the end, his head looked no less as if it had rolled in a freshly made flower bed than mine.

That's what his *no* is protecting—the way we are with each other, all the slowness that extended into this morning.

For Will, giving away the cornflowers would be like giving away a part of our home, of us. My covert romantic.

I fight the urge to jump into his arms right now. It's only Emma's response that reminds me of where we are and what we're doing.

"Oh... I didn't ask her." Emma isn't easily dissuaded by reason, but she saw a kid at school whose face puffed up like a blowfish within seconds after taking a sip of milk. She knows what an allergy is. "I'll ask her, okay?"

"Love." Will won't let go of the matter. "*I'*d like to keep our cornflowers." His words are emphasized and slow. "They remind me of the time we saw them first, when we bought our *Lilliputian Chalet*."

Our home.

Will's eyebrows are arched high and his head slowly nods up and down as he speaks, looking at Emma. "*I* don't want to give them away to anyone. Okay?" He's confirming, not asking, and Emma knows it. It's rare for Will to insist on anything with the kids, but when he does, there's no negotiating.

I wish I could shout at Will, over the kids' heads, how much I love him. That I finally get it. I want to share with him the future of the Ford family tree tapestry. I want us to firmly sow the foundations of it right now.

Emma scrunches her little face and tightens her lips, the bottom one extended far in front of the upper. She goes back to facing the shed like that.

I wish to squeeze her tightly in a hug, transfer to her my knowledge that nothing matters except for what's here, right now. But I keep still. If I let myself loose, I won't be able to stop. Like I used to be when I was her age.

Emma bends down to lay her sprig of rosemary in front of the shed's door without Mariah's prompt this time. She clears her throat like an adult and then shouts out an angry "Ugly, thank you!"

She looks at me, her lips pouted. I bend down and kiss the top of her head before she stomps back into the line.

Mariah steps forward. She takes her sprig of rosemary from her front shirt pocket and lays it next to Emma's. She quotes, "'Give me now leave to leave thee,' good Ugly. I thank you for all your years with us." She takes a deep bow like a ballerina and then steps back in line.

I step to the front, all lightheaded. "Ugly, thank you." I had more prepared, several silly exchanges between the Clown and the Countess from *All's Well*, but little Mara Popovic bubbling inside of me threatens to take over. I need to keep her in check. So, I don't say anything further.

Will looks at me, but Mariah's voice redirects his gaze.

"Pa, it's your turn." She sounds more at peace now.

Will picks up the shears from the grass and steps toward the shed. He straightens up tall and raises the gleaming shears like a sword directed at the shed. The shears flash light into my eyes as he gesticulates. "I declare Ugly-the-Shed suspended from its duties and banish'd from the land of our *Lilliputian Chalet*." The rhythm of his voice sounds as if he's reading a proclamation from a scroll, standing in a medieval town square.

Our Lilliputian Chalet. Our home.

Will moves the shears up and down, as if inviting the shed to a duel. "'If I were thee, I'd throw myself away.'" Then he twists his torso sideways, as if evading a sword. "'Pray you, stand farther from me!'" The shears still up in the air, his voice deepening like a bassoon with every phrase. My Will, whom no one can outshine when it comes to quoting his namesake. Will, whom I could not love more. "'I do desire we may be better strangers!'" he calls, as if in the middle of a sword fight, moving his torso around to dodge the imaginary attacks. "'Let's meet as little as we can.'"

The kids laugh, like they always do when their pa recites Shakespeare. My heart is bursting with hope.

Will lowers his shears, calms his movements, and adds in a regretful, quieter tone, "'All which it inherit, shall dissolve.'" He pauses. "We all know it, good Ugly."

I won't let the thought of the letter from this morning spoil this moment. Or the thought of Nora's mother. I remind myself to stay in the moment, in breathing the future of the family tree tapestry. But despite this, the thought of her grates at me. My stomach churns, the sensation dragging at my elation.

*

Now we go on with step two: dismantling Ugly.

We pick up our safety gloves and goggles from the toolbox. Emma's sparkle-twinkling gloves catch light and blink, just like her dress and her Mary Janes. Once our safety gear is on, Emma and Will step right up to the side of the shed. Emma reaches for the metal shears from Will, but he loops his left hand around her left fist, holding the handle with her. Her hand is invisible inside of his. With his right hand, Will lifts the metal sheet wall from the bottom and eases the back blade of the shears underneath. Then he loops his right hand around Emma's right fist, they press the handles in together, and the first cut is made.

Emma's all pride when the shears snip the metal.

Mike, our next-door neighbor, appears from his side of the fence. He's in his tight-fitting bicycle gear that matches Emma's shimmer. He's getting ready for his Saturday "Tour de France" around one of the Western Washington lakes. The selection of razor-thin bike frames hanging on hooks in his garage astonishes me. Like in a bike shop, they're all aligned sideways with the exact same distance between each of them. He takes each bike out into his yard every Saturday morning, checks the brakes and the tires, trues the wheels, and tightens the seats. It reminds me of how Grandpa used to check newborn calves.

Pulling down the shed is of interest to Mike, since the view into his backyard will now be left wide open. I can't imagine it's a welcome change, though I don't expect Mike would ever utter a word about it. *It's a Ford decision*, he said when Will asked him a while ago if he had a color preference for our fence dividing the two plots. Land ownership is sacred to Mike, and he's sure to respect everyone's choices on their own turf. If he doesn't like what we do, he'll do something on his side.

"So, the Ford shed's gone?" Mike asks and leans his palms onto the fence.

"Look, Mr. Mike! I'm taking Ugly down first." Emma tries to gesture with the shears, to show where she cut the metal sheet, but Will's grip is not letting go of the shears in her hands. His hold prevents her from waving the blades around.

Mike gives her a serious head nod with knitted brows and pursed lips to acknowledge her accomplishment. "Ugly is all done up now," he says, as if uttering a philosophical thought, then throws his fist up in the air and shouts, "Viva Mar-Em, down with Ugly!"

Emma and Mariah giggle. They like how he fuses their names into one, even though they know he does it because he can't tell them apart.

"Hey, Mike." I wave at him before quickly snapping my gaze back to the metal tips of the shears, and to Emma's and Will's hands. The metal is sharp. Rust is everywhere on the shed, I'm sure of it. *Their gloves are thick, it couldn't go through*, I comfort myself, but still keep my eyes on both their hands.

"Greetings to you, lad," Will says, without taking his eyes off of Emma and the shears. "Bravo, Wem." He loosens his grip so Emma can let go of the shears' handles—first one, then the other. He smiles at Mike for a moment and then hands the shears to Mariah. Mariah cuts the shed sheet on her own. Will only holds the metal end bent, so that she can fit the shears underneath and continue Emma's cut. "I'll see next week if I can plant some small firs here."

"That'll be nice... if the soil's good." Mike uses his foot to scratch a line in the dirt, making a shallow rut. It lifts a bit of dust from the dry ground. There's been over a week with no rain in Seattle this spring.

"Great job, Masha. Well done." Will takes the shears from Mariah. "Aye, that's what I'll need to see. It looks like clay deep in, but we'll see."

"Let me know if I can help." Mike pushes himself upright against the fence. "I'll leave you to your work now." A moment later, Mike's back in his garage and invisible to us again.

In all the years we've known Mike, he's not once spoken a single sentence that was either unwelcome or too long. We often spend evenings together with him, usually in the backyard when days are warm and the kids are asleep. He seems to add perfect repartee to every sentence, and is unfailingly courteous. But what I like the most about Mike is that he never pries into our former lives. For him, we're just neighbors, ordinary

Americans like everyone else.

After I get my snap of the shed, Will takes over, and we watch the large metal shears cut around the nails. Far simpler than I'd imagined—even uneventful, I'd say.

*

In the end, it takes less than an hour to collapse the walls and fold down Ugly. At first, Mariah and Emma follow Will's moves like hawks, exclaiming *Wow* in one voice every few minutes. But halfway through, they jump on the zip line, which Will ran along the other side of the house two summers ago. The kids are now pushing each other down the cable, in and out of our sight. The shed demolition is a bit disappointing to them, I know. They expected a lead ball, a firefighter ladder, and a horn to signal when the swung ball would crash into the twelve-by-ten-by-ten-foot corrugated metal walls. Instead, engineer-Will cuts around the nails, and the shed folds in on itself. No glamour, no sense of *Elvis has left the building* for the expectant kids.

I keep alternating between looking at Will's hands, at the metal rust lurking around, and back toward our Lilliputian Chalet, our *home*. I do my utmost to keep my heart from trying to explode. To not think of who is coming at four o'clock.

After the final wall falls, I urge the kids to go back inside and to get their room decorated for the sleepover. I need them to get some rest when they finish. I know I'll need some time to prepare myself for her arrival, to think it through, and to formulate a response if my homeland comes up. But I convince myself that I'm not as troubled anymore, now that I have *our home* within me.

Will collects the dismantled walls and ceiling, takes them without any effort to the back of the garage, then loads them into the bed of the rented pickup truck. His tall swimmer's body moves slowly, as if feeling rather than seeing the space, careful to keep the parts of the shed from scratching the garage siding. Or himself. His green denim shirt is woven so tightly, I'm pretty sure a nail couldn't pass through.

Wait, *green*? I squint to see better. Will's shirt is *green*! But that's just impossible. He never wears green, just as he never wears orange or purple, the colors he'd been born into. But this one does look green. A regular collared, long-sleeved denim shirt, one that matches Mariah's. Now when I think of it, he had this same shirt on when he snatched the letter from me this morning. How did I not see its color earlier? Huh. He must've bought the shirts yesterday when he went with the girls to pick up birthday decorations, as I was layering the cake at home. *Green.*

I can't think about it right now, though.

I continue picking up the metal scraps lying around, but I mostly watch Will. He's careful, he's always been careful, but accidents can happen even without the new boys' threats. They can happen despite his thick *green* shirt, Doc Martens, gloves, and goggles. Even despite his up-to-date Tetanus shot.

Now it's only the shed's wooden base that's left to be taken apart. Half an hour of work at most, I gauge.

I'm getting ready to go in and help the kids when Will's axe hits right onto the base of a nail. The zing of the two metals, axe on nail, is followed by growling from below the top board of the base. A warning. The sound is almost like a human yelp.

It stops me dead. Will pauses. Then he knocks on the top board with the back of the axe. He's gentle.

"Go in and close the door. It's a raccoon maybe," he says to me.

He waits while I nod an acknowledgement. The growl again, soft and warning. I go in and keep the back door propped open just enough to see what's happening.

1982: Kosovo,
Uncle Bekim and Aunt Fata

'Ayde u planine, zelena livada, nane mila
'Ayde u planine, zelena livada.

Mom and Dad stop humming when Grandpa walks in tonight from Uncle Bekim and Aunt Fatima's. I twist around on the couch to better see him. As I move, the bags with sliced potatoes soaked in vinegar to lower my pneumonia temperature crinkle on my feet. I sure hope vinegar won't leak and stick to the leather in the couch! If it does, when I'm able to smell again, I know I'll *so* dislike the stink. Mom says vinegar odor evaporates, but I can smell it long afterward. Every spring, when Mom cleans all the oak furniture with baking soda and vinegar, we must keep the windows open at night so that I could sleep. Mom says that I can smell like a fox. That Katarina has the eyesight of a hawk and I have a nose of a fox. I wrote that down in my diary.

When I look up at Grandpa, who's sliding off his shoes, I notice that he looks older than before. I worry for him a little bit. He's a grandpa, I know, not a dad, but he looks so much older than before I got sick with pneumonia. The bad leg he hurt at that work party, when he was laying bricks for the post office building where Mom and Uncle Sima now work, looks like it could buckle under him even with the cane. I don't like that he looks this way.

I'm not yet sure if I'll write in my diary about how sad Grandpa is. I'll talk to my cousin Simonida and see what she thinks. Simonida has read all six of my diaries several times over. I used to give Grandma every entry to read and to approve of, but since she died and Grandpa is so sad all the time, and Mom and Dad are always busy, Simonida is my only reader. She has her own diary, too. She's a family story repository for the Markovics on Uncle Sima's side, because I already have the Popovics on Aunt Vera's side covered. But Simonida also wrote down in her diary stories Grandma told us about Aunt Vera when she was little. Aunt Vera was such a proper and well-behaved little girl, nothing like the *little rascal* Dad was, Grandma said. I can sort of imagine Dad as a little rascal, and I like it. Sort of like me.

Simonida sometimes copies my diary entries to her own repository when Grandpa's stories include the Markovics. For instance, how when Uncle Sima's dad, Grandpa, and Uncle Bekim went to the work parties together to build our Kosovo, they sang songs around the bonfire and teased each other about their young wives. Those are such happy stories! Grandma always chuckled when Grandpa would look at her with such a smile, then they would stare at each other in that way of theirs. Grandpa would say how Uncle Sima's dad called Grandma too smart for her husband, and how Uncle Bekim defended Grandpa by saying he'd sure have to develop some smarts to keep up with her. How everybody wanted to marry Grandma. I so loved being with Grandma and Grandpa when they were like that, staring at each other and smiling. Those were such joyful stories for my repository.

But now, when Dad asks Grandpa what they say at Uncle Bekim's, Grandpa's whole face crumples, and he sighs through his nose like he intends to keep no more air inside him. Both Mom and Dad look at Grandpa. They have their worried eyes and wrinkled faces on, and I *so* don't like it when they all turn this way!

Just as Grandpa is about to say something, Mom quickly waves her hand as if swatting away a swarm of flies, and the three of them all look at me. Even though I have pneumonia, I'm upset that they all think I'm too little to be trusted with anything. I want to remind them that *I* am the family story repository. But I'm too weak to complain.

"Fatima sent some chicken soup for Mara," Grandpa says and lifts the pot in his hand. When Mom nods, Grandpa puts it on the table that is covered with clear vinyl.

Mom started laying a clear vinyl cover over the crocheted sunflower tablecloth. *Until,* she says, *Mara learns to stop wiping her hands on it.* I just like to feel the thread under my fingers, to make the tips of my thumb and index finger meet in the center of the thin loops, to wrap my fingers through them. I don't know why I like it, but I do. I'm sure all the kids who grew up before me in our home with our sunflower tablecloth loved it just as much. But Grandpa won't admit it, and Dad neither, not even Katarina. I don't know how it's only *my* fingers that leave stains. But if Mom had grown up in this home with this sunflower tablecloth, she would've understood why I love it, whether she'd admit it or not. And just so it's clear, I do try to remember to touch it *only* when my hands are clean. I forget only sometimes.

"How's Grandpa's dove?" Grandpa asks, bending to feel my forehead.

I just look at him. I don't know what to say.

"Still has the fever," Mom says, exhaling a lot of air and shaking her head left and right.

Grandpa knits his eyebrows. "Aunt Fatima says she'll bake you Zhito cake when you get all well," he says to me.

Grandma used to bake Zhito cake for my birthdays, and Aunt Fata and I helped her prepare the layers. Aunt Fata's Zhito cake tastes the same as Grandma's, I know for sure. She made it for us this past Christmas because Grandma had already died.

Grandpa's heavy, rubbery hand weighs down the top of my head. "You must get well to eat your cake, you know that." He raises his eyebrows and nods, staring at me. "Aunt Fatima says you can have the whole cake if you want."

I've never been allowed more than a piece at a time, because Mom and Grandma were always afraid I'd get sick to my stomach. Luckily, Dad saves his piece and lets me have it in secret. But when I look up at Mom now, she nods. If I didn't have pneumonia, I think I'd be jumping as high as the eagle's nest on top of the cedar tree at the edge of the clearing.

Grandpa looks at Dad with a scrunched-up face again. Dad sighs, then moves my legs off of his lap and onto a cushion. When he gets up, he kisses me on my forehead, and he and Grandpa go into Grandma's bedroom, where Grandpa sleeps alone now. I'm afraid Mom will leave, too, but she just follows them with her eyes as the oak floor planks groan underneath their feet, and they close the heavy door behind them.

I trail the silky thread on Grandma's blanket with my index finger. Cross-flower- rhombus. Cross-flower-rhombus. The whole Zhito cake for me.

Oh, how I looove my Aunt Fata!

Aunt Fata and Uncle Bekim are not *really* our aunt and uncle, even though we all call them that. They call Dad their *sinovac,* and Katarina and me and Petar and Simonida their grandkids. You call someone sinovac, your little son, when your brother has a son. That way, if something happens to your brother, you care for your brother's kids as if they were your own kids. That's what Grandma explained to me. Sinovac for a boy and *sinovica* for a girl, and they're really your son and daughter.

But Uncle Bekim and Grandpa are not *really truly* brothers. They are *brothers-by-milk*— oldest and best friends. When Uncle Bekim's mother died in labor with him, Grandpa's mom, who'd just had Grandpa herself, took to nursing him. That's how they grew up together and became brothers-by-milk.

Uncle Bekim went to the Second War with Grandpa and Grandpa's younger brother, my great-uncle Yovan. Their eyes always water at the same time when they mention Grandpa's younger brother. Grandpa and Uncle Bekim dug a grave together with sharp rocks and their own hands somewhere in Greece for him.

I don't like it when they talk about my great-uncle Yovan. I don't know where to look when their faces turn that sad. I imagine them putting this boy Yovan into the muddy ground and then I start crying, thinking about my cousin Petar in a grave like that. Or Dad, whose name is also Yovan. It scares me that Grandpa named his son, my dad, after his dead brother. But I still wrote all that down in my diary. We must not forget Great-Uncle Yovan, even if it makes us sad.

Aunt Fata is Uncle Bekim's wife. As soon as she and Grandma married Uncle Bekim and Grandpa and then moved to their husbands' homes, they became besties. I guess they're still besties, because you don't stop loving people just because they die. Like Grandma said.

But anyway, at our family gatherings and their family gatherings, we're always all together. They really are like family.

Grandpa told me once that he and Uncle Bekim each wanted to be best man at the other's wedding, but neither our bishop nor Uncle Bekim's imam allowed it. Grandpa said that would've made them real brothers, not just brothers-by-milk. *That's an old tradition from way back, and we'd both honor it—when you are best men at each other's weddings, your two families become one family.* That's what Grandpa told me.

But Grandpa also told me that would've made Uncle Bekim's grandsons my real family, like cousins, and then I wouldn't be able to marry either of them. I don't even want to marry Abdul or Ismet! They're not even in first grade yet, and they always pull on my shirt to ask if Simonida and I will take them wherever we're going. I'd be happy to be a real family and to never marry them.

When I asked Grandpa why our bishop and their imam didn't let them become one family, Grandpa told me it's because our religions are not the same, and in a wedding, you need to pray the same, cross yourself the same, or bow the same, so you can make a proper promise to God that you can be best man.

I think, though, that our bishop and their imam thought that Grandpa and Uncle Bekim were already brothers, because they look so much alike. I guess that's what happens when you nurse from the same milk, like Uncle Bekim's twin grandsons, Abdul and Ismet. I said to Grandpa that our bishop and their imam probably thought it was not proper for them to become brothers twice-over as best men, but Grandpa said that both the bishop and the imam were in the wrong.

*

'Ayde u livade, dva bela chadora, nane mila
'Ayde u livade, dva bela chadora.

The buzzing from Mom's voice is coming back into me again. I move my head a little to have one ear completely on her chest. I like feeling her voice from the inside.

When I move my head, I see the workroom door is open. It makes me very sad. Grandma died two months ago already, and there has been no *poselo* with the other village women this winter at all, but the workroom is still left just as she always had it. It's the most colorful room in our home. Tapestries hang on every wall, ones that show the same landscapes in different seasons. I know all those landscapes by heart. I just need to look through the windows in the winter, the summer, or the spring, and they're all there, just like on the workroom tapestries.

But my favorite tapestry is the one with our family tree. The names of twelve generations of Popovics are spread across the whole wall. Grandma added Katarina's name and my name to the tree, forty days after we were each born. Mom will have to add our husbands' and our kids' names. That's the tradition—if your grandma's alive, she adds the people you marry and your kids to the tree, and if not, your mom does it.

I'm a little upset at whichever great-grandma many times over started the family tree tapestry long ago, though. She should've used smaller stitches for the first generation's names and left more space for all the generations that were coming after them. When Mom adds the names of our husbands and kids all the way on the bottom, they will be so small, I fear no one will be able to read them without Grandpa's magnifying glass. Katarina and I will have to marry men with short first and last names, because our last names will change when we marry, so there needs to be space to stitch them in, too. And we'll also have to give our kids short names, so they can all fit. I wish the great-grandma who started it all had thought of us more.

Grandma said to me that maybe she and I could start a new tapestry, to be ready for Katarina's grandkids and my grandkids to add their names to it. But then she died, and I have yet to learn to weave a tapestry. I'll do it, though—start a new one with small letters, so that my great-grandkids many times over won't be upset with me. I'll just need to get well and eat my Zhito cake first.

From the couch, I can see all ten shades of dyed yarn drooping on metal hooks in Grandma's workroom. They're all dried now, since it was Grandma herself who hung them wet, a week before she died.

I described Grandma's workroom in my diary. I know that's silly, because the workroom will stay like this forever, and everyone will always know about it, but I described it anyway. I like to remember Grandma in it.

I can't see her woven baskets from here, but I know they stand ready with yarn next to the wooden loom. I know that the loom smells of cedar, like the long branches Dad saws into logs after his May pruning. The legs of the loom are so smooth and slick that I love gliding my palms along them and smelling the cedar close-up. But my hands and face need to be washed first—Grandma made me remember, so the loom wouldn't spoil for many generations after us. I've forgotten to do it only sometimes, but I'll be careful all the time from now on.

This is the same warp-weighted loom that Great-Grandma used when she weaved Grandma's cross-flower-rhombus blanket I have covering me now. Great-Grandma was Grandma's mom from Orahovac, but she died when Grandma was a little girl, and because Grandma was her only daughter who survived, she inherited both the loom and the blanket. That's how we have them now—the loom in the workroom and the blanket on me.

The yarn on the loom is weighed down by stones with holes drilled through them, to keep the wool threads taut, and to prevent them from knotting. Grandma explained all this to me. But I've never been allowed in the workroom on my own because of the *thunder*. They censure me as soon as the door creaks open, and I have to sneak in when no one is looking.

The heavy loom weights hanging off of the long yarn threads sound like thunder when you clink and clank them against one another. But I never-ever wanted to knot the yarn or break the stones, I just wanted to create thunder. And I for sure never wanted to mar my nails purple. It's so silly of them all to ask me if that's what I wanted, to hurt my fingers so they ached for days afterward.

Only Dad never asked me that. I think Dad secretly wants to create thunder, too, but he's a grown-up and he has to behave. He told me that when I asked if he wanted to chase each other through the puddles. I told him I don't want to be a grown-up if I'll have to behave all the time, but Dad says I don't have to. He says I can be any way I want to be, and I'll be just right. Even if I break loom weights to create thunder. *I'll just dress your fingers in broadleaf plantains to heal, like Grandma always did for you.* That's what Dad told me, but in secret, so Mom wouldn't get upset with us. Mom wants me to behave all the time, the way Katarina does.

When I sneak into the workroom now—I mean, when I don't have pneumonia—I just sit on Grandma's stool. It almost feels like she's there. Maybe that's why I saw Mom pretending like she didn't see me go in last week. She knows I haven't broken a single stone since Grandma died. I want it all to be there forever, just as she left it.

I wish so much that Grandma and all her poselo women would come back. I promise I'd be patient and let Grandma and all of them teach me how to embroider and crochet and stitch. I'd learn how to weave a tapestry for the new family tree. I really would! And I wouldn't break anything ever again! I promise with my proper *Pioneer's word*.

I'm really sorry I never listened to Grandma and learned how to work with my hands when she was alive. She used to slip in the suggestion, between my blanket-calculation lessons, that it was high time for me to get busy with my own dowry.

Katarina, fully ten years old, has already embroidered herself two pairs of perfect pillows, with the multi-colored message *May the Good Lord Bless Us with Health, Harmony and a Houseful of Children* stitched on each pillowcase, which Mom sewed out of dazzling white cotton. The pillowcases are already starched and deposited in Katarina's dowry chest, and she's now working on matching bedsheets.

But my Mara, Grandma used to say to me, *you'd prefer to jump into a rainwater barrel full of tadpoles.*

Now I wish I listened to her better and was less of a *little rascal.*

No nice boy will ever marry a girl who can't crochet a lace tablecloth, Child. Grandma would point at our long oak table draped with the sun-flower-lace tablecloth, now covered with a clear vinyl because somehow only the stains from *my* fingers stayed on it, and she'd tell me that's what I need to learn to make in order to marry a nice boy.

The Nestorovic girls, with their dowry chests full to the brim, will snatch the nicest boys from all of you, she'd say with raised eyebrows. But Slavica and Sonya Nestorovic are practically grown-ups already at twelve and fourteen, four and six years older than me, so how can I possibly compare to them!

Then Grandma died, and now I don't know how to learn to make all these things. Mom will teach me, but she works at her post office job and doesn't have as much time for me as Grandma did. So I worry about it a little.

Now, I twist my head a bit lying on Mom's chest, to see our dining table better. I promise myself that I'll never-ever again put my greasy fingers on the sunflower tablecloth. I promise that when I get well, I'll count the hooks and the number of stitches and remember exactly what Grandma said about the *tablecloth crocheted to perfection.* I'll count the hooks and then make it. I promise with my proper Pioneer's word.

I must learn to crochet to perfection, because I need to marry a nice boy. I'm scared that if I don't fill my dowry chest, I might have to marry one of these new boys in the village. And I need to give Simonida the same warning, otherwise she and I will be in real trouble.

When Grandma died in October, Mom folded away the sunflower tablecloth, spreading Grandma's blanket on the dining table instead, and then Dad laid Grandma on it. I asked why she wasn't covered with her blanket, instead of putting it underneath her. *It's protecting her from the draft,* Dad said. But Grandma was so cold and yellow-pale, I worried for her very much.

Two days before she died, when she couldn't get up from her bed anymore, Grandma told me to remember what Simonida and I promised to our Saint Nicholas. She said that death is a part of life, that she'd be all right, and that she'd look after me from wherever she was. But when she was laid on our table, I still couldn't stop worrying for her. I held her hand to try to warm her until Dad said it was time to put her in the casket.

After Grandma was buried, Mom thrashed and aired Grandma's blanket under the roof of the log shed, and now it's mine. *As a catch-up for Mara's dowry,* Grandma said to Mom before she died. At least I have something now for my dowry to help me marry a nice boy.

When I don't have pneumonia, I can smell Grandma in her blanket, like a whiff of valley flowers on a cool spring day. She told me once it was her mom's smell, but I know it's Grandma's. I wish I could smell it now, but I can't even smell the vinegar stink from my wrapped feet.

*

'Ayde u chadora, bolna moma lezhi, nane mila
'Ayde u chadora, bolna moma lezhi.

Mom stops humming when we hear the pull on the handle on Grandma's bedroom door. Dad walks out into the main room toward us, looks at Mom only for a moment, and I can feel how Mom holds her breath. When she sighs, her sigh is all cut up, like a sob-sigh, and my head bounces on her chest in the same way my fingers bounce down Grandma's old washboard.

Before Dad closes Grandma's bedroom door, I see Grandpa, standing in front of the cross hanging on the wall beside their bed where Grandma used to sleep. He's praying. Grandma's dad carved that cross out of *orah*, a walnut tree branch from his own yard in Orahovac. He wanted Grandma to have the cross as a piece of Orahovac, to protect them in their married life.

Grandma told me that when she felt homesick for her girlhood home, she would touch the cross and feel that she was back there, with her dad and mom and brothers and their families, and with everyone back in Orahovac.

Since Grandma died, I sneak into her bedroom when Grandpa is at Uncle Bekim and Aunt Fatima's and touch her cross. Then I feel like Grandma is back here with me. But I won't write that in my diary. It's our secret—Grandma's and mine.

1995: San Francisco
Love Story

Will sits next to me at my first Barsync, and I try to cover my embarrassment from staring at his bare belly a moment ago. I know there's no hiding it—it's inscribed in my burning face. I don't know where to look, so I just smile aimlessly at everyone. Then I see Eric two seats from Will, his eyes fixed on me. I don't understand his look, and I feel an urge to just leap up and leave.

Ace of Base is playing loudly, and it's a relief that I know the lyrics. I sing along inside me as a girl telling a boy not to turn around to see her heart torn apart as he's leaving her. I try to disappear within the words and melody.

Will says something to me, but the song is so loud, we have to lean in toward each other before I can hear him. I have to fight the musk around him that makes me want to lean in closer.

"I've never been to Kentucky," he says into my ear. "How did you like it?"

It takes me a moment to understand the question, feeling his breath on my face. "I liked it... I liked it very well. It's slow there."

He gives me that sudden, hijacking smile, and I wonder how I could've ever pegged him as an intruder.

"Aye." He nods, cocking his head sideways. "It's nice when it's slow."

It's too intense looking at him and being so close. My breathing speeds up and I instinctively turn toward Isabella again. She and Stacy are laughing about something, and as soon as I look their way, Stacy pulls her chair toward me and leans over Isabella. I regret turning away from Will.

"I'm telling Isabella what I bought today." She stops for a moment, and then adds, barely controlling her laughter, "I bought a calendar… with Georgia O'Keeffe's flowers."

The first time I saw Georgia O'Keeffe's flowers in my high school art textbook, I rushed so fast to turn the page that it accidentally ripped. There was no way, I thought, that the printers obeyed education rules with such explicit pictures.

Isabella's and Stacy's heads bob in the same laughing rhythm as I remember my high school textbook. They look like teenage girls conspiring to do something they would never get parental permission for. After a moment, they calm a bit.

"For her *boss*." Isabella raises her eyebrows high and nods.

Stacy snorts, prompting Isabella to roar with laughter, all control escaping them again.

I smile, all the while wishing I could turn back to Will.

"She got Georgia O'Keeffe's flowers for her sixty-three-year-old—"

"Today!" Stacy injects. "It's his birthday today."

"Sixty-three years old." A pause. "Today…"

They nod at each other, stifling more laughs.

"Married, with grandchildren, boss." Isabella lifts her index finger to emphasize *boss*.

Their bodies shake with spasm-like quivers, as if they're possessed.

"Whoops." I open my eyes wide and grimace, cringing for Stacy. "Yikes."

It's wonderful to witness this laughter, this complete abandonment with people that belong together. I don't recall laughing like Stacy and Isabella since Milan, a boy from our village back home, caught my cousin Simonida and me peeing on the creek embankment. Long ago, before everyone started leaving.

But it's Will's presence I feel, half an arm's length away.

"I thought I was so cultured, getting art for him," Stacy continues. "His wife works for the GAP headquarters, and she was the one who lobbied to get the original Lichtensteins for their cubicles."

"She did, yea." Isabella adds, "Their grandkids love comics."

Stacy nods and continues, "He always talks about the Lichtenstein above her desk, and I thought... oh dear!" Her head shakes left-right, left-right. "I was rushing this morning, just in-and-out of the store, and look." She extends her hand, like offering something to Isabella and me. "I handed it to him, all wrapped up with a bow on top"—she mimics making a bow with her hands—"thinking it was a Lichtenstein calendar that his grandkids can see when they come to his office, and when he opened it, in front of everyone... can you imagine... I..." she pauses, gasping through laughter. Her palms go up to the sides of her head over her ears. "*Black Iris*, *Blue Flower*, *Red Cannas*." Her head and her whole torso shake as she tries to articulate.

Isabella's tears are streaming down her cheeks now.

"The whole office saw it," Stacy concludes.

Everyone at the table is now listening. Rob, who is sitting to Stacy's other side, describes how she nearly cried on the phone after it happened, how she told him she was quitting and moving to another planet. Isabella and Stacy laugh even harder, and everyone at the table is laughing with them.

I take advantage of the clamor to pull my chair a notch away from Isabella's and turn slightly back toward Will. I sneak a peek at him. He's smiling, though he doesn't seem engulfed in Stacy's story.

I lean against the back of my chair, completely facing forward. I put my forearm down on my armrest on the side toward Will, without realizing his arm is already on his armrest, aligned closely with my own. When my arm comes down, it feels as if his arm moves ever-so-nearer to mine, enough to feel each other's skin. His arm hair silky and tingly.

I instinctively shrink myself in my seat and move my arm away just a touch. He couldn't possibly be that near deliberately, I'm sure. It's like when someone's knee unexpectedly leans against yours under the table, and you know that if you let it be, once the other person realizes your knee is not a part of the table, it'll be clear that you attributed meaning to an accidental touch.

But I immediately regret moving my arm away. I stare at the center of the table, glued to my seat. I'm aware that everyone except for Will and me is caught up in the calendar affair.

Then Will says something to me. I turn to him, and we lean toward each other once more. For the second time, I have to take a moment to understand his words.

"Who's your favorite Yugoslavian author?" he repeats.

His face is close to mine, and it feels as if he's inhaling me with each breath. His arm hair is brushing up against my skin again, and I'm not sure whether it's because I moved closer or he did. I remain perfectly still, holding my breath, knowing that I'll choke on my words if I try to speak. I feel how the music, laughter, and words around us gradually seep out of my consciousness. It's just Will, his musk, and his arm hair. I distantly realize that his mention of Yugoslavia doesn't sound invasive or threatening. As if it's not a country in the headline news.

I guess he sees I'm unable to say anything coherent, so he continues, "I heard of Andric." He pronounces Andric with a *ch* sound at the end, the way it is originally spoken.

"Yes." I nod, trying to sound casual as I form a thought. "He won the Nobel for Literature." Then I look back into his eyes, and again I don't know what to say.

"Are you familiar with Oscar Wilde?" he says suddenly, as if his own words come out of thin air, all on their own, surprising him.

"Yes!" I pull my head back from Will and spark back into my senses. I still have to nearly shout and strain to hear him, but now I can think. Our arms stay still against one another, though. "I've seen his plays at the Belgrade National Theatre."

Will cannot know how much I love Oscar Wilde. That his collection of plays was the first book I ever read in English. A lifetime ago, when Simonida and I were in second grade, our teacher, Teacher Danica, put up a school show of *The Importance of Being Earnest*. I was Gwendolen and Simonida was Cecily. For months afterward, Simonida and I imagined ourselves as Gwendolen and Cecily taking tea on the haystack in front of our homes.

"He's so funny, how he satirizes his society," I say.

"Aye. He's a master of wit, he is." Again, that hijacking smile you cannot but smile back at. "'Ignorance is like a delicate exotic fruit; touch it and the bloom is gone.'"

"*Earnest*, I know. Mrs. Bracknell. She's my favorite character in all of theatre, I think."

"I like Miss Prism, too." He makes a stern face, his eyebrows trying to connect over two vertical cleaves squeezing the bridge of his nose. "'The good ended happily and the bad unhappily. That is...'"

"'...What fiction means.'" I jump to finish his quote, and we propel each other into laughter.

"There was a good turn-of-the-century theatre scene in Belgrade, too."
I feel like he's screwed in a fuse, and I'll never stop talking now. "We
have a few great satirical playwrights, somewhat of the Wilde sort. I
remember an anecdote about when one of them, Nusic, in the early
1900s, crossed the River Sava into the Austro-Hungarian Empire, north
of Belgrade, Yugoslavia today, and when the Austro-Hungarian border
officer asked him his occupation, he said he was a writer. The border officer threatened him with arrest if he continued monkeying around and
ordered him to better declare what he did for a living. Nusic repeated
he was a writer. The border officer, seeing that Nusic was dead serious,
turned around to his scrivener and waved the writer away as a lost cause.
'Record: Unemployed.'"

We laugh again, but Will is looking so intensely at me that I feel like he's
swallowing my thoughts. I drop my eyes to his shoulders and think about
how their width could wrap you invisible in them. His shirt entirely un-
successful in its attempt to disguise the rounded muscles underneath.

"Not a respectable profession... to be a writer."

I nod. "Do you write?"

"Nay," he says with a slight head wave. "I read, though." His *though*
sounds like *thoy,* and I think I've never heard English so soft and mellifluous. "You?"

"I used to. Diaries. But now I have no language anymore."

He nods in understanding. "Language is a curious thing, I've noticed, so
different from everything else. It takes years to acquire a new one and
almost no time to lose the old."

I wish I'd been able to explain it that way.

A waiter moves around our table, and I realize that everyone is ordering
drinks, the laughter has subsided, and the talking groups have split up
again after discussing the calendar ordeal. Eric's gaze makes me feel
uncomfortable again, but I don't linger on it. When the waiter steps behind us, Will raises his arm that was brushing against mine and opens

his palm toward me, an offer for me to order first. When he lifts his arm, I immediately wish he'd put it back.

"A Fuzzy Navel, please."

"I beg your pardon." Will's eyes open wide, his eyebrows lifted in question, his full smile at the ready.

I blush all over again, realizing for the first time the meaning of the drink name as I remember his exposed belly. "Peach schnapps… I mean, orange juice…"

The waiter lifts his head up from the notebook where he recorded my order and tells Will, straight-faced, "A cocktail name, Fuzzy Navel."

I regret ordering it and make a mental note to not order it again with people from work. When a college friend gave me a sip to try in Kentucky, the smell reminded me of the peach brandy Dad brewed in Kosovo. I generally don't like alcohol at all, and if I ever order a drink, it's only this one. But it had never occurred to me to think about what the name stands for until this moment.

"I'll have the same," Will says, and extends his arm back along the armrest, where mine lies in waiting.

I wish this moment would never pass.

Rob breaks it, however. He asks the whole table if we are up for dancing after this drink. I keep quiet and so does Will. The rest of the people say yes, and propositions for the place start being shouted around the table and over the music. I don't know any of the places they mention, I just feel the hair and the heat from Will's arm. And his musk. A place is decided on.

"It's a block away," Eric shouts out. I feel this directed at me, rather than anyone else.

Then Lizzy's boyfriend shows up, and we all squeeze a bit closer to make space for another chair. I fasten my gaze to the center of the table, barely breathing. I fear turning toward Will, but my arm is not moving. Neither is his. Isabella asks me something about a blouse I have on, and I tell her I bought it on sale in a store on Fillmore. The drinks come, Lizzy's boyfriend orders his, and we all cheer, glasses clinking in the middle of the table. Will's arm is away again, but his body is so close, I smell it and feel its heat even as I'm turned to Isabella.

Will and I don't look at each other again until we all put money on the table and get up to leave. I pull at my chair, but the back leg is stuck against Will's chair. My chair tilts and I tilt with it. Will's hand is on my arm to stabilize me, and his warm palm on my bare skin sends a surge through me. I feel for a moment his thumb stroking my arm as he's holding it, like he's taking a small tactile taste of my skin. But his caress is so short, I wonder if I imagined it.

I notice Eric's face and register his annoyance. It seems irrelevant. I only know I want more of Will's hand on my arm, just as I know I should know better than to want it.

*

When we're outside, Eric is next to me, telling me about this club where we're going and about what cool world music it plays. He was there with his pals and that's why he suggested it. I'm sure to love it, he says. He speaks quickly, as if trying to make up for lost time. I smile and nod and say I'm sure it's a great place.

I turn around when we get to the crosswalk and see Will walking alongside Lizzy and her boyfriend. Their heights and sizes make them look like matryoshka dolls. Will is the big one that can fit them all. I felt his eyes calling to me even as Eric spoke and we walked. I remind myself to be discreet, that I need this job.

The club is really just a few blocks from Market, and I'm relieved to realize I'll know how to get back to a bus stop.

When we go in, the club is not crowded. It's still early, and the music reminds me of belly dancing. We get drinks and take over a small bar table with three stools. We pile our purses, backpacks, and jackets on them, and I follow everyone to the dance floor, a glass of mineral water in my hand. When I get to the dance floor, I notice that Will is still at the table. I look at him, and he shakes his head left-right-left-right and mouths *No dancing.* He sits on a stool, another Fuzzy Navel in his hand, and looks in our direction. It's hard to move freely with his eyes on me. I can't tell for sure he's looking specifically at me, but I feel it.

After a few songs, I'm exhausted. Too much excitement for one day. *Enough,* I tell myself. *Know thy measure.*

We're all dancing in a circle. I smile, as do all the others, and after I finish my mineral water a couple songs later, I point at the restroom and leave the circle.

The club is filling in with people now. The girls in tank tops, phosphorus on them glowing fluorescent in semi-darkness, make the place look like an act in a magic show. I put my empty glass on one of the shelves alongside the wall. After the restroom, I squeeze through to our table, tell Will I'm leaving, dig out my jacket and backpack, and wave goodbye to everyone on the dance floor. I do it all quickly but still notice Eric's look of surprise.

Will asks me if he may walk me out, and I don't really know what to want. I'm spent, but I'd also like whatever this is with Will to go on. Besides, it'd be nice to have someone walk with me to the first Muni bus headed up to California, I think.

I shrug my shoulders at Will as an answer, and he grabs his leather jacket and flaps it onto his back. I push really hard on the black metal exit door, but it resists any movement. Will steps to my side, his arm grazing my hair, his warmth radiating everywhere, and he thrusts the door open. We walk into the unusually warm spring night and I shiver.

"Here." He places his leather jacket on my shoulders before I can refuse it. It's weighing down on me as his musk, exuding from the jacket, enwraps me speechless. I don't know if I say anything in thanks.

"To where?"

"California and Fillmore."

"You lead."

That's all the exchange between us before we get to the streetlight at Eighth and Market. I know I'll take bus number nineteen to my place from here. I spend every Sunday afternoon around Market and Hyde, so I know this area well. But I still wish for Will to walk with me a little farther.

We stand and wait for the streetlight to turn green.

"What do you do when you're not working?" Will asks.

No one has asked me this question since high school.

"I like farmers' markets." When I realize what I said, I look at him, half-expecting him to laugh at me. "I like roaming through them." The way his eyes are on me, I wonder if he hears my words. "I like the smell of fresh vegetables. Tomatoes... I like tomatoes," I continue, straining to explain.

"Aye." His voice seems to say he expected no other answer. "There's something about it, the scent of tomatoes."

When I was little, we all grew tomatoes, but Uncle Sima and Aunt Vera had a whole orchard bubble with *yabuchar*s. My cousin Simonida and I would pick the squiggly heirloom giants, rub them against our clothes, and bite into them like apples. That's what I seek in farmers' markets.

"And sage... and rosemary," Will adds.

"And sage, and rosemary," I confirm. I'm guessing his mom or his grandma baked bread, too.

"So, you go to markets to smell herbs and tomatoes?"

"Well, there's a lady there." I point behind Orpheum Theatre in the direction of the Heart of the City Farmers' Market. "I go to her after church. She's very kind."

She has the warmth of home. But I don't tell him that.

Will looks in the direction I point. From where we stand, it's impossible to see the statue of Simon Bolivar where Mrs. Jane sets up a stand on Sundays.

"And she sells tomatoes."

"Yes."

"I see."

When we cross Market, we turn left on Grove and up Larkin, left on Eddy and up Polk, following the bus line I plan to take once Will thinks of rushing back to the club. On Polk and Post, bus number nineteen stops right in front of us, but Will makes no move to usher me toward it, and I'm relieved. We continue to walk slowly and speak slowly. I know he'll think of a bus any moment now, stop at the next bus stop, wait for me to board, and head back to be with the others at the club. But as long as he doesn't, I'll enjoy this. Whatever it is.

"You're from Belfast?" The moment I say it, I know I'm a fool.

He responds before I can ask something else or make amends.

"Aye, Belfast." A pause. "I'm from the grand city of *Beal Feirste.* Belfast." He sighs as if his meaning is ironic. "And you're from Beograd." He pronounces it as it's meant—*beo grad*, the white city.

"Yes," I say, and for the first time ever since Dad died and I switched to the Belgrade accent, I feel a pang of guilt for lying about it. I rush to continue before I can think through the following words: "When I was little, Dad read to us about the Troubles."

He sighs and turns his head away from me. I imagine his thick eyebrows nearly connecting.

Full stop, Marica! Full stop, right there! I don't apologize, I just go quiet, hold my breath, and walk. *Curious, prying, that's all he sees.*

"All the world's been reading about it," is all he says after a pause. He doesn't ask for details and doesn't provide any, but there's a lifetime of weight in those words.

Like all the world is reading about Yugoslavia, I think. Like all of Serbia was reading about us, the Kosovars, back then.

For some reason, his tone makes me feel weightless, as if he recognizes beauty in all that pain, beauty in having had a past. As if this Will and I are of the same flock.

We continue walking without words, slowly, together. We take a left on California, and the traffic stops us at Octavia.

"Isn't this pretty," I say, pointing at a Queen Anne house with a turret on the corner.

"Beautiful."

I look at him to say that this is the spot from which you can see the mountain range for the first time. *Just look down California, straight ahead toward the Financial District.* I want to point out the exact spot at the intersection from which the city looks like it's rising out of the mountains, almost as if carved out of them. I don't know why, but I feel he'd like to know.

When I look at Will, ready to say all this, I see his smile directed at me, and I forget all about the mountains. *Beautiful.* Despite his heavy jacket on my shoulders, I shiver again. The wide shoulder epaulets bend down toward my elbows, and they warm and weigh me down at the same time. I just keep quiet.

The cars are gone, and we continue across the street.

When we reach my building, I thank him for walking me, unlock the entrance door, and go in. I don't turn back. I've never learned how to take leave of anyone, I know that about myself. I guess it might be true what the doctors said after Dad died, about separation anxiety. Or it was the abandonment issue? They feel the same to me.

I run up the steps to my apartment, then realize that I still have his jacket on. I run back downstairs, jerk open the entrance door, and find him not ten steps away. He's not rushing to get back to the club.

"William," I shout, and he turns back before I sound the second syllable of his name.

I take his jacket off of my shoulders, fold it over, and hand it to him. He extends his arm to take it.

"I'm sorry, I forgot."

"No matter." As he's pushing his arm through the sleeve, and the jacket collar bends toward his face, he puts his nose into it, and for a split second, he closes his eyes.

I get the shivers again and feel like my legs won't hold me.

His jacket is on him, and he looks at me with a smile—not hijacking this time but fulfilling—somewhat in a daze and simultaneously all present, in the moment.

This is how he looks when he's being intimate, I think, and quickly look down to the pavement, afraid he can read the thought in my eyes.

"Thank you," he says.

I know he's wrapping up our time, but I have no strength in my legs to turn around and leave as quickly as I did a minute ago. I just linger there.

Then he breathes in deeply and breaks the spell. With the exhale, he says, "Catch you Monday, then."

"Yes, Monday," I confirm.

He waits for me to unlock the entrance door again, and he pulls the door open for me, his body very close.

I'm inside, not running up the stairs, just putting one foot up in front of the other. I don't turn around to see if he's still standing there.

Today: Seattle
Another Family

The kids are in their bedroom, putting up the ornaments for Emma's birthday party. Will had begun breaking down the base, the last part that's left of Ugly, when an animal growled from below the top board. I now stand inside the house, looking at Will through the slight opening of the back door.

Will's baritone calls out toward the fence, "Mike, there's an animal coming your way, lad!" Then he hits the board with the back of the axe again, along the planks, to prompt the animal to race out. He heads toward the garage, where he opens then closes the door. I close the back door and wait behind it.

Then Mariah and Emma start yelling and banging at their bedroom window that overlooks the backyard. I rush to them.

"Pa went into the garage—"

"So the animal can escape! But it's not! Look, Mama, look!" Mariah's voice overpowers Emma's.

"Let me tell her!" Emma is annoyed.

"But you always talk and never let me say anything!"

Emma rolls her eyes at her sister, knowing full well that Mariah will let her tell the tale today. It's her birthday. Emma continues, emphasizing every other word, opening her eyes wide and speeding up as she goes along. Her words merge into one sound by the end of the sentence.

"Mama, Pa hit the board with the hammer and then went inside the garage, but the animal isn't moving, see?!"

And indeed, the growling creature is staying put, stubborn, not accepting the gift of a safe escape. The three of us are looking through the window screen when Will comes back from the garage and strikes a blow at the end of the plank again. He hits it harder, but away from the animal. He's cautious—he doesn't want to injure it, he just wants it gone. Then he steps away again, toward the garage.

We hear growling again but see no movement.

Will comes back to the shed base and looks at it. He goes into the garage and returns with the gasoline canister for our lawn mower. He sprinkles several drops of gasoline on the very end of the board, away from the sound, and lights it. The fire smolders for a few moments without burning through the top board, and the animal's sounds grow louder, but it stays staunchly underneath the base. The animal is firm even in its assaulted lair.

Emma fidgets in front of me and I realize I've been holding my breath. I put my hands on her shoulders and breathe. Will's hammer taps along the planks again, but the animal is not moving. The smoldering fire causes more growling and nothing else. I close the kids' bedroom window overlooking the yard, confirm it's locked tightly, order them not to open it until I say so, and go to the backyard. As I come out, Will is scratching the back of his head.

"What now?" he says to himself. His eyebrows are knitted, and he's biting one side of his lip. He says louder, "Mike, what do I do now? I don't want to hurt it." He thinks for a moment. "I can't light it anymore, it could be scorching underneath there."

"Hmm." Mike is standing right by the fence, looking over it at the base.

"Oh, I'll pour a wee bit of petrol inside the cracks. Maybe the smell will get it out."

"Yeah, okay, that might work," Mike reasons.

Will spills a few drops of gasoline in between the cracks in the top board, several feet from the place where the sound is coming from. "Go back in and close the door," he tells me before he retreats into the garage again. "Mike, you should go in, too."

I go inside the house, close the back door, and rejoin the kids in their bedroom. The three of us are at the window, expectant. Several minutes pass without anything happening, and I start heading back toward the kitchen and the backyard. Just at that moment, the kids shout:

"It's a raccoon! It's a raccoon! Mama, come, it's a raccoon!"

I turn back and see the biggest raccoon I've ever seen in my life. It's almost the size of a small brown bear I once spied on through Grandma's bedroom window, way back. This raccoon takes a few steps toward the fence and Mike's plot, then it stops, all the while looking at its homestead. When it sees me, it starts back toward the hole under the board. I unlatch and open the window, grab the first loud toy, an old toy guitar that plays Hannah Montana tunes. I turn it to the loudest volume and beat on it, too.

"Go, shoo, go!" I yell.

The raccoon looks back at me and starts retreating. Then Mike's gentle shooing comes from his side of the fence. He's at his back entrance, ready to close the door to safety inside.

"Come on, raccoon, come on, baby. To the bushes. Come on."

Will comes out of the garage and stands in front of the shed base, not allowing it to return under the panel. The raccoon seems like it's debating which way to go—back to the lair or to the bushes. It unwillingly and slowly climbs the tree trunk on our side of the plot, and from there, goes to the garage roof. Then Mike tells us he sees it step into the bushes behind the garage.

As Mike tells us the raccoon is in the bushes, Will starts whacking away at the board again. After re-latching the kids' window, I come out of the house to watch him do it. At once I see something furry.

"It's a baby! It has a baby!" I shout.

Will freezes mid-strike. He takes a few steps back to look. "No wonder she didn't want to leave," he mumbles. "What do we do now?"

"Maybe get a box and put it in there," Mike says as he leans over the fence to look.

"But we can't touch it! She might not recognize the smell of it if we touch it! Like a cat," I say in a rush, afraid for the baby and its mother.

"I would maybe wear gloves?" Mike says, his voice deliberate and composed, as if calming a child.

Will gets a box and some paper towels from the garage, and I get my safety gloves from the deck table. I look up at the kids' bedroom and warn them with a finger wag to keep the window latched, to stay put and not come out until I let them.

I'm afraid of what the raccoon might do. I know I'd defend my young ones, so why wouldn't she? Mariah and Emma are staring, wide-eyed and open-mouthed, at the crack in the base where the baby is hiding.

Gloves on, I pick up the baby by the skin of its neck. It has almost no weight—it's brand new, but its eyes have opened. Then I see three more. They're all lying there, with completely spread-out legs and surprisingly long claws. They are the size of six-month-old kittens and not moving.

"Should I call the SPCA for you?" Mike asks. "Or that animal removal place, what's it called?"

"No!" I don't intend to shout. It just comes out that way. "Let *her* find them. *She* is the mother."

I lay them all in the box and put paper towels around them for heat. I hand the box over the fence to Mike, and he lays it, half-open, close to the bushes where she had gone.

"She's near somewhere, I promise you she is," he says gently, looking at me as he comes back to the fence.

Then I look up, and she is right on the ridge of the garage roof, half her body on one side, and half on the other. She must have missed the transfer of her babies and just come out as Mike took the box over. The way she looks, she could be crying. I don't know. She's all sagging, lifeless, as if just looking to see what's happening. Like she's thinking, *they're gone, I know, but I still need to see.*

Then the babies click. Her fur perks up first, then she stands up, looks down at her gouged-out home, then behind her, and with the next click, she disappears from sight.

The box is empty within minutes. Mike retrieves the box and hands it to Will, Will breaks it down and throws it along with the paper towels into the yard waste. I just stand there in front of the remains of the wooden base.

"Relocation. It's okay," Mike says, as if hand-picking each word. "She'll find a new home."

My eyes go to her exposed lair. Cozy, with wood shavings, and the concave area the size of her body. How safe she must have felt there.

"No, lad, not relocation." Will's voice is somber. "Ethnic cleansing."

Mike's expression takes a moment to turn to discomfort, then to disbelief. His face is frowning as if witnessing something distasteful, impolite. He abruptly turns around, like he's looking for something.

"But not genocide," I add, more to myself than to Will and Mike. "Ethnic cleansing, but not genocide."

Will puts down the axe on the serrated shed base, takes off his gloves, then comes to me. He puts one palm on my back and the other at the back of my head and draws me to his body.

When we separate, Mike is already somewhere out of sight, and the kids have come out to the backyard.

1983: Kosovo

Leaving Home I

It's only March, but the bear family has already come out of their lair. I'm so lucky, because now, for a whole week before we leave, I get to spy on the three cubs while they're still brand-new babies.

I have my shiny new binoculars Uncle Sima and Aunt Vera gave me for my ninth birthday last October. Simonida got her binoculars for her ninth birthday, eight days after I got mine, so now we both spy on the animals. We didn't get to have our birthday celebrations again this year, as last year it was Grandma's year of woe, and this year it's Grandpa's, but we still got our gifts.

These binoculars are the best gift ever! That's what I wrote in my diary number nine: *The best gift ever!* And they will stay the best gift ever, until next October when I turn ten, and Dad teaches me how to carve my own shepherd's flute. He promised he'd teach me despite Mom's raised eyebrows and her warnings every time we mention it. *Mara's still too little for those carving knives, Yovan.* But I know Dad will teach me. He always keeps his promises.

For now, with my shiny new binoculars, I get to spy all the way from Grandma's room on the bear cubs and all the animals sneaking through the forest. If things were normal in our village, Simonida and I would become official livestock and poultry guards. We've already designed badges for the two of us to pin to our school uniforms. And we'd deserve them, too!

Last Tuesday evening, for instance, I spotted a fox slipping into the Yovanovics' chicken coop. I bolted outside to tell them and to save the chickens, but then, even before Mom shouted an order to get back inside, I remembered that the Yovanovics were already gone. Like we'll be gone next week.

Simonida and I invented this spying game because Mom and Aunt Vera want to confine the two of us inside our homes all the time now. Since Grandpa died, then Dad stepped on that terrible nail when he was chasing me in the valley and his blood got poisoned, but especially since the whole summer thing, Mom and Aunt Vera have changed-unrecognizable. Everything is a deadly danger to them now, like we'll drop dead any minute or something.

They've been restricting everything we do. Like, we have to come home straight from school now. With Katarina and Petar! Simonida and I are not allowed to walk to and from school without my older sister and Simonida's older brother anymore. And we can never be outside our fenced yards. Ever! Except when we're at school. We can't even run to each other's homes without a chaperone anymore. Five houses over!

This makes us constantly get into trouble for having to figure out ways to sneak out, just to be together and run around the village. It's becoming especially hard for Simonida. Aunt Vera's eyes are everywhere, I swear, especially because she's not distracted with packing like Mom is.

But even when we manage to sneak out, everyone we see tells on us. Not the new families, of course, they don't care. But everyone else who's still in the village, Serbs and Albanians, they all tell on us. It's no fun at all.

When Simonida and I protest being made to stay inside the fenced yards, even Katarina and Petar give us lectures. *You two don't understand, can't you see the village is not the same anymore*, blah blah blah. So annoying. Simonida and I know very well how to recognize danger. We're only two years younger than the two of them, but they act all grown-up with us, like we're just little kids who need to have our hands held. So annoying!

They'll see when Simonida and I become the family story repositories for the Popovics and the Markovics. They'll see when everybody knows that it's Simonida and I who are not letting anyone be forgotten in our families!

I didn't write any of this in my diary, though.

But this new spying game is good, and I wrote all about it.

When Simonida and I can't be together, we spy on the animals and record everything about them. We write down their descriptions and spots and colors, all in detail. We even draw them, though Simonida's drawings look very perfect, and mine don't even look very much like animals. But never mind that. We record the time of day when we detect them, and we record all their movements. Then, when we can see each other, we exchange our records.

That way, if I saw a lynx lying in wait to hunt a grouse, for instance—which I'm very upset about, because the grouse is the most beautiful bird that has ever lived, with its feathered feet and wooing dance, and why wouldn't a lynx find a rat or a snake to hunt instead!—Simonida can track it another day, and I can track a chamois or a wild boar or another grouse burrowing into the snow, if she saw them first.

But we both look out for the bear family, of course. We spied on the sow in late October and spotted where she made her lair, so we've been looking out for her tracks every day since it started thawing last week. Then yesterday morning, a whole week before I leave, she came out with her three cubs. How lucky is that!

Dad says this is what scientists do, that scientists observe nature. Simonida and I would much rather be the village guards than scientists, but we decided it's okay to observe nature for a while. Until I return and things get back to normal.

Nothing has been normal in our village. Simonida and I know that very well. We go to school, we see things. But we'd never admit that to Katarina and Petar! And I'd never write about it in my diary.

Ever since August, when all eighteen new families came to our village with all their kids—more than eight in one family sometimes—and then the Serbian families started leaving, we've been playing mostly Serbs with Serbs and Albanians with Albanians.

I'm sorry for Uncle Bekim's twin grandsons, Abdul and Ismet. They just started first grade in September, but the new boys told them on the first day of school, in front of me and Simonida, that they'd break every bone in their bodies next time they saw them hanging around with the Serbs. They're only little kids, Abdul and Ismet. I don't know how these new boys could say such things, even if they're lies.

But Abdul is such a fighter, as little as he is. He shouted at them that he'll be like his Uncle Yovan when he grows up—he'll work in our Trepca Mine and his Uncle Yovan will teach him how to be a mine engineer.

The new boys slapped him on the head, laughed at him, and said that Dad wouldn't ever teach him anything, that he'd never come back from the hospital, that he'd die from the poison in the nail, and then Trepca Mine would be all Albanian. They said that no Serb would ever so much as sniff in there again. *We'll take your homes, dig up your graves, burn your monasteries and churches!* they shouted at Simonida and me, using very bad words. *You'll-be-no-more!* they yelled, and I could feel their spit spray all over my face.

When I told them they were liars, that Dad is recovering and coming home, they said that even if Dad recovers and keeps his leg, which they somehow knew the doctors said might be cut off, he'd get *cancer* from the poison and die.

I had to fight to not cry in front of them. Dad was in the hospital the whole of August and September with that nail poisoning after I badgered him to chase me, and I was very scared for him.

Then Simonida called them liars and stupid, and told them that *cancer* is an animal, not a disease. They called us *Serbian hors*, the way they call all of us girls at school, even Nedzada. Then Simonida shouted that they are stupid and pulled me and Abdul and Ismet into the school building. *Kosov-a, not Serbi-a! Kosov-a, not Serbi-a!* they shouted after us.

Simonida and I worry for Nedzada a lot. She's the only Albanian girl who still goes to school. None of the new families' girls go to school because their dads won't let them. This is what some of the nicer new boys told Simonida and me—that the girls are not allowed to study. And now Nedzada is the only Albanian girl left among us.

Her grandpa, Mister Farid, brings her to school every day and waits for her after the classes are over, but she cries every morning and begs him not to leave her. When her grandpa leaves, the new boys shout into her face that they'll kill her along with the Serbs if she comes again tomorrow. She just stands there, shrinking into the collar of her uniform, and cries with no sound.

Simonida and I tell Nedzada these boys are liars, but she now runs away from us, too. We used to jump rope and play hopscotch together all the time, but now she won't even stand with us.

Of course, Simonida and I know things are not normal in our village! How could Katarina and Petar think that we don't!

Dad is almost all well, though. He still hobbles, he's weak and slim, and he can't lift me up yet, but he walks on his foot, and his toes are not black anymore. His skin is still a little yellow, like Grandma's and Grandpa's skin when they lay on the table for their wakes, and that worries me a little. But three days ago, when he went for his six-month checkup, the doctors told him that there is no poison left in his body. It just needs to heal.

"So then," Mom's been asking, "why is it that we have to rush and leave, when the rest of the family is staying?"

But Dad would say nothing to that. Only that we must.

Uncle Bekim brings his healing herbs and teas for Dad three times a day.

He says it's good that we're leaving. But when he says it, his eyes turn so sad, like when he and Grandpa used to remember Grandpa's younger brother Yovan, the one who died in the Second War and they had to dig a grave somewhere in Greece for him with their own hands and then Grandpa named Dad after him. I don't think that Uncle Bekim really truly believes it's good that we're going.

Aunt Fatima is even sadder. She comes every day, too, bringing us soup and stew and lamb meat, even when it rains, and she walks with a cane as small and thin as she is, through mud and slush. Then she just sits with Mom, holds her own face in her hands, and cries and cries without a sound, only her bent back trembling.

When Aunt Fata doesn't cry, she speaks of the times when the three of us, Aunt Fata, Grandma, and I, used to make Zhito cake for my birthday and Dobosh cake for Abdul and Ismet's birthdays. She asks me if I remember how they used to tease me about my future husband and about my future mother-in-law, and how we used to laugh and laugh and laugh.

But then she turns all sad again, wanting me to promise that I would never forget those times. That I would never forget her and Grandma and all of us here. I try to assure her that as a family story repository, I have it all written down in my diary, but then she puts her head into her hands and starts crying again. Then I get so sad, I sit with her and just cry, too.

I'm not happy we're leaving! Not a smidge! Belgrade, as vast as it is, with as many people as it has, will never-ever be home. Not even for a little bit. This is home. Grandma's Kos-and-Met, Kosmet. Where Simonida and I can run around and become the official livestock and poultry guards with badges pinned to our uniforms.

Well, I wrote some of it in diary number nine. I did write about Dad's poisoned foot and the two months at the hospital, about how Uncle Bekim now comes every day to help him heal and Aunt Fata brings us food even through mud and slush, and about how we are leaving for a little bit. But I didn't write anything about how sad Uncle Bekim and Aunt Fata are. I tried, but then I would cry the whole time as I wrote and then smudge the fountain pen ink. I know I'll remember it all just when I look at the smudged pages.

*

I lay my shiny new binoculars on the windowsill and get ready to sneak out and meet Simonida. I'm a little sad that my binoculars will have to stay here when I leave, but Mom has already said that she won't let me take them. I'm allowed to take only one suitcase with my things, and I know that Mom will make me take my schoolbooks and clothes and whatever, but not my binoculars. Or my diaries! There are too many, Mom says, and they'd take too much space in my suitcase. I need to just remember it all, she says.

Ever since Dad came back from his six-month checkup three days ago and said we'd be leaving next week, Mom's been constantly folding and unfolding things in the main room. She's made three piles on the table, leaving only a small area for us to eat on. *What we'll have to leave*, *what we'll have to take*, and *what we'll take if it fits into the suitcases* take up almost the whole oak table. She sighs over the piles all the time and asks Dad a million times a day how she is to pack up everything into only six suitcases.

My shiny new binoculars and my diaries are in the group *What we'll have to leave*. It's okay. They'll be safe here until we return.

Well, no matter what Mom says about it, I'm going to take Grandma's blanket with me. I'll wear it as a cape instead of my winter coat.

Mom says I have to have my coat during the trip, and that the blanket can't fit into my suitcase with all the other stuff she's making me take. But I choose Grandma's blanket instead of the coat, no matter how angry that makes Mom. It's warm, it's pretty, it's Grandma's. It's a catch-up for my dowry, like Grandma said, so that I can marry a nice boy.

I'm taking Grandma's blanket with me, and that's that!

1995: San Francisco

Will Leaves

The weekend following the Barsync Friday when Will walked me home is passing somehow. Very slowly. I hope Will might call, but he doesn't. He cannot possibly have my phone number, I reason, it's not yet printed in the white pages, since I just moved here. But something still gives me hope.

I call Katarina and Mom on Saturday, as I always do. The calls are expensive, so we can never talk for long, but even five minutes a week with each of them feel like a lifeline. It's my Saturday morning and their Saturday night. All three of us can imagine what each other's lives look like with these calls: I'm beginning my weekend, Mom is getting ready to watch a movie or read a book before bedtime, and Katarina is getting ready to go out. These calls confirm that we still belong together despite the long three-and-a-half years we haven't seen each other. I miss them so much. It's an understatement to say I miss them.

And yet, Belgrade is a never-again for me. Ever. Wherever I turn there, I remember Dad, sick and dying. I witness the memories of us, as we used to be, wiped out like a disease. There, we have no familiar meals, no songs from home, no traditions. Even the adults' accents from home have deviated into something not-from-home. Nothing is the same. The family that fled to Belgrade has been doing its best to *overcome*, as my therapist advised Mom after Dad died. *Help Marica overcome.* Overcome Grandma's Kos-and-Met, Kosmet, like it had never been. Like we had never been.

Uncle Sima put it in a proverb-like saying one time, telling Mom when he thought I wasn't listening, *Sometimes you must let the past die to help the future live.* I guess that's what families do, like Grandpa used to say—take care of each other. My whole extended family collectively decided to let the past die, to save the present. And I get it. I do.

No one needed to explain to me, even when I was ten years old, what caused Simonida to start peeing in her bed for a year and have to repeat fourth grade. Why it took just one mention of Grandma's Zhito cake for her to start trembling like she stepped on a loaded power line. Just one reminder, then six months at the hospital, missing two-thirds of her classes, and all the rest that came along.

They try to let it all disappear for me, too. Especially when they know I stopped sleeping again. I don't tell them anymore. They never ask me directly, only if I'm rested, what time I go to bed, if it's loud at night where I live, but I've stopped telling them when the months of sleeplessness come. They cannot help, like they could not help me back in grade school and high school. If they know, they only worry more. I deal with them as best as I can—*tough it out*, as Stacy said when describing her and Rob's backpacking trip. I just make sure I'm always cheery on Saturday mornings.

This *overcoming* is the new boys' prophecy coming true: *You'll be no more.*

*

This Saturday morning, after Will walked me home from my first Barsync, I tell Katarina about him. About sitting together at the bar, his silky arm hair, his face so close to mine. How we walked to my place, slowly, his *beautiful*. She rejoices with me like only my Katya knows how to, partaking in my hopes, excited as much as I am.

"Well, listen Mara, many people meet at work. Why not you and Will?" That's how she responds to my fluttering voice. Her excitement professed within reason, as always.

I know what she means, even if she doesn't say it. Mom and Dad met at work before Dad became a mine engineer. So did Aunt Vera and Uncle Sima. She means that it's in the family, and I can't escape it even if I try. Katarina means this, I know it.

I could stay on the line listening to her high hopes for Will and me, even if I had to miss all my meals today to pay for this phone call. Her hopes that he's *the one* after just one evening of this walking together to my place.

But I don't mention to her that he's from Belfast. I don't want to remind her of us all back then, of watching the news with Dad, Grandma, and Grandpa, of the young Belfast saleswoman overturning the clothes to look for bombs.

After the phone calls, I clean the apartment, go buy groceries for the week, and then rummage through the angled shelves of the City Lights bookstore on Columbus.

At the bookstore doorway, I slow down and take a second before I push the door open. I savor the anticipation. Like when I'm in a theatre right before a play begins. The room goes dark, I close my eyes, and the suspense right before I escape into the story is all that breathes in the whole universe. I never close my eyes before stepping into the bookstore, of course, but I inhale the feeling all the same.

There is something extraordinary about bookstores in San Francisco. They seem to be made to stun you into wonder before you even look at any books. Their entryway mosaics, vaulted passageways, age-darkened oak floors, warmth-emanating colors, images of famed people past and present. All are overtures for the promise of stories and the flight into them that you seek. City Lights, in particular, is such a bookstore. So much love, so much hope bestowed upon the building of this city.

Saturday passes. I go to church on Sunday. Against all reason, I expect Will there as well, but he doesn't appear. Right after church, I run by my apartment to change into normal clothes, then go to the market to be with Mrs. Jane. I stay to help her pack up at five o'clock, as I've done the past two Sundays. Being with her distracts me a little, though I don't mention Will. In the evening, I can't focus on anything. I only listen to music and look at the clock. I don't sleep much.

Monday finally comes. But it comes as an antithesis to all my hopes, a balloon-deflating experience. Will is shut away in his office all day, and Eric doesn't hide his annoyance at me. I get a sense that Eric is a hard enemy to have, that he could bury you alive, and that I should be careful around him.

At some point in the morning, Isabella stops by and whispers a question, asking what happened between Will and me.

"Nothing! Nothing happened." *Why do people stick their noses into other people's business?* "He walked me to my building, that's all."

I see she's regretting the question, and I'm sorry to be brusque to her. I wish we were not colleagues. I so wish I could tell her how I long for him, how his arm hair felt on my arm, about his musk and his voice and his smile. Isabella would be a wonderful friend, I know, and I so want to tell her all this. But we work together, and I cannot risk my green card.

"He didn't return, and I thought maybe… you know, you guys hooked up." She stops and then adds before she turns to leave, "He's a great person, you know." She doesn't wait for me to respond.

When Will doesn't show up at all for the whole day—not in the kitchen, not on the path leading from his office to the restroom, not anywhere—I decide to stop listening for his voice, to focus on work, and to forget about Friday. Dan, my haven as ever, is my one safe person.

It continues on like this for the rest of the week, and I start thinking that maybe Will is on a business trip, or out sick, or something. It's hard to hide yourself so effectively in a small office space like ours. If Eric invited me to go and see his *cool stuff*, I would go. But he doesn't. When we see each other, Eric looks at me as if I've offended him.

*

Toward the end of the week, I feel so lonely, I just trudge through the days, hauling myself around, feeling even my eyelids too heavy to hold up. I wish I could call in sick, but I have no sick days. It's only my fifth week since I started at Blazoning Inc. *I'll manage*, I repeat to myself. *Ten months and three weeks is all there is before I get my papers, Will or no Will.*

But I still hope, every hour of every day, that he'll seek me out to continue whatever happened between us. In spite of all my reason, I anticipate this all the time for the next two weeks. But when I know he must show up for our company meeting, his chair next to Rob-the-CEO is empty.

In fact, an hour before the meeting, he walks toward the kitchen in front of our cubicle area just as I get up from my seat. It's like he willed me to look his way, when I had no reason to stand up. This is the first time I've seen him since the Barsync. He's in a blue-gray striped suit, looking as if the very idea behind a man's suit was devised for him and him alone. He stands like he's pausing on a runway, modeling for me. I blush and don't have enough sense to respond to his "Hi."

Harry, whose desk is across the aisle to the left of mine, stands up as well.

"To a funeral or an interview, lad?" Harry, as always, imitates Will's accent when speaking to him, and I wish to slap him for it.

Will looks at him, then again at me, and smiles. "Aye." He lets the answer levitate between us.

I sit back down with fog overtaking my mind.

When the IT report comes on the agenda during the company meeting, Rob gives it in Will's place. Eric offers to do it, even though Lizzy is his senior and she's keeping quiet. Rob thanks him, a bit snappishly I'd say, and continues on. As he gives the IT report, at some point Rob looks at me, then pauses mid-sentence, like he's lost his train of thought. His look triggers my green card alarm, and for the rest of the meeting, I stare stiffly at the Blazoning Inc. logo.

The logo seems like the reason in and of itself. It's embossed along the center of the conference room table, and I follow its galactic colors bursting out in reds and blues and metallics, the blinking that shoots the whole Milky Way upward. Like a shimmering reflection of Christmas tree lights in a windowpane at night. Like we had back home, when we were all there. The embossed relief of the logo calls my fingers to trace it, to feel it under my fingertips. Like I used to feel the ornaments' rough and cool spiraling shimmer on our Christmas tree. I have to suppress the urge and hold my hands tight on my lap.

The logo helps the meeting pass, interrupting a constant downward eddy of emotions.

*

I don't see Will again until the following Friday, when the next Barsync comes, a whole month after Will walked me to my place. This time, no one comes to specifically invite me. As we walk to the same bar, neither Eric nor Will stands next to me. I walk alongside Isabella. I try to smile and nod at whatever she's saying. She looks at me with a frown, but then immediately softens her look, smiles, and continues walking as if she observed nothing unusual. I'm grateful that she's not asking me anything. Though I so wish I could tell her all about it.

Eric makes a point of being as far from me as he can. Harry and he are trying to outshout each other about a football game, but every block or so, he throws a glance at me as if asking what I'm still doing there.

Will walks with Rob and Stacy, chatting about what, I can't hear, and seeming completely unaware that I am here.

It feels that even the building facades on Market Street are part of a set with everyone on it, except for me, an extra who'll never be called in to act.

At the bar, I sit next to Stacy, and Harry sits next to me. Will is next to Lizzy, whose boyfriend doesn't show up. I catch her explanation that he's on a trip visiting his parents in Iowa.

I bear through the time at the bar, smiling at everyone even as Will looks like he's reading Lizzy's lips. His arms are on the table, however, away from Lizzy's, I notice. But he's all engaged in her words, whatever they are talking about. When Haddaway's "What Is Love?" song plays, he looks at me as the singer calls out to his baby not to hurt him. I freeze and feel the muscles in my throat tightening. *I will not give you the pleasure, William Ford.*

Lizzy's two dimples in her cheeks say she knows only happiness. It's true, I've never seen Lizzy without a smile, and I normally think it's nothing but charming. Now I wish I won't have to do so much as greet her ever again. But I know I'll have to. I need this job.

I try to be animated with Harry and Stacy. I focus on them, each in turn, though strings of words come from them in the form of noise inter-twined with ever-more menacingly loud music. I nod and smile, hoping it's an appropriate reaction to whatever they are saying. I count the min-utes before I can leave. They decide to go to another club this time, and before everyone else gets up, I dump the money for my mineral water and the tip in the center of the table. The bills are all wet and crumpled from the way I squeezed them in my hand, which must be obvious to everyone, but I don't care. I hurriedly tell them I have something going on and must leave.

"It was fun, thank you," I say, looking between Rob's eyes. Rob, whom I wouldn't describe as particularly friendly lately. *Who knows what's go-ing on in his life*, I think. *It's not easy being a CEO of a startup.* I know I can think this only because the lawyer called me this morning and told me my immigration process is going according to plan. I can decide, at least for now, to ignore Rob's mood and decide it's not mine to wonder about.

I turn around quickly from the table and catch my foot on several chairs on the way out. Will doesn't stand up to offer to walk me out. I don't know if his eyes are following me.

I walk to my apartment, my feet grabbing the asphalt. When I take a left on Sutter, I look around to confirm it's the right street. I got here so quickly, too quickly, passing Tenderloin without seeing Brad and his German shepherd on a sleeping bag at the corner of Hyde and Turk. Or Anne walking Hyde with her big garbage bag covered in ice cream and star stickers. For a moment I think of turning around. Then I remember I see them on late Sunday afternoons, when I return from Mrs. Jane's. This is a Friday night, and they must be looking for shelter elsewhere. Still, the thought that I could've made them feel invisible makes me cringe as I continue toward California. I know what it feels like to be different.

I lose my breath on California before Gough Street, not from uphill exertion but from anger. When I get to the intersection of Octavia and California, I see the Queen Anne house with a turret and remember his *Beautiful.* How I wanted to share the view of the mountains with him. My throat tightens and I rush on. It's all either flat or slightly downhill from here to my building, and that's for some reason more upsetting than going uphill.

He could be married, with children back in Belfast. A philanderer. How many has he charmed with that smile of his? Beautiful, indeed!

There's something nagging at me, something that says it just cannot be, that it's impossible he could be so false. But I know what I've seen, and there's no way it could be anything different. I must stick to reason, I remind myself.

You are done, Marica, all done with this charade, I say to myself. *Green card, work, career, that's all you need.*

As I step over the three slanting stairs toward the entrance to my building, I promise myself that in the future I will not imagine men as they are not. I'm glad my neighbor Sharina is out. She'd not let me out of her sight, this upset. She'd see it right away and insist on knowing what happened, as any friend would.

The clock inside my apartment greets me with its handles overlapping at six thirty-three. I hear Katarina's singsong voice inside my head: *Clock handles meet—someone's thoughts are on you.* "I don't think so, Katya," I respond out loud. "I don't think so."

I realize I covered two miles of some of the steepest hills in San Francisco in just twenty-seven minutes. I don't even know why I remember it was six minutes past six o'clock when I left the bar, but I do.

*

I act strategically on Monday and Tuesday. I avoid noticing everyone who passes by my cubicle, I block out trying to isolate his voice from the other sounds, I rush out of the office at the end of the day, after checking that there's no one in my path toward the exit. By the end of Tuesday, I've trained myself to not think of him.

Lizzy comes to my cubicle on Wednesday, when Isabella is off, and asks if I want to go to lunch together.

I don't mean to be brisk when I say, "Sorry, can't do."

Her whole being seems so genuine, I have to work hard to dislike it. But her face loses its smile and I know I've overdone it.

"I'm sorry, Lizzy."

She smiles a *No problem.*

"I just have a lot on my mind."

"Of course. If you ever want to, let me know. I'll always be happy to go together."

Then, all at once, Will is everywhere. I get a sense that something changed again but discipline myself to not wonder about it. He walks past my cubicle several times every day in the next week. He has things to ask of Dan and Harry, both of whom he'd never asked anything of since I took over my cubicle. He doesn't come to ask me anything, but I think he slows down whenever he passes by and looks in toward me every time. If our eyes meet, which I do try to avoid as much as possible, I smile a distant smile. I sure never say a word.

With the rest of the Blazoning Inc. people, however, I manage to speak smoothly, without choking on my words. No one looks at me as if something's wrong, so I assure myself I look and act normally.

Whenever I accidentally run into Rob, he takes an extra moment to look at me as if there's something he'd like to ask, or say, or confirm, but he never does. His look is not unfriendly anymore—it's more curious, but it still strikes me with a feeling of chilled sweat and a mental picture of me on an airplane back to Belgrade. The mechanism I practice within me as a quick reminder that nothing has changed in my job or my green card application mostly works. I try to avoid Rob as much as I can, though.

As for William Ford, with every new day I'm prouder of myself. He won't have the pleasure of seeing me hurt.

*

The next three weeks pass somehow, and for my third company meeting, I come into the office last, sit closest to the door, stare at the logo, and take notice of no one. *Three months done, nine left to go*, I remind myself as I take a seat, mentally patting myself on the back for having made it this far.

Rob announces that Will is giving his final IT report, and then he lets Will introduce a new IT principal, a stranger I didn't even notice in the room. Will says he's giving the man an orientation and training, in advance of his own departure next Friday. This man is Will's replacement. I can barely take in any of Will's words, and I don't catch the name of the man. Others seem to be in a state of shock as well, though Rob, Mark, and Lizzy appear calm, and Dan minds his own business, as usual. Everyone else is looking at each other for an explanation. Dan wishes Will a great future and asks if any adventures lie ahead for him.

Before he answers, Will looks at me. So does Rob. I move my eyes as quickly as I can to the logo.

"I think so… I hope… so." Then he pauses. "It's another startup I'll be helping to build, but I'll miss Blazoning." That's all he shares.

I don't know if Will looks at me again or not, because I don't look up from the logo. I have to consciously squeeze my hands tight below the table, as I'm afraid they'll follow the instinct to try to reach for the shimmer of the carved wood. As soon as the meeting is adjourned, I slither out of the room.

Right after, Eric bursts into my cubicle. "He's canned, you know. He's canned, because Rob saw he should've bought the software like I told him. There's no friendship in business, you know. Rob's not dumb."

Glee is oozing out of him, and I wish I could shout him out of my space. But I stay unresponsive, and he leaves to whisper in Harry's cubicle. Harry responds back with his snarly murmurs. I dig into my work.

*

Until next Friday, I don't take notice of Will even once. I pop ibuprofen instead of coffee again, I don't eat lunch—I'm not even hungry—and I rush in and out of the office as if the workday is wedged between urgent meetings. If he's standing in the pathway, as I sometimes hear his voice nearby, I hunch over my desk papers and make sure to not instinctively stand up.

Finally, his last day arrives. *I'll be free today*, I think. *It's getting easier already*, I encourage myself. *Every day I'm better.*

But then, just as I'm getting ready to rush out for the day, Will's tall figure leans over my cubicle wall. I feel myself freeze like an animal ready to attack, before I look up at him. He has a happy grin on his face as he asks if I'll go to his last Barsync. *What now, making peace with a former colleague? Want to be remembered with grace?*

"No, I am otherwise engaged, but I thank you for the invitation." I speak slowly, squeezing the words through my teeth, staring at a spot between his eyes.

"Aye," he responds, "but come anyway."

I rush to turn my face to the computer screen, to avoid screaming at him to go screw himself. Over two whole months of acting as if I don't exist, and now *Won't you come to honor me.*

But I'll soon be free of him, I remind myself. I force my body to slow down, the benefit of being in therapy from when you're nine years old.

"You seem happy. I'm glad for you." I say it without looking at him until the very end of the sentence.

"Aye... I'm happy."

"I guess you're going into a bright future." I'm as flat as I can be. "I'm sorry I'll have to miss your..."—I look for the word—"celebration to-night." I remember the business lingo I've heard used in such circum-stances. "I do wish you all the very best in your future endeavors." I don't care where he's going, if they offered him more money, if he's a CEO, or whatever the reason is. I don't care. I return my gaze to the screen to show the conversation has ended. But he just won't leave.

His voice is now soft and imploring. "It'd be a craic if you'd come, Mari."

I'm stunned when I hear my name rolling down his tongue. As if it be-longs to him, as if he said it a million times, as if it's the most natural thing for him to name me in his own particular way. As if that's my name—Mari. It rolls down his tongue like Mom's sweet cherry syrup she used to make when we were all together and had a home. No one, not anyone, has ever called me Mari. Not Dad, nor Mom, nor Katarina, not anyone in the family, not any of my previous boyfriends, not any of my Belgrade or Lexington friends. No one. They all call me either Mara or Marica. That's what I've always been to everyone. But he rolls *Mari* down his tongue like an Irishman speaking French, *Maw-ree*. Intimate, personal, like something to hide from everyone, something to protect.

I think he sees the shock on my face, so I bend my head closer to the papers on my desk. *Don't be a fool, Marica*, I repeat to myself. In the background I know Will is saying something, but I cannot hear him over the noise sirening inside my head.

When my body is calm and I'm ready, I look up again, and he's still there, smiling and looking at me. He's leaning over, his torso threatening to break down my cubicle wall, thickened by my carefully written, pinned-up Post-its, noting all that I need to focus on, that I must not forget. My whole future, a pathway to my green card, it's all on those Post-its. If they come down, I tumble with them.

"Craic?" I try to sound as if that's the key word in all he said. I don't correct my name.

His eyes are so gentle, I must look away.

"Exceptional..." He lingers on the word. "In your case, anyway."

His words are soft, almost inaudible, and I make the mistake of looking up again. His whole face is alight.

"Oh." I have no mind present to say anything at all. I wish him gone, that's all, but he keeps on leaning over my wobbly parapet. I want to tell him to back off, to go away, to watch out for my wall and my pinned-up future. That I have work to do, immigration status to earn, and a life to tend to.

"Come, Mari... please, come tonight."

I look straight at him, and all that I've tried to keep under control rises up inside of me as I squeeze the words through my teeth. "I wish I could, but I cannot. And it's Ma-ritza!"

His facial expression finally changes. I'm so done. *Leave, leave, leave* is all that's in my mind, and in horror, I realize I whisper it out loud. I jerk back my chair, nearly stumbling, and the rolling chair thuds heavily against the floor. He jolts into my space, grabs the chair by the top and me by my upper arm to stabilize us both. I smell his body scent again.

We're standing so close to each other, it would take almost no movement to kiss.

Harry, who's been on the phone speaking like he's alone in the office, shouts from his cubicle without standing up, "Is everything okay there?"

I push against Will's chest, my palm curving on his taut flesh, so imminent and warm as if there's no shirt between his skin and mine. I squeeze out of the cubicle and march down to the bathroom. His scent makes the muscles in my throat tighten more. The sensation of his chest still burns on my palm, and I need to count to breathe.

Check yourself, Marica. He's just playing with you, and you know it.

Today: Seattle
Good Uncle John

The broken-down shed walls and base all lie on the bed of the pickup truck. They're ready for Will to take them to the dump before Emma's friends come for her birthday party at four o'clock.

Mariah and Emma are still in the backyard with the two of us. They have abandoned prowling around the bushes with hopes of getting another glimpse of the raccoon mom and her babies. It's been almost an hour since she picked them up out of the cardboard box and carried them away.

Will is in his quiet place, raking corduroy patterns in the soil of the former raccoon family home. The soil is barren of their presence, and is sifted through like sand in an hourglass, purged of all memory of its past. Like the raccoons have never been. Like the new boys promised to Simonida and me a lifetime ago: *You'll be no more.*

He absentmindedly touches his front jeans pocket, his mind deep within. *No matter what's in that letter, we can deal with it*, I reassure myself. I'll talk to him about it tonight.

Will's rake is graphing lines in the soil so straight, it's as if he's tracing the ruled page of a notebook. Quiet and precision go together for Will, like one feeds off of the other as he's formulating some certainty.

Over the years, we've put into the compost hundreds of notepad pages with perfect geometric shapes, which he draws as he contemplates lines from his green volume devoted to the Bard's tragedies. I'm convinced his mind doesn't even know what his hands do when he's in his state of quiet.

I've always left him be in it. I've never interrupted whatever it is that he's thinking through. But ever since the Belfast suitcase arrived, and he's started gliding from his quiet into calls for "healing," I've sought a way to shield myself and to escape these calls. But now I know this "healing" is meant for him alone. When the kids go to bed tonight, I'll tell him that he can talk to me about any of it. He just needs to be more careful around the kids. We *both* need to be careful saying anything in front of them. They'll just be asking for more, and before we know it, something unintentional will slip out.

I walk around the backyard now, looking for whatever leftover shed pieces I've missed still on the ground. I can't leave him to his ponderings, I need to remind him it's time to leave for the dump. I don't know what, but there's something in his movements, his hand reaching for his jeans pocket, and his quiet, that chills me.

I bear the air around Will's quiet. *Relocation. Ethnic cleansing. Genocide.* The contesting concepts, they weigh heavily. And Nora's mother's arrival. I try to grab onto the *home*-making idea, but I feel it slowly suffocating within me. I'm grateful for Mariah's and Emma's excitement that assails the throttling of air I feel.

"She was this big!" Emma spreads her arms as wide as she can to describe the raccoon mom. "But the babies were just itsy-bitsy." She measures against her palm with her index finger and thumb to show the size of the babies.

"Well…" Mariah starts correcting Emma's assessment, which to her is clearly slipping into the imaginary, but then she thinks again. "You know, Emmie, they did have to be really tiny when she had them, so they could be born in such a small space under Ugly."

Will doesn't hear a word the kids are saying. I'm glad I'll need to remind him soon to look at the time, to wrap up his raking, and to go to the dump.

All of a sudden, Emma's voice pierces the heavy air like a needle spears a balloon.

"Pa, tell us another story about our Good Uncle John."

Her words stop the very blood within me. I freeze, bent down on the way to pick up something shiny that seemed like a nail head, but turns out to be a shimmery bead fallen from Emma's dress. Still bent over, I jerk my head up and stare at Will. His raking doesn't so much as falter at Emma's question. *He hasn't heard her.*

I straighten up and take a breath before I'll be ready to tell Emma to go in and to start getting their room all done for the party. But in the exhale, I feel a word nettle me: *another*. Emma said, "Tell us *another* story." Since the suitcase arrived, he's told them about his schoolmates and his teachers, but not about John. Never about John.

Another story. *Good* Uncle John.

I stare at Will in a new state of shock, as he combs the soil without the slightest rhythm change to indicate that Emma's request has reached him.

"Emma, go in and get your room…" I rush to say, but Will interrupts me.

"Aye, your Good Uncle John…" His voice sounds like it's coming from the depths of his mind, dreamy and melodious, responding to a question of his own, rather than Emma's, like he's not really aware that his words are being spoken aloud, or that they interrupted me. He stops raking when he gets to the end of the line in the soil, sighs with his full torso, and keeps his eyes on the rake.

The kids run to him in the way they run when I shout that their ice cream is on the table. They stop by the very edge of the square where the former shed stood, right where the beams used to frame it. Mariah's arm lands around Emma's shoulders, and Emma's arm hugs Mariah's waist.

I stare at them as if witnessing a well-prepared playacting that I'm still in the process of understanding. Not yet sure of the plotline or of what to expect.

Will throws me a glance briefer than an eyeblink. He feels his jeans pocket, smiles somewhat of a pained smile, nods at the kids, and lifts the rake to his shoulder. He's ready to tell his tale.

The kids' faces are all anticipation of the joy from this forthcoming treat, a treat they seem to know well. As if *John* stories are a habit that fills our dinner talks. As if they've ever been spoken out loud.

I just stare at the three of them, from the outside. Still connecting their words and gestures into meaning.

"Let's see. He had this huge dark beauty mark above his lip." Will curls his fingers into a ball to show an exaggerated mole above his lip. "Like this." He smiles at the kids. "Did I tell you this? A handsome lad with a handsome mole."

The kids laugh.

"All of us wee lads from our estate loved your uncle. But you know that already." Will's voice is composed, deliberate—he knows what he's saying and to whom. Not dreamy anymore. He throws me another short glance.

The kids clap their hands and then resume their positions with their arms wrapped around each other.

"Pa, tell us again how he was your general."

"Yes, Pa, tell us, tell us Pa, how he was your general!"

The *home* feeling I tried reenacting through my being just a moment ago rapidly chills over, nerve-by-nerve, starting from the tips of my toes, icing up toward my brain. I try to breathe as I stare at my family.

Will's voice now reflects Emma's and Mariah's cheer, sounding as if John could be expected to drop by anytime to visit his nieces. "We, the wee lads, we followed him around everywhere"—he enacts a goose step in place with the rake over his left shoulder—"like his personal entourage, as if he were our general." He straightens out like a flagpole and salutes with a palm out against his forehead.

The kids mimic him.

"He'd climb up a lamppost to tie a rope for us to swing around it. He'd pay the ice cream man to give each of us a wee bigger scoop. 'For my Willbo's mates,' he'd say."

"Oh, I so wish Uncle John would pay for my ice cream scoop!"

Emma's voice and her loud sigh bring me back to full awareness.

"Both of you, go inside right now and get your room ready. Right. Now."

The kids turn to me with surprise on their faces, as if my very presence is unexpected. An intruder in their private joy.

Emma starts a complaint with "Maa-maa! It's my birthday and I want to hear—" but Mariah looks at me for a split second longer, with her eyebrows furrowed, then whispers something to Emma. After the whisper, the two of them walk inside without another word. The back door thuds as Emma jerks it shut behind her. I'm sure she looked at me as she did it.

I feel myself plunging into a new abyss.

"*Another* story!" I hiss when the kids close the back door. "*Another* story, William!" I shake my head left-right-left-right in disbelief. "He's dead, Will. *Dead.*" I point at the back door where the kids disappeared. "And they are *little.*"

Even before I spew these words at him, I know I shouldn't. I know I cannot make him keep his past inside. If he wants to share it with the kids, there's nothing I can do to stop him. They're his as much as they're mine. I know all that. But doesn't he understand that they'll just want more? That we must be careful what we're putting into our kids' minds?

I know I shouldn't ask him anything right now. Especially not what's next: Spilling open his Belfast suitcase in front of our little children? Showing his happy family photos in front of a *Sniper at Work* sign, with the soldiers and their guns casually pointing at the feet of the kids in the picture? A fine way to enjoy ourselves as a family, he thinks?

I know I shouldn't, I know, but I ask all this anyway.

He just stands, leaning onto the rake, watching me with that "healing" look in his eyes, like *I* am the one who's lost the way. It's that look of his that pushes me over the edge. That, and his hand still on his jeans pocket.

"Or better yet, why don't you first let them read their grandfather's letter? Then you can unfold John's bloody shirt to present the authentic exhibit: 'Here, kids, this is the shirt your granddad and I pried your *Good Uncle John*'s body parts out of when they brought him back to us, blown to pieces. See the blood stains? A fine memento, don't you agree, lasses?'"

I know I shouldn't say any of it. What I should say is *This is not the way to make a home, Will. The kids need a carefree childhood, not stories from their father's infernal past.* But I say all the other things instead.

Even as it all comes out of me, I'm aware of what I should do instead: Stop, calm my body, send him to the dump, wait it out, and think it through before I speak. But I panic. For being barred from their stories. For not being trusted to signal a warning. *The kids are sure to ask for more, he must know it. There is no going back once you start on the stories. They will only want more of them.*

He doesn't say anything. After I don't know what else to add, he lays the rake on the grass outside of the square of soil, takes off his gloves, comes to me, and hugs me tight. But I don't want his hug. I want him to tell me he'll let them be kids. To tell me he'll be careful with what he puts into their minds.

But instead, he says, "We need to heal, Mari, we need to let go."

I should not fall into this "healing" trap, I know it. I should respond with *Fine, let's think through what you can tell them about John. The happy parts only. No pictures. No deaths. No bombs. No shirt, ever.* But I don't. I call him *careless* instead. *Negligent. A cruel father.*

I try to squeeze out of his hug as I say it, but he doesn't let me go. His hug is smothering me, making me unable to keep the words inside. Locking me in place with his voice whispering into my ear, "All's well, Mari. We'll be all well."

The top button of his green shirt rubs my face raw, calling up the tears. Like the wound he's ripping open.

His arms feel like a noose, tightening, snaring the old life in me, me from way away. I do my utmost to breathe and to prevent the tears from responding to his words.

"We need to let go. We need to forgive," he continues, trapping my past, resurrecting the losses, unsheathing the pain, exposing the broken parts. "We must heal," he continues with his whispers, trying to lure the former me into uniting with the former him.

Not the way to make a home for our kids, Will. Not the way to happiness.

What is it anyway, to "heal"? To tell the kids about the new boys in my village? About the nail? About Simonida's face when she arrived at the Belgrade train station with her one-way train ticket—her nine-years-old eyes like there was nothing left in life to hope for? About Dad? About *home*?

I know I shouldn't ask him this: "Is it 'healing' what you're doing? Impregnating our beautiful, peaceful present with your apocalyptic past? Step one: Let's tell the kids the happy memories about their *Good Uncle John*. Step two: Let's show them his stained shirt. Step three: Let's describe the grief that killed their grandma. One-two-three: 'Heal.'"

He responds to all I say with an even tighter hug.

I turn my voice flat and low. "Let go of me, William!"

He takes a moment and then drops his arms. He stands back and I see his face. All that I said to him is on it. His eyebrows weigh heavily on his whole being, like it's Judgment Day. Quiet. He stands a little bent over, like he could use a prop to help hold him up. I see all this. He looks like only he knows how to look through me, then he turns around and starts toward the truck.

Then he touches his pocket, stops, and turns around. He looks at me, mumbles about having to do something before he leaves, unties his Doc Martens, and goes inside the house.

I don't follow him. I stand outside of the raked square, looking at it. It's bereft of any sign of life, of a home.

A few minutes later, Will comes back out. He ties his boots, nods at me, and leaves without a word. His steps seem like he's plodding through heavy snow.

1983: Kosovo
Leaving Home II

Mom and Dad are in the main room, making it almost impossible to sneak out. I'm meeting Simonida behind the school building to exchange our animal-observation records as soon as I can get there. I spy on my parents like a hawk from Grandma's room. The records are tucked inside my sweater already. As soon as Mom goes into Grandma's workroom, and Dad hobbles after her, I tiptoe to the front door and slip into my boots. I don't put on my coat because Mom would immediately see that it's missing from the hook.

I know I can't write any of this in my diary, because if Mom reads it, she'd be very upset.

I run as fast as I can toward the school, past the Yovanovics', the Zharkovics', and the Nikolics' homes. They're all empty now. It's only the Milosavljevic family on the way to school that's still there. I shoot like a bullet by their home. If they look through the window, Mister Milosavljevic will rush straight away to Mom and tell on me. He's done it so many times already. *For your own good*, Mom says when she censures me. What-ever! But no one will see Simonida and me behind the school building today, on a Saturday. The only thing I need to do is get there as fast as I can.

The last house before the school, the Nestorovics' home, is also empty. They left a week ago exactly, a day after Mister Nestorovic came back from a month at the hospital. I run by, but I still glance toward their house. Simonida and I are sort of the special guards of Slavica's and Sonya's dowries. When they left in that huge rush, they didn't take their dowry chests with them. But it's okay, because Simonida and I make sure no one will touch them. Especially not with dirty hands!

Past the Nestorovics' home, I'm almost at the playground when I see one of the new families' dads and his four grown sons coming toward me. I'm not afraid of them. But then I recognize the new dad, the one who sent Mister Nestorovic to the hospital. His youngest son who goes to the lower grades with Simonida and me brags about his dad beating Mister Nestorovic broken, so we all know who did it.

As they walk toward me, the new family's dad wields a crowbar, his oldest son carries two shotguns over his shoulders, and his next-oldest son jiggles a box of matches. All five of them walk like they're part of a parade or something, like a cheerleading squad and a marching band I saw on TV for the Youth Day celebration.

I stop running and repeat to myself that they wouldn't hurt a kid.

They all fix their eyes on me, and even though Simonida and I said we would no longer greet the new families like we always used to greet everyone in the village, I still call out a "God be with you." When they hear me, the dad swings his crowbar, and for a moment I think he'll strike me with it. He spits right on my boot instead, and then all four of his grown sons do the same. The sons then stomp their feet hard right in front of me and shoo me away like a feral dog.

I run to the back of the school building and hide behind it. I wipe the top of my boots against the grass and say to myself that they are just plain not nice, but they wouldn't hurt a kid. But I can't stop shaking.

Then Simonida scurries around the corner, all flushed. "Nestorovics' entrance door is open," she whispers quickly. She pushes her animal-observation records into my hands, grabs my records from under my sweater, and sticks them inside hers. She doesn't have a coat on, either. Then she pulls me by the hand and we dart behind the Nestorovics' barn.

We're both worried. What if someone steals Slavica's and Sonya's dowries? Everything they'd worked on for years and years, so that they could snatch the best boys in the village from all of us? What if their dowry thieves marry the nicest boys instead? What will Slavica and Sonya do when they come back from big-city-Belgrade?

When Simonida and I sneak behind their home and peek through the side window, I recognize the same family I just met on the road. They are inside the Nestorovics' home, and now the youngest son who goes to the lower grades with us is in there as well.

We see, through the window, the four grown sons carry the two cedar dowry chests. They carry them downstairs from the top floor and then through the front door.

Simonida grabs my arm, we look at each other, and we sneak around the house, to where we can see the front yard. I bend down so Simonida can see over my head.

Slavica's and Sonya's dowry chests are heavy. We can tell from the way they swing between the grown sons before being laid down next to the horses' trough.

Simonida clutches my upper arm.

The new family must have dragged the trough from the stable because a path furrows through the grass in a jagged line. Mister Nestorovic would never drag it this way. Now he'll have to reseed the path because of this careless new family.

The trough is standing between the front door of the house and the gate. Not filled with water, though. Fire burns inside it.

Simonida and I watch as the two eldest sons unlatch the chests and open the tops. Then, with their hands—unwashed, I'm sure of it—they tumble through Slavica's and Sonya's dowries.

I hear Simonida breathe heavily, and I squeeze her other hand that's not holding my arm.

The boy from our grade gets to Slavica's chest and picks up a blouse. It's the one that she was so proud of, with stitched maroon peony flowers circling around a cross in gold and green silk threads. I'm sure she stitched it that way just because she loved the pattern on Grandma's blanket so much. Slavica's grandma brought the blouse to one of our poselo gatherings when Grandma was still alive, to show how her *not-yet twelve-year-old granddaughter could stitch in such an even hand.*

The boy from our grade unfolds Slavica's blouse and looks at it. Then he crumples it like a piece of paper and throws it to his father. His father catches it and wraps it around his hand like a bandage. I can see the gold glimmer of silky crosses catch the sun as he moves his hand. He then rubs his hand wrapped with the blouse against himself, rub-rub-rub, right where you're not allowed to look. All his sons laugh.

Simonida grips my upper arm so hard it hurts.

I'm almost happy when the fire flashes through the blouse inside the trough. I remember how Simonida and I weren't allowed to touch it with our hands when Slavica's grandma brought it to show it to us. We wouldn't wash our hands, so we could only look with our eyes. Katarina's hands were clean, and she was allowed to move her fingers across the stitching.

Watching it burn in the trough, I imagine how the sleek thread must've felt, like a silky stream of water pouring from a cup over the tips of my fingers on a hot summer day. I wish so much that I'd had my hands clean when Slavica's grandma showed it to us. I wish I could have always remembered how it felt under my fingers.

Simonida and I stare as they rip through Slavica's and Sonya's dowries. The sleeves and dresses and bed sheets drag through mud and slush as the new family's father and his sons cheer and play ball-toss with them. I remember how the Nestorovic girls carefully folded every piece inside, ironed and starched first. All by themselves.

Simonida's hand is wet over mine.

When the chests are left empty, the four sons take them back inside the house. Their dad and the youngest brother follow them.

Simonida and I don't move.

When they come back outside, they carry the Nestorovics' old tapestries, wooden crosses, and many smaller and larger icons. Everything beautiful that could not fit into the Nestorovics' car a week ago. The new family dumps all of it into the fire after rubbing themselves with the crosses and the icons. I close my eyes, I cannot look as they do it. But I hear their cheers. Like it's a celebration.

I get really cold all at once.

The tapestries seem to have doused the fire, but then the new dad stirs it with a long stick. The fire simmers back into life, flickering through the icon of Virgin Mary holding Christ, thrown face-up on top of the burning tapestries.

In the end, when all has burned through, the dad and the oldest son take their shotguns that were leaning onto the house. They aim at the Nestorovic name on the plaque at the top of the house at the count to three, then shoot. We hear how the slugs chip the stone at the same time.

This causes Simonida and me to step right out from our hiding place, not thinking. After two rounds, all that's left from Nestorovics' name is *Ne to o i.*

Simonida sobs aloud and I put my arm around her. She looks down, and I do the same, to see a stream of pee coming down her pants.

The boy from our grade sees us first. Then he and his brothers start shouting the words Simonida and I had never heard before they came to the village. They laugh at Simonida and point at her wet pants.

Their father rubs himself like he did with Nestorovics' girls' dowries, the icons, and the crosses, only without anything in his hand this time. He stares at us with eyes that scare me. His sons then charge at us, and Simonida and I sprint back home, she to hers and I to mine, our animal-observation records flying out from under our sweaters. We don't stop to collect them or say goodbye to each other or plan another meeting. We just run, each to her own house.

I hope Mom and Dad will be inside when I run into the main room, but they're not. I go inside Grandma's room and wrap Grandma's blanket around me really tight. I'll be taking it no matter what Mom says. It's my dowry catch-up to marry a nice boy. Grandma said it and she's older than both of them. They ought to listen to her even if she's dead. I *can't* marry one of these new boys.

*

Grandma's blanket soothes me a little, but I can't stop shivering, thinking of the Nestorovics. What do they have to come back to, now that all their things are burnt and their family name shot out from their home? It's like they had never been. I wish I could ask Dad. Or anyone.

I'm scared to remember Mister Nestorovic's face, all broken-up, toothless, and lined with scars, like the body of Simonida's dog Zhuyko when the tractor hit it.

He should've kept quiet! I know I'm a kid, but even I know he shouldn't have said anything to the new families' dads. About the work parties and the years and years and years of the villagers building Kosovo with their own hands and money. He should never have said any of it!

The new families don't care about all of the families that laid bricks and dug kilometers-long trenches for the telephone and electricity wires to *build Kosovo's future.* Or how they built Trepca buildings. Or how Grandpa almost lost his leg when a pile of bricks fell on it and Uncle Bekim carried him all the way to the clinic and then Grandpa had to walk with a cane afterward. Mister Nestorovic shouldn't have said anything. He especially shouldn't have said that the new families were not allowed to threaten the villagers out of their homes. Maybe then they wouldn't have burnt all their dowries and crosses and tapestries and shot out their name.

What are they to come back to now?

I wrap myself in Grandma's blanket even tighter. repeating to myself that the new families wouldn't hurt a kid.

Where would we come back to if they move into our home when we leave? If they burn Katarina's dowry and our tapestries?

I tighten Grandma's blanket around me again. I'm not leaving it here.

Dad said last night that I don't need to worry about our home. That all of the Popovic family line and Uncle Bekim and his son will take care of it until we come back. *No one would dare touch anything here*, Dad had said. *It's our home, Popovic's home. Sava Popovic built it over three hundred years ago. The plaque he chiseled our name into proves it.* I believed all that last night. But what about the plaque with only *Ne to o i* left on it now?

I wrap Grandma's blanket around me tighter yet. I take one of Grandma's handkerchiefs from her dresser. It has her initials embroidered in sky blue, and a wavy sky-blue threaded hem. It's snow-white, starched, crisp-ironed. It was probably Grandma who washed and fixed it herself before she died last fall.

I stick my nose into it and smell her there. I smell her in her blanket, too. I pick up Grandma's hairbrush by its wooden handle, so slick and warm, its grain lines beautiful to just look at. I press my palm into the bristles made from horsehair, and they tingle my palm. I want to remember forever how it feels. I can't take it with me to big-city-Belgrade, Mom said.

I lay my first baby shoes, which are soft like a lamb's belly, on Grandpa's pillow. I put them next to Grandma's white baby shirt that her mom sewed for her. Then I lie down on Grandma's pillow and smell her in it. Her spring valley smell. I look all around the room where I've put our pictures together, and I see her. That makes me stop crying.

I arrange on the side table my small icons from all the very, very old monasteries. Grandma told me when we visited them that these monasteries were built in the Middle Ages. All in Grandma's Kos-and-Met,

Kosmet. I cross myself and kiss each of them. Then I flank them with Grandma's and Grandpa's icons.

I do my secret ritual, even though it's not nighttime.

Every night, after we say our prayers all together, Dad, Mom, Katarina, and I, in front of our family icon of Saint Nicholas in the main room, I secretly say them again in front of the cross hanging on the wall beside Grandma's bed. I started my ritual when I inherited Grandma's room after Grandpa died this winter. I don't tell anyone about it, not even Simonida. It's our secret—Grandma's and mine. *We don't stop loving people just because they die*, Grandma said. She also said she'd be looking after me from wherever she is. I know that's true, because I feel she approves of my secret.

I say my prayers now, cross myself three times, kiss Grandma's cross, then kiss each of our icons again.

I wrap Grandma's blanket tight around me again and open diary number four, the one with Grandpa's story about Sava and Milka Popovic. How they lugged the rocks from the mountain to build our home here in Kosovo. The chips off of the mountain.

I so wish I had a new happy story to write in my diary.

"Mara!"

I close my diary, put it in its place—number four—with the other diaries. I wipe my face with my sweater sleeve and go to the main room. I don't take off Grandma's blanket.

"Mara, come. You need to try on some things, so I know what to pack for you."

I come out of Grandma's room, rubbing my eye to pretend like I have an eyelash in it, but Mom doesn't notice my face. Dad looks at me a little long and knits his eyebrows, but he doesn't say anything.

The six suitcases are open on the bench alongside our long oak table. All of them are so full, not even Popeye the Sailor Man could close them. I can see my schoolbooks and my clothes in one of them. My winter coat is right next to it.

The sunflower tablecloth lies folded on the side of the table. I'll have to remember exactly what Grandma said about the perfect thread count, so that I can begin crocheting one in big-city-Belgrade.

Mom's handing me a pair of snow pants that Katarina's outgrown, to try on. Why would I need snow pants, when we're going in the spring?

"I'll pack my things, Mom. I know what I want to take."

"Mara, please." Mom looks at me like she has no strength inside her to say another word. Her voice is completely empty of its usual melodious-ness, nothing like normal. Then she looks at Dad with those same eyes and lets the pants fall on the table. "I can't, Yovan. I just can't."

Dad limps to her, hugs her, and she sobs in his arms. I hear her even after I go back to Grandma's room and close the door.

Before I leave, and while Dad is holding Mom in his arms, he turns to me. "Mara-my-sparrow, Mom needs to pack for us all. She knows best what we all need to take." Dad says this with his soft voice, but I know he won't discuss it anymore. "We can't take all that we want, only what we can't be without." Then he sighs. "Until we come back. Soon."

The way he says *soon* makes me really worried. Well, I'll be taking Grandma's blanket no matter what either of them say.

1995: San Francisco
The Market

I stay in the bathroom stall for who knows how long after William Ford invited me to his last Barsync. I take my time, and when I come back to my cubicle, he's not there. I'm the only person left in the office, and I finish my week's work in peace.

I walk to my studio apartment, five hilly blocks up California. I don't look at Grace Cathedral to catch the magic of memories from the monasteries in Grandma's Kos-and-Met, Kosmet. I don't look to the sides of Mason Street to see the world dipping into the water and being pulled back up by the mountains. I just trek up without pausing.

By the time I make myself go to bed, the apartment is so clean, every curve of each one of my three faucets can serve as a mirror. I go to bed without turning on music or getting a book. *I'm okay, I'll be okay, he's not The One.* If anything, I can be rational. I know that about myself. *It's better that he's leaving.*

In my prayer, I ask Dad if he's proud of me for not letting Will hurt me again. But I don't feel Dad's response. For a long time, before tentative sleep grants me some relief, I feel like I'm in a dark bubble, alone as a void.

Saturday passes. I speak with Mom and Katarina while feigning that life is normal. I don't mention Will. Katarina stopped asking about him when I told her about how he sat with Lizzy. She knows I'll tell her if anything important happens. Last Saturday, I just mentioned he had quit. She'd said, *Maybe that's for the best. At least you'll be able to breathe again, not expect anything.* My wise, wonderful sister. I wish so much she could be here to sit with me. To talk me out of this.

On Sunday after church, instead of going back to my apartment to change into a pair of pants and a sweatshirt, I head straight to the farmers' market in my dress and heels. I need to prevent myself from sulking in bed all day like yesterday.

Mrs. Jane, the lady that sells vegetables from her garden, packed me a flat of tomatoes last Sunday. She tried convincing me to wait a week for the sun-ripened ones to come into season, but I'm sure she'll be happy with Mom's tomato sauce that I made from this batch. I'm bringing her two jars of it in my backpack.

I'll spend the whole Sunday afternoon lingering around Mrs. Jane's stall. She's the closest person I have to a relative in the US, my feeling of *home* in America. She's the only person here whom I've ever told that I come from a farm where we tended a vegetable and fruit garden. Mrs. Jane is in her sixties, lives inland on her farm around Stockton, is a widow, her kids are grown. A big-bosomed and wide-hipped woman, she's like a picture of primordial motherhood. When she hugs you, your worries disappear within her body's embrace. Just like Grandma.

She tries to refuse my money every Sunday, but I threaten to never come back. Still, there is always extra in the bag she prepares for me. Red peppers, bunches of spinach and kale, fennel roots. I picked up a fancy lemongrass hand lotion at a boutique for her two weeks ago and gave it to her last Sunday. I don't indulge myself with anything so extravagant, but I like how it smells on her. Like the wildflower valley in the spring, back home. There is something Kosovar about Mrs. Jane. I know that's impossible with her fifth-generation English American origins, I asked her. But there is still something I know as Kosovar inside of her—motherly, soil-bound, whole.

Mrs. Jane and I talk about all kinds of things. I don't tell her about Dad and Grandma and home. Of course, I don't. I tell her about my work, she tells me about farming and her life. About her cattle that she calls *rother*. A calf that was born with a bad leg, and the cow nuzzling it, trying to hobble on her three legs to teach her calf to move as it can. Mrs. Jane had no heart to slaughter it after seeing the mother. She speaks of that cow and her calf like there is no difference between a parent and a child in any world. It reminds me of how Grandpa used to say that even trees have parents who feed them through soil. That all families are the same, looking after one another. I think that Mrs. Jane and my family, as we used to be back home, would agree on everything.

Mrs. Jane is the one I need this morning. I need her to say how worried she is that I'm too pale, too sad, and don't eat enough greens. I need to tell her it's all fine, she's exaggerating, but I love her nevertheless. I almost expect her to pluck a broadleaf plantain and soothe my hurt. Like Grandma used to do when I'd mar my nails purple after making thunder with her loom weights. Mrs. Jane makes me feel like I can do anything, like I can survive anything. She reminds me of how it used to be, how Simonida and I used to be, before the one-way train rides.

From Hyde, I can see the right half of her stall, the left half still hidden by Simon Bolivar's statue, and I already feel at peace. She is handing a full bag to a customer facing her and cannot see me yet. As the customer turns to go, she offers a glossy red pepper to a hand that extends to accept it from behind the platform below Bolivar's horse's right hind leg.

I come to a dead stop.

Then I debate whether to turn around and go back to my apartment. But I've already brought Mom's tomato sauce for her, so I'll just drop off the jars and leave. I can say I have errands to run, if a reason comes up to say anything at all. I won't disturb her with her visitor. I'm aware I have no exclusive rights to Bolivar's concrete pedestal. Or Mrs. Jane's Sunday afternoons. All I need are my immigration papers, and I'll manage that much on my own.

As I inch closer, I see the whole stall and the visitor's legs standing on the bricks. Jeans and low black boots with yellow stitching, the rest of the person still hidden. Mrs. Jane doesn't see me yet, as she is talking to her visitor. I still take steps toward the stand, a chill warning me to turn around and leave. Then the figure stands up, back turned to me, and I know it's Will. There he is, in his dark jeans and a leather jacket, his hand holding a red pepper.

I'm startled in half a step. I pivot, almost slipping in my dress shoes, and rush to disappear back toward Grove Street. But it's like he smells my presence. He leaps away from Mrs. Jane's stall, and he's right there in front of me.

"Mari." His whole face is a smile. "You're here."

"Why are *you* here?" I don't understand. "You left." End of conversation. Nothing more to say.

"Aye, left," he confirms, with a wild delight in his voice.

For a moment I think he must be ill. No one with any sense acts like this.

"I wanted to ask you out."

Then the fury inside of me starts anew. *Can't take a refusal to his last Barsync, is it? No one refuses William Ford?* I keep the words within me, but I know my eyes are scorching him.

His voice sounds like he's unaware of the message my eyes are launching, however. "Blazoning… there's a rule. No employee dating." He sounds apologetic, but the smile doesn't leave his face. Like he's embarrassed to admit something and simultaneously unable to disguise his joy. "I have my papers," he adds almost inaudibly. "My granddad came to America." Then he pauses before he speaks again. "Please Mari… will you go out with me?"

I don't move, don't say anything, don't understand anything he's saying.

"Mrs. Jane here." He turns to point at her. "She told me you come to her. So, I waited."

I look at Mrs. Jane, and she waves and points at a brown bag she's prepared for me.

"I asked at every stand with tomatoes if they knew you. That's how I found her. She told me you call her Mrs. Jane. But she said you don't come before one." He looks at his watch and then at me with a smile blitzing his face. "You're early. I'm glad of it."

Nothing makes sense.

"I… I don't know," I finally say, though I'm not sure myself what it is that I don't know.

"That's grand," Will responds, as if he's sure of whatever I meant. "Let's meet in front of your building tonight at five, and let's go for dinner."

I guess I agree, as his shining eyes become like slits from the smile that overtakes him. He pivots on his black boot's heel with a "Ciao" and walks from me to Mrs. Jane. In a big swoop, he snatches his red pepper from the edge of her stand like a trophy with its cap bitten off. He leans in over the stand and tells Mrs. Jane something, to which she smiles, replies, and nods in approval. He bows to her like a nineteenth-century prince, with extended leg and arm, then walks away along Hyde toward McAllister, in the opposite direction from me. When he's about thirty feet away, he stops for another moment, turns around, and looks at me once again. No wave, just a look, like he's taking a mental picture to keep within. Then his long legs stride away.

I continue standing where he caught me on the sidewalk, until I realize Mrs. Jane is beckoning to me.

"Marica, come love, I have your tomatoes."

I walk to her, unsure of everything around me.

"Will is a nice boy," Mrs. Jane says as she gives me the bag. Then she comes around her stall and puts her hand on my arm, warm and soft. She looks into my eyes like she wants to make sure I'm paying attention to her words. "He'll be good to you."

I take the bag from her and leave, feeling like a windup doll. I don't know if I thank her. If I say anything at all. When I get to my apartment, I realize I still have her money and the two jars of tomato sauce for her. I didn't stay with her today or help her pack up. I know I should go back, pay, give her the sauce, but I cannot make myself get off my bed. *Think through this*, I keep repeating to myself, but I stay in a daze the whole day, staring at the clock.

Employee dating rule? Where do people meet, then?

*

Cycles of vacant thoughts cascade through me until it strikes four. At four o'clock, I take another shower, put on my jeans and a T-shirt. I don't want to dress up. I put no makeup on. I want to look normal. I don't want to let myself descend into hope. I only half-believe he'll show up, anyway. *That's grand.* What did that even mean as a response to *I don't know?* I wish I could call Katarina, but it's already past midnight in Belgrade, and she's working in the morning. She'd know what to think.

He does show up, waiting for me at five o'clock. I see him from my window before I come down. I roll up my blinds ever so slightly, only to see the street, and there he is staring up toward my window. As I come downstairs, holding tight onto the railing, I still believe I might have dreamed up the whole encounter, and I won't really find him there.

But he holds the door for me as I push it open from the inside. He looks at me in a way that makes me wonder if he'll lean in very close. He doesn't. Instead, he starts speaking as if continuing a conversation we'd just paused a moment ago. As if this is not a transcendental moment, as if it's the most natural thing in the world for a William Ford to quit his job as principal engineer and CTO at the company he started with his friend, the company he even named, in order to go on a date with a Marica Popovic, an assistant web designer without a green card. His voice sounds like all this is to be expected, and there was nothing that could have prevented it. I wish to scream at him to start acting like a normal human being. And to let me feel his breath on me.

"How about we go to a place I discovered last week?" That's his greeting.

He doesn't try to hold my hand or kiss me, or anything. We take a right on Fillmore and just walk next to one another. I try to keep my senses present. As we walk, he tells me how he read Ivo Andric and enjoyed his novel, how he went to a world music store and bought some CDs from Belgrade old-time *tamburitza* bands, and how he is now reading Nusic. Like he's giving me his productivity report.

I just keep quiet and walk. I'm unfit for anything else.

We step inside a Greek bakery about a ten-minute walk from my apartment. I've never been in it before, though I've been planning to try their cheese pastry from the first day I moved into the neighborhood. Every time I pass by, I slow down to smell its scent. I think it might taste like Grandma's cheese pita as I remember it.

The bakery has three small round tables and two webbed metal chairs to each table. They stand on the shiny tiled floor, alternating rows of sky-blue and white. A man with a heavy Greek accent and a belly comes to take our order. I ask if they maybe have cheese pita on their menu.

"Of course we have *tiropita*!" His thick knitted eyebrows come together. I guess I should feel censured, but his frown feels warm. "It's Greek staple, tiropita." He looks to make sure I understand. "How many pieces?" He points with his roller knife at the pan with pita, lying inside the glass vitrine.

"Two please."

"You?" He turns to Will.

"Same, please."

"Yogurt?"

"Yes, please." Then I correct myself. "For me."

"Me, too," says Will.

The man turns around, and his lower body disappears behind a four-foot-tall parapet dividing the kitchen from the restaurant. He emerges with cutlery wrapped in rough paper napkins. He places them in the center of our table without a word and then goes back, his bottom half invisible behind the parapet. Within a minute, and before Will and I say anything to each other, he returns with our orders.

"I thought you might like this place," Will says, not taking his smile off.

"I do, thank you." Grandma made cheese pita with creamy *kaymak* and cheese from our cows. Kaymak that melts in your mouth, finger-licking divine. The yogurt this man serves from a pitcher must be homemade. It's almost like Aunt Vera's. She made the best yogurt and sour cream. But I don't tell Will any of this.

"This is heavenly," I say to the man who's now bending over the worktable behind his wall.

"Of course. It's Greek." He looks at us and grins, as if uttering a joke and an unquestionable truth, all at the same time.

Will and I laugh without reservation. I like this man. No falsehood around him, around this place with tiropita and homemade yogurt.

A moment later, he's focused on his hands' work behind the parapet. I wish I could watch him unroll the dough disk, slather it with butter and cream, and sprinkle droplets of cheese over it. I'd like to see if he layers it like Grandma used to.

"My wife rolls out dough, and my mother makes the cream and cheese. From her cows." He speaks without lifting his head from his work.

Will and I listen.

"You two have accents." The man is all matter of fact.

"I come from Belfast," Will responds, "and Mari comes from Belgrade."

The man's hands pause on the worktable, and he lifts his head up, his thick eyebrows meeting. He looks first at Will and then at me, taking his time with both of us. Then he looks down, but his arms stay still. "Your people suffer. I'm sorry." There is a sense of weight overcoming the room. "I have no one in Belfast, but I have a friend in Beograd. He has little kids." He bites his lip on one side. "Who's there of your family?"

All the Greeks I've ever met, then and afterward, have been like that: direct, warm, and genuine. Always all about family.

"Everyone," I respond.

"How do you send them money?" He comes to the side of the parapet where we can see all of him. His fists are on his waist apron. He's trying to contain the dough in his hands and save the fabric.

I'm alarmed to realize I've never thought of it. In Lexington I'd used library books and never bought a single textbook. I ate on a budget smaller than given. I did all this to save enough for the ticket back to Belgrade, if it came to that. There was no one who could have helped me with the airplane fare, and it was hard to save on a student stipend. But now I've started earning, and still, helping Mom and Katarina hadn't occurred to me.

Will, as I soon learn, has always sent money to Belfast. *A family tithe*, he calls it. *Once a month.*

As I say nothing, the Greek wipes his hands on his waist apron, lifts a notepad to the top of his wall, and writes something in it. He rips out the piece of paper and hands it to me. The paper is doughy, sticky, and sprinkled with flour.

"Here's the bank name. They're a rip-off, take twenty percent of every transaction, war profiteers they are." He shakes his head. "But I couldn't find a better way."

I thank him, look at the paper, fold it, and zip it in my purse.

"I'm Ioannis," he says and offers his hand to Will first, and when I extend mine, he takes it. His hand is gooey like Grandma's when I helped her spread and roll out dough on our long oak table.

Dad's name, Yovan, is a Greek variant of Ioannis. Like Grandpa's younger brother who was buried in Greece during the Second War. The one whose grave Uncle Bekim and Grandpa dug with their own hands. All these lives connected by names, soil, and blood.

I tell Ioannis my full name and Will says his own. Ioannis pronounces my name just as it's intended, *Ma-ritza*, and Will's as *Vel*.

When we're all done eating, Will insists on paying, and Ioannis nods in approval. When he tells us to come again for more *real food*, Will responds that we will. We wave at each other like three people who have a bond, and I realize that Will and I are starting anew. The time between the first Barsync and this morning disappears.

*

We stroll aimlessly, close to one another, but not hand-in-hand.

Will asks who my favorite artist is.

"Right before I left Belgrade, there was an exhibition with a few of Ilya Repin's pictures, a Russian painter."

"Aha."

"I only saw several of his portraits." I look at him, not sure how much information he wants. "For the aristocracy, you know, nineteenth century."

Will just nods without a sound, leaving space for me to go on.

"But I remember a big picture of a woman by the piano." I fear for a moment that I will bore him, so I cut my explanation short. "I liked it."

"Why?"

"Well, I didn't know anything about her, really, but she seemed to be a fancily dressed, you know, entertainer. But the way she looked at you, it was daring. I just liked it."

This is what Katarina and I discussed when we were in the Belgrade gallery, looking at this piece. Katarina liked Repin's other paintings better, but I couldn't draw myself away from the woman at the piano.

"Why?"

"Why what?"

"Why did she appeal to you so much?"

Because she was all exposed, and yet she seemed to show no broken parts to her. She let no one see how their edges rubbed against her flesh and tore it. She was convincing in her peace, in her self-assurance.

But I can't explain all that. Instead, I look at Will and shrug my shoulders. "Her eyes seemed to say, 'Here is what I am.' Unafraid, dignified. Like she was in charge, and people like her... women in her position are never in charge."

Will stops for a moment, I follow suit, and he looks at me like he's trying to read something in my face. "Have you seen Manet's *Olympia*?"

"No." I do recognize the name, but I don't recall seeing the picture in my art textbooks. "I know his *Flute Player*. And I really like his Roma woman portrait. But I don't know *Olympia*."

"I think she'll strike you."

"Why?"

"I think she's also in charge."

"Have you seen her in person?"

"No, not in person." Will starts his slow walking again, as do I. Then he adds, "We'll go to see her together."

"Oh." I thought I'd know when European masterworks came to town.

"When is she coming here?"

"Nay," Will says calmly. "She's not coming. *Olympia* is in Musée d'Orsay."

"Musée d'Orsay... Paris?"

"Aye, Paris." He looks at me, smiles and nods as he says it.

We, the two of us together, will go to Paris to see Manet's Olympia. There's something reliable in his words, however absurd they sound.

*

For the rest of the evening, we partly walk, and partly bus and tram, around the perimeter of the city. The Embarcadero, the Rotunda. I hope for his arm around my shoulders, but it doesn't come. We walk very close to each other, in step, but not in a hug. We come to the foot of the Golden Gate Bridge below Marine Drive and sit on the hill overlooking Marin County. There is no one around us, as if the two of us are the only people on Earth.

The Pacific swishes like my River Ibar, as I remember it from the summers when Dad, Katarina, and I swam in it. Mom had never learned to swim, so she just watched us from the bank. I don't know anything more soothing than being enwrapped by water, billowing in its expanses, not touching any solid ground, and still knowing you won't be hurt. Dad taught Katarina and me to love the water, to feel the bliss of it and our own power in it. I wish Mom would have let herself feel the same. Allowed herself to trust another to help keep her afloat.

"When I was eleven years old, John, my brother, took me to a shipyard one time." Will almost whispers, as if talking to himself. "Where the Titanic was built... Harland and Wolff."

We sit motionless, staring at the ocean where the hills and the lights from across the bay roll with the stars.

"The Pacific smells like it."

"He's much older than you, your brother?"

Will takes a long pause, enough for me to wonder if he heard me. I look at him and see his face muscles flexing up for a moment. Then he releases them with a half-sigh, like he's holding onto the rest inside.

"Aye," he says barely above a whisper, "he used to be. Eight years older… Not anymore, though." He pulls his knees against his chest, his arms tight around his knees. "There's only two left." His eyes stay fixed on the water. "I'll be older than John in two years."

Panic hammers inside of me. A clear call to escape that I intend to honor.

I slide my hands under my thighs in a jerky move and feel a broken pebble cut into my flesh. I flex my hands, toes, and gut in one breath. Hard.

After I check my urge to run, I take my hands out from underneath me and sneak a sideways peek at Will. By the way he sits, completely still with arms wrapped around his knees, I can tell that he remains in his own thoughts. The cut in my hand stings, but it's small. I turn away, like I'm stretching my neck and my arm, and lick the cut clean.

Then I pull in my arm next to Will to look at my watch. I graze him with my elbow to wake him out of his trance. "It's past midnight, I should go. It's a workday tomorrow," I declare.

Will takes a moment to respond. When he does, his face tells me I need not worry—the tale is done being narrated, alarm or not. He stands up from the hill overlooking the Golden Gate Bridge, he dusts off his pants, and I wish we weren't leaving.

*

As we walk back to my apartment building, Will asks, "Tell me, Mari, what's the most unusual thing in the Serbian language?"

"Calling your daughters your sons," I say without thinking. Then I laugh.

"What do you mean?" He stops and stares at me with a smile of disbelief.

"I know, it's funny, isn't it. You would often hear people call their daughters *sin*, son, rather than *cherka*, daughter. I'm not sure why."

"That's unusual, indeed."

"But there's also a word, *sinovica*. It refers to a brother's daughter. Isn't that funny. A daughter is cherka, but the name for your brother's daughter is based on the word *sin*, meaning son. Odd, is it not?"

Will narrows his eyes at me, then he looks up over my head, into the distance. He frowns. When he looks back at me and asks, "What's the name for a brother's son?" his question feels urgent, like much depends upon it. Almost like it's a dare.

"*Sinovac*. Its root is the same as for the word son. Sin, Sinovac."

He drops his gaze to the ground, doesn't say anything. He scratches his head in a nervous move I've never seen him make before, chilling the air around us. He starts walking quickly, as if I'm not there. As if he's trying to leave the conversation and me behind.

I follow him and fill the silence, trying to turn it lighthearted. "It's completely different from the way you call your sister's kids. Sister's kids come from the root for the word sister, *sestra*. *Sestrich* and *sestritchina* are her kids, nothing to do with the word for son, sin."

Will is eerily quiet, and I continue, not knowing what else to do.

"It's because there's a tradition, if a brother dies, then the living brother takes the kids as his own. I think it must exist in other cultures, too, I just find it interesting that it's so clear in the Serbian language. Like you know what your role is."

He walks without words. It feels like his steps are even faster. We get to my entrance without another word between us. I can't understand what changed.

At the entrance I just nod at him, thanking him and wishing him a good night, all in one breath. I turn around quickly to unlock the door and leave whatever this is behind. But he lays his warm palm on my upper arm, and I stop. His face is gentle again, and I think he'll lean in and put his lips on mine. He doesn't. He just looks into my eyes, not rushing to move, but not reaching closer, either. Like he's reading something in my eyes. And then he slowly takes his hand off my arm, takes a step back, and breaks away.

"Friday at seven." He points with his index finger to the ground between us. "Here."

Okay, I think. *Friday at seven.*

Today: Seattle
What is a Home?

The next thing I hear are the pickup truck tires scraping the gravel in front of the garage. Moving away, slowly, like an accusation.

The sun's rays are hailing down onto my body, scorching the hollowness within. I just stand, staring at the parallel soil tracks.

Home is such a hesitant concept, anything can crush it. Levying the past in particular. The weight within us—we inter it within us, we don't weave it into our future. I wish Will knew that. You can't build a home if you inject it with all the pain that has been. You can't revive hurt to build happiness. You just can't.

Only an hour ago, the vision of the Ford family tree, a clean slate, a fresh start with Will and me as the great-grandparents many times over of all the Fords that come after us—our version of Sava and Milka Popovic, a thread to connect us all to one another—it glowed glory within me. Our home. Belonging. Sown roots. The Fords' future.

That vision feels like a curse now. *May the Lord giveth and then taketh away*.

I wish I picked better words, didn't say so much. I wish he hadn't kept persisting. *This is not the way, Will*, I wish I'd said to him.

I feel blood surging into my brain, dizziness threatening to topple me. I know I must not think of it now.

When the screeching sound of the pickup tires has entirely faded away, I take a deep breath. I stand still like a sentry and make a plan: I have forty-five minutes before he returns from the dump. That means I have forty-five minutes to practice a welcome speech for Nora's mother, the *not from Serbia, from Kosov-a* one. A welcome for the new boys' kin. I try to evade the picture of her in my mind, of her in a chorus with the new boys all those years ago, shouting into our faces: *You'll be no more.*

I force a stop onto my body to quit the thought. One thing at a time: Prepare the speech. My hope of making a home is gone, a non-issue now. No purpose thinking about it anymore, like when Dad died. Focus on what is.

*

I step to the side of the kids' bedroom window to hear what's going on, but to avoid them seeing me. Their voices are raised, Emma's more pronounced, with an argument brewing.

"No! I want to show my friends where Mama and Pa are from! I'll tell them to be careful!"

"It's a five-hundred-piece jigsaw puzzle, Emma, and you'll never set it up. It takes hours and hours."

"Well, Ma-riah, even if it takes hours and hours, my friends are smart and we'll still do it! It's my birthday, you know! I get to decide what we do today!"

I know how they'll be staring at each other, Emma defiant and Mariah thinking through her options. She loves this puzzle that we put together as a family, and she wants all five hundred pieces intact, in a box, left in the attic until her sister's friends are gone. How to get this to happen is the question she's figuring out.

"How about I give you my world map, and you can show them where Mama and Pa are from?"

"No! I want us to put *this* world map together!"

If Mariah doesn't find a way to convince Emma to pack up the puzzle and put it away, their argument is bound to grow into a fight long enough to prevent them from having time to get some rest. If Emma doesn't have some quiet time before her friends overwhelm her with excitement, she'll have a meltdown in the middle of the evening. We all know it'll happen, we've all had the experience. But Mariah won't let go of the puzzle. If her reasoning doesn't succeed, Emma will only get more upset, derailing the schedule.

I can stop this right now. There are almost two-and-a-half hours before Emma's friends come, and if I stop this argument now, they'll have time to pack up everything else they don't want Emma's friends to play with, and then get some rest. I just need to veto the puzzle and take it to the attic. Emma would be upset, but not for long. I just need to go into their room and solve it.

But I cannot. I have no mind left for arguments and explanations. I must conserve what I have for practicing the speech. Focus. Don't botch that up as well today.

"But Emma, we'll never be able to put it together again with Mama and Pa if your friends scatter the puzzle pieces all around the house and yard like they did last time with the flower-valley-and-mountain one. Remember how we never found *sixteen whole pieces*." Mariah's voice is rising now, as well.

I walk all the way around the house, cut across the front lawn, and get to the back door from the other side, so I can avoid walking in front of the kids' bedroom window. I can't have them notice me right now. I step onto the deck and head to the back entrance without a sound.

Before I step over the threshold, I look once again at the dirt square, the flawlessly combed wound cleansed of all its inhabitants.

I see Mike mounting one of his bicycles in front of his garage, now entirely visible with the shed gone. His back is turned to me, but I can still see in my mind the contortion on his face when his suggestion of *relocation* was met with Will's *ethnic cleansing*. How serene it would be to be Mike. To be shocked at these terms. To disbelieve them. To find them distasteful. To not connect them to anything you know.

How serene it would be to believe in a simple move, not one that tears apart everything that you are, that deforms a life into another warped identity. Forever.

Relocation. It's okay, Mike had said to me when we found the raccoon babies. *She'll find a new home.*

As if home could be found just like that. How I wish that Will and I could possess such belief.

"Maa-maa!"

Emma's call shakes me back into the moment. I must get ready for her. For Nora's mother.

I rush inside the house and cross the living room, avoiding the creaky floor planks. Take twenty-seven steps from the back entrance to the attic stairs, as Mariah once counted. Halfway up the fourteen curving, narrow steps, I bend my head to avoid getting a head-bump from the low ceiling, and I'm at the opening to the attic. My *box room*, as the kids call it, is to the left of the stairs. Their playroom is across from it, to the right. I sense calm around me.

*

The box room is a white-walled attic storage space, full of boxes set in two rows with a narrow pathway between them. It looks almost like an antithesis of the kids' playroom. The two attic spaces, the box room and the playroom, were originally built as mirror images of each other, but they now each have an entirely different sense of space. The playroom's vast, the box room's practically non-existent.

The playroom's walls are painted in pink and lilac with flowers drawn on top, and within the playroom, a bookshelf Will built out of cedar planks that still smell like the tree they were felled from, a sky-blue beanbag, a pink plastic table with two small chairs in light green and yellow, and a pink, yellow, and lilac toy stove with matching pots and pans. One of Mariah's friends once described it as *a fairy-tale room.*

The box room is filled up to the low, slanted ceiling with the same type of boxes—clear plastic with blue tops. They line both sides of the room, in two columns and two rows deep on each side. I've never counted, but there must be around fifty boxes in this small space.

One of them is just mine, hidden on the bottom right against the wall.

Even without a door, the sounds from downstairs miraculously never reach up here, into my box room. I sit down in the middle of the narrow path between the two rows of boxes and start to seek *my* healing.

I squeeze my arm in between the first box row where I sit and touch the plastic behind it. My sunflower tablecloth hides inside. My sunflowers never come out of the hidden box unless I'm alone in the house. But when I touch the plastic of my box, my fingers can feel the sunflower thread. I know how my sunflowers feel, my stand-in for Grandma's blanket.

All those years ago, Mom made me put on my winter coat and leave Grandma's blanket on the couch as we were leaving home. I screamed for it all the way to the train station. I didn't know that Dad went back inside and without anyone seeing him, snatched the sunflower tablecloth from the oak table and wrapped it around his body under his coat. Like gauze dressing a wound all the way to Belgrade. He was already skinny, his clothes too big for him, enough to hide the tablecloth, but not big enough to hide Grandma's blanket. Dad's last gift to me. Our secret.

When I touch the box where my sunflowers lie, I am affirmed. I know I had Dad. I had a home. I belonged with the roots in the soil that bred me from the flesh and bones of my ancestors. My peace. My healing.

The scene of my welcome to Nora's mother comes all on its own. My mind is processing, adjusting, memorizing.

We're on two sides of the fence, I am inside, she is not.

Welcome, welcome, wonderful having Nora over, I'm Emma's mom. A quick wave, no handshakes, no names, just the roles we hold over the fence. *Nora-dear, come on in, the girls are waiting for you.* The gate opens only for the child. I keep my eyes on the mother, keeping her on the other side, clear that she's not expected to cross over. I close the gate as the girl comes in.

Does Nora have any allergies? Oh, okay, good to know. Say it all in one sentence, like there's nothing else in the world but the care and joy of this celebration. Be a bubbly, cheerful American mother excited for her child's birthday. Be nothing else.

You're welcome to pick her up in the morning, between nine and nine-thirty, we're going to church afterward, so the timeline's kind of tight. Shoulder shrug, eyebrows up, an apology. *Or, if Nora doesn't feel comfortable staying for a sleepover, you're welcome to pick her up tonight at eight-thirty. They'll start watching a movie then, and I'm sure Nora won't wish to leave in the middle of it.* Plan for the minute she'll be back, eight-thirty, don't be caught unprepared.

Then get my cell phone out. *You have our phone number, correct? Please give me your number, just in case I need to contact you.* Say it out loud while typing it into my phone: *Nora's mom.* No name, just the role. Look up at her, *Ready for the number when you are.* Repeat the numbers as you type them in. *Okay-good, I have it now.*

Then another wave and a carefree smile. *Thank you for bringing Nora. Emma is very excited to have her.* Busy, cheery, quick, over within a minute. Turn around and go toward the celebration. All done.

Act like Kosovo is not in my veins. Like there has never been a stone home with twelve generations of Popovics in it. No tapestry with our family tree. No chips off of the mountain. And no new boys shouting a prophecy.

I pull back my hand that was touching the sunflower box. I need to write all these things down. Plan every step and then rote-memorize it like my multiplication tables on Grandma's blanket.

The box to the left of me, across from the row with my sunflower box, is full of the kids' old notebooks, pens, and markers. I flap open the notebooks box to get a piece of paper and a pen. As I pop the lid off, the notebooks box slides toward me, pushed by the Belfast suitcase behind it.

A chill runs through me.

The suitcase had been set hidden against the wall, shielded by its own row of boxes. Like my sunflowers across from it. I know where it was hidden, I did it myself two months ago when Will asked me to find a place for it before the kids saw it. It looks like someone's moved it.

I push the notebooks box to shove the Belfast suitcase against the wall, to push it back to being hidden. But it won't go back. I thrust at it again, burning my palm with a slap on the plastic. I have no time for this. I must prepare for Nora's mother.

The awkward bent of my torso and the act of sitting on my legs and twisting to push and push the stubborn notebooks box against the Belfast suitcase is making my back hurt. The more I shove it, the more they both slide back toward me.

I pause.

An unwelcome, intrusive thought forms inside of me. What if I opened it—would this morning's letter be there?

I lift the suitcase toward me and suspend it above the notebooks box, without really thinking about what I'm doing. I breathe.

I notice that both latches are unfastened. One of the locks had already been broken when the suitcase arrived, but when I hid the suitcase, I bolted the good lock and folded over the rings of both locks to latch them. They held fine. Now both latches are undone and the suitcase holds only with the good lock.

For a moment there, I shudder, thinking that the kids might have gotten into it. Then I realize that's impossible, as there's no way they could've kept quiet about it, and I'd surely know. And then I realize that before he went to the dump, Will came back inside. He must have done this.

I lean the suitcase against the notebooks box and try to still my breathing. To think it through. But I have only one thought—the letter might be inside.

1995: San Francisco
Love Story Take Two

When Will comes to pick me up next Friday, it's a repeat of Sunday, the first day we spent together after he intercepted me at Mrs. Jane's. We stroll, we talk, we eat, and then we part ways until tomorrow.

There is one change, though—we don't meet on Sundays, my day for church and Mrs. Jane, we meet on Fridays and Saturdays instead. Other than that, all is the same for the entire month of Fridays and Saturdays that follow. No kissing, no touching, no holding hands. He waits for me in front of my building on Fridays at seven o'clock and Saturdays at noon, and he doesn't reach for my hand, doesn't wrap his arm around my shoulders. We just walk and talk and sometimes eat. Yet more non-dates.

This Saturday morning, the most recent one in a string of potential sameness, I wait for the noon hour. When I spoke with Katarina this morning, she said that maybe Will is shy to take the next step, and he needs time for courage to build.

"That's *really hardly* possible for me to believe," I said to her.

It just cannot be the case with Will. He seems so determined, so assured in his steps, like he knows exactly what he's doing. He left Blazoning so that we could *date*. He told me that in so many words on the sidewalk in front of Mrs. Jane's market stall. There is no way he didn't think long and hard before he decided to leave his own company. He *started* Blazoning with Rob, his best friend. The two of them, their mission, their years-long work since college. Even the name *Blazoning* was a concoction of Will's own mind. The flaming Milky Way in its logo, too. There is no way Will would've just abandoned it all without being sure that we, he and I, were in it for the long run. The very last adjectives I would ever ascribe to Will are *indecisive* and *impulsive*. There's just no way he did it without a thorough consideration.

That's what I said to Katarina this morning. But if that's all true, then why is he holding back?

"Maybe he needs *you* to be ready. To know that *you* are ready." Katarina said.

I cannot understand this. How could he not feel that I long for his hand to hold mine? For my lips to feel his? When he looks at me, his eyes are the very reflection of my longing, so how could he not recognize it in me? It's just impossible.

Katarina insisted this morning that he might need to *really* know it. She made me remember all the signs he'd been giving me all along before he sought me out at the market that Sunday a month ago.

The signs you missed one-by-one, every single one, she said. *He hid away in his office for two whole weeks after the first Barsync because he had to think it through. Then, when he finally showed up in that striped suit, he'd already sorted it out with Rob. He'd already decided, passed the climactic point, no turning back.*

I still gasp when I think of him in that striped suit.

He was going to an interview, and he came to show it to you, Katarina reasoned. *But you didn't get it.*

That's true. Even when Harry asked him where he was going, to a funeral or to an interview, and Will looked at me in that way of his, as if sending a message before he answered with *Aye*, I still didn't get it. I knew that no IT worker in San Francisco wears suits except for when going to interviews, and yet, I didn't get it.

Katarina said he must have assumed I would've known. That I would've realized *why he came to pose for you in that suit*. And also why he missed the company meeting, why he then started coming around my cubicle all of a sudden, looking in, being everywhere, and then why he left Blazoning. *But you got none of it. Maybe that's what's stopping him now*, she said. *He's there, but he can't tell that you are. That's why he's holding back*.

I wish so much to be one of those big city girls who can kiss a boy first. To tell him I like him. To tell him he's in my being before I open my eyes in the morning, and the last to leave it before sleep overtakes me. That I can barely take a breath without him inside it.

This morning, as she sensed how disheartened I was by all his reservation, Katarina tried for some comic relief. *Just imagine what Rob must have thought when he told him!* She chuckled to herself. *Utterly silly, delusional even. He must've asked Will, What if Marica turns out to be a psycho? What if she's secretly married, or has someone already?*

I can imagine Rob disbelieving Will. *Leaving your own company for a girl you once— once!—walked to her apartment?* Katarina's certainty about Will's intentions has rubbed off on me somewhat.

Still, I don't get Will. A whole month of just hanging out. That's what my Kentucky college friends called what Will and I are doing, *hanging out*. We're hanging out on Fridays and Saturdays. Nothing else.

And yet, it's not really just hanging out. It's like we're a couple somehow. Like he's paving the way to something with his questions, with the way he looks at me like he wants to slowly, piece-by-piece, get to know me as deeply as if I were a part of him. Wants *me* to know *him* like that, as well.

When he bends down to hear me in the crowded Ghirardelli Square, I don't know that he hears any of the words I say. He just looks into my face like he's breathing me in with his eyes, with all his senses. Like he wants to know how my lips form an *A* or an *O*, how I take my breath, how my breath sounds going in and out, how my eyelashes move as I blink, how my throat moves when I swallow. Last Friday he watched me smell a rosemary bush. I had bunched up a sprig gently, to not disturb the bees or the flowers, like Dad taught me, and when I looked back at him, it seemed like the blood within him had stopped coursing through. Like he was going to take my hands in his and smell the rosemary on my skin. But, he didn't.

In between our times together, we read the same books. He said he'd like to read anything I'd like him to read. That's what he said: *Whatever you'd like me to read.* The way he said it, it was as if he asked for permission to see into my soul, to let him inside, to open his own to me.

Our first book was the biography of a Uruguayan junta leader's lover. Katarina told me about it. The lover knew the exact scope of evil the junta leader participated in, which even affected her own family, disappearing two of her cousins, yet she'd stayed loyal to him all the years after his death, accepting her punishment for it. A siloed, lifelong isolation for not even being a wife. He had a wife and children—she was just *a side thing* for him. Still, she'd never denounced him.

That whole Saturday, Will and I wondered whether it was possible to love with such abandon, to love someone cruel, to love without the ability to judge any of it. To watch but not see. Could such love really be? How?

I could tell he thought a lot about it. Coming from the Troubles, it's not surprising. War and violence are inseparable, people become ruthless, and yet, love is always there in all its forms. Like the four ancient Greek words for love. They're all there—in war, in violence, in life.

Last night we talked about Anna Karenina. We wondered how it might be excusable that she left her young son so that she could be with her lover. That she destroyed her infant daughter's future. We wondered just how much vulnerability is excusable. If a need to be as you are can be pardoned even when it means you abandon all who depend on you.

We never come to any conclusions, we just wonder. But Will's questions are creating this sense of understanding between us that I've never known, except with Katarina. Understanding of me, of him, of life. We never, of course, we never-ever mention our own experiences. It's always all about the characters in the books, all hypothetical. There has never been a single insinuation that anything applies to either of us in any way. These are just our thoughts, discussions, philosophizing.

When we aren't spending time together, I cannot shake off the questions and the answers. I talk to him in my mind as I sit at my cubicle desk, as I walk to and from work, as I read. He's always there, always around in my mind. As if the world does not exist outside of the two of us.

And yet, what Will and I do is not dating, even if it's not exactly just hanging out.

When we spoke of Anna Karenina last night, it occurred to me that maybe his family is objecting to me. Family is everything, and if he's the only son left, it shouldn't surprise me that his parents might want him to be with a woman from their homeland. Curiosity, a raw need to know, overtook me, and I had to ask.

"Is there any family left in Belfast?" I was unable to make myself look at him as my words came out. I wanted to know, even though I was fully aware I would come across as prying. Curious. Intact. But I had to know.

We were on the way to dinner at the Stinking Rose. He'd made reservations for us, I don't know how, since they're known to require them six months in advance. I stared down Columbus Avenue, my question hanging uneasily in the air.

When he heard me, he turned his head away and looked toward the traffic in the street. I'm sure his eyebrows came close together and his breathing sped up, though I couldn't tell. His voice came out delayed, in a single word. "Father."

One person in all the family. Father.

To soothe the intrusion of my question, I offer my scripted answer. I told him that Dad died when I was little, cancer, that I barely remember him. That Mom and Katarina and the big extended family are all back in Belgrade where we're from. I narrated it all as I'd done before, almost as if filling in a form: *Where are you from? Parents? Sibling(s)? Living? Dead? Cause of death?* I feel a pang for lying, but then I think I didn't even lie about most of it. I *was* born in Belgrade, my passport says so. Mom's difficult pregnancy accounted for her long stay in a big Belgrade hospital. Dad's death certificate does say *cancer*, not blood poisoning. It was almost all true, what I told him.

"Do you miss your father?" I asked.

He didn't respond for a long time, for almost a whole block. Then he said, turning his head to look down Columbus, halfway toward me, "I miss John. My brother. I miss Ma."

I didn't feel resentment directed at me for asking the questions, I felt raw grief. Like an open wound, a stinging pain with no end, even if hidden from view. If I'd let another urge take over me, I'd have leaned into him. But I didn't. We just walked into the noisy restaurant and Will told the host his name.

*

That was last night. But as the noon hour creeps closer this Saturday, I'm starting to understand another thing that Katarina said this morning. As I'm getting it, a sense of my naivete burns through my gut. A boiling sense of humiliation.

I'd have gladly accepted anything else, anything other than what I now know.

This morning, Katarina helped me understand it all, though of course that was the very last thing she wanted to do. She intended to comfort me by saying that I finally don't need to worry so much about my stay in the US, because Will has his citizenship, so if anything goes wrong with the Blazoning sponsorship, I can just marry him. She wanted me to know, in spite of everything, that we were a couple already.

But the idea wedged me dead as I realized that was exactly it. That was it. I stood, waiting, until the complete thought had formed inside of me. *He thinks I'll use him.* How did I not see it before?

At first, I thought I should tell him not to worry, that I can take care of myself, I always have. I thought acknowledgement would relieve the concern. But then I realized something more—he's regretting leaving Blazoning. I noticed a while ago that he never mentions his new job. Now I get why—it must be because it's not fulfilling. It's the very opposite of the dream he worked so hard toward with Rob—the dream I prevented.

This whole morning, I've been thinking through our time together, and I'm now realizing that all I've been seeing between the two of us is an illusion, figments of my own imagination. It's only the way *I* feel.

I remember how he spoke with Lizzy during the second Barsync, like he was reading her lips. That's how he is with everyone—attentive, focused, present. And so that's how he is with me. Nothing different. It's just the way he is, endlessly courteous. He's being courteous, while I'm dying to be with him. That's the imbalance.

As the morning wears on, I understand better and better. He committed himself to spending time with me, and he's trying to bear it as best as he can by sticking to his sense of honor. He wouldn't stray from his chivalry if it killed him. I don't know how I know, but I know that about him. I also know now that he must have changed his mind. He's not holding back—he's just trying to make it tolerable with interesting books and philosophizing and discussions. Nothing personal. He's biding his time until an honorable exit becomes possible. That is, until I get my immigration papers.

The eternal curse of reliable people: You do what you say you'll do, even if you change your mind. Will promised me Fridays at seven and Saturdays at noon, and now he must go through with them. A reliable person never breaks a promise or leaves someone in need.

This is what I finally understand, this morning. I now know that all I'd believed he felt, all that I'd seen in him, I in fact invented. I've invented it. In my wish to understand why he's held back so long, my focus on dissecting his looks, his words, his behavior, I've missed the key—he changed his mind. Will does not feel the way I do any longer. That's what I finally see.

As I'm awaiting the noon hour, I almost wish I could be on an airplane to Belgrade. With all the losses and pain, at least no one there will feel pity for me.

Then the anger rises up. William Ford should know that all of my life, ever since Dad died, I've stood on my own two feet as best as I could. Alone, I researched universities, the requirements, the scholarships; I studied for TOEFL every day at the Central Belgrade Library for two whole years of high school and passed with 673 out of 677 points, and six points out of six for the written test. I'd like to ask him how many people he knows who've passed TOEFL with that score. Certainly not many.

I rut my life's path, and no one has ever done it for me, not since I was nine years old. I know what I need to do and I do it. I'd found a job when I needed money to pay for all the tests, applications, and later, the airplane ticket to Lexington. I was the only high schooler I knew who had a job. I went completely alone to Lexington, finished my studies with honors in a foreign language within three, not four years. No summer breaks for me. I've managed all of it on my own. I'll manage my immigration papers just as well. I wish William could know all that. That I'm not a person who needs his pity.

I'll be done today. That's my comfort. I can't just cancel on him, as it would be rude, but I'll end it this evening. I still don't know how, but I will. There's nothing to hope for. Pure chimera. All of this *the world doesn't exist outside of the two of us* is my own invention. My own desire. His is to get out of it all.

Not to worry, Will, after today you'll be all done.

I write my decision on a Post-it slip and pin it up on the board above my folding table: *End today. Non-negotiable.*

*

A few minutes past noon, I come downstairs, where he waits for me. I've never been late before, but I'm not exactly in the mood to care for etiquette. I'm tempted to tell him to pity in his gentlemanly manner whomever else, I'm not *that girl*, but I'm conscious that I must control myself. Be courteous, like him. I open the entrance door, stumble over the threshold coming out, and don't look at him.

He says his normal "Hi, Mari."

I nod in response, and I'm annoyed even more, feeling his examination of my face.

"I thought we could try a place I heard about, Ti Couz?"

I don't say anything, I just start walking down Fillmore, not sure if that's even the right direction to this place he mentioned.

What sense of honor does he get out of this? Like he's courting a maiden from Victorian England, just missing a chaperone, while never intending anything. I wish to remind him that such conduct was indecorous even then. You either want or you don't want. But you never give false hopes to anyone. *What a vain need for chivalry. A savior syndrome.* I feel so degraded, I wish I could just turn around and never see him again. *I can take care of myself, William Ford! Green card or not. With you or not.*

As we walk, I realize I'm chanting "No, thank you, William."

"Sure. Where do you want to go?"

"I'm sorry." When I realize I've said it out loud, I try to smile and look at him. "I was thinking of something else."

"I know."

And there, again, there is that sense that nothing exists, only the two of us. That he cannot possibly be feeling what I know for a fact that he's feeling. But I check myself. *He's only courteous, Marica, nothing else.*

I don't respond to him, just walk.

"What would you like?" he repeats.

"It's okay, let's do that place you mentioned."

We walk down Fillmore towards Market. It's a long walk, many blocks, to go without sound. Tears well up in my throat, angry and sad combined. *This is it, the end.* I imagine tomorrow, after my anger disperses. I imagine longing for him. The steps I'll take, trying to overcome it. I imagine leafing through a Berkeley Extension booklet with courses that I'm already late for. I can always take a few in the evenings and stay busy catching up over the weeks. *I'll decide tonight, after this charity "hanging out."* The tears are at the corners of my eyes, starting to fog up my vision. I have the urge to go back the way I came, rush into my apartment, avoid all this, and save myself.

On the corner of Fillmore and Fulton, I look toward the Old Holy Virgin Cathedral. I come to it often after work, just to walk by and put my hand on the wooden door planks. It's never been open when I've come by, but a while ago I made a plan to come here one Sunday for a service, instead of going to St. John's. *Maybe tomorrow*, I think. I look up through the tall trees from the corner of Fillmore and Fulton, toward the icon with the open arms and the angels above. I make a plea: *I'll need Your help tomorrow.*

When I look back at the streetlight to see if it turned green, I realize Will is not beside me. I turn around and see him standing more than ten feet back on Fillmore. I extend my arms out and open my palms upward, as if to say *What now?*

For a moment, he doesn't move, just looks at me with that look of his and a smile. Just looks. Then he takes very slow, measured steps, coming toward me, anchoring me to the ground.

I look back at him for a moment, but unable to move. Then I feel my throat so tight, the air is struggling to get through, in or out. His footsteps come as if in slow motion. I feel everything around me—the wind streaming through my hair, a leaf cradling down to the pavement. I know the leaf would be spiky on its edges if I caught it in its flight. Brittle. I can almost feel it in my fingers. I smell a nearby lavender bush. I feel no ground under my feet, a breeze could topple me over. I recognize this moment for what it is.

Will is coming slowly, smiling that smile that overtakes his face like he knows what no one knows, the joy of this moment. The very existence of it.

When he reaches me, he takes my face into his hands. It feels right. Stabilizing. I smell his musk. His palms are so soft and warm, cupping my cheeks. His eyes are fully open as he looks into me, just looks, holding me. Then he bends toward me and his breath reaches my face with his words. His lips, thick and wide, come very close to my face.

"I fancy you, Mari," he whispers.

Dizziness overtakes my mind. I just feel his body so close to me, his lips hovering above mine, his breath on my face, his musk I want to absorb, his hands on my cheeks and neck. I have no lucid thought inside of me.

"I fancy you very well."

I don't even remember the anger. It disperses like a balloon, raw longing spilling directly into my veins. I can't breathe for want of his warmth on me. I have no guard against this wanting. I reason nothing, my senses only feel for him.

His movements are very slow. He kisses my eyes first and I feel the tears release. His lips follow their flow to reach my lips. His palms guide my face. I don't know if my lips respond. He stops for a moment, not letting my face out of his hands, his eyes happy. Then his lips go to mine again. I don't know how to stop the shivers taking over me. His arms envelop my body, pulling me into his own. His head is leaning against mine like it's always belonged there, only there. We don't move.

"My Mari," he whispers.

He pulls back to look at me again, and I hear people next to us, waiting for the light to turn green. "That's love, man," says one person. "Yeah baby, love," says another.

Will turns to them, one arm wrapping around my shoulders, and his other hand taking mine into his. "Love, indeed," he responds.

They laugh, hearing him, and the tears still stream down my face. I have no real idea where I am or what's really happening. I just feel.

When we finally step into the street to cross it, I look toward the icon again. The open arms and the angels above.

Will doesn't let my hand out of his own the whole day. Like he'll never let go of me. We walk down Laguna, cross Market, and walk into Mission. We don't talk, and we don't pass a block without stopping, my face in his warm palms.

"I'm starving," Will says when we get to 16th. "You?"

I nod.

"Let's go to Ti Couz."

If I had to describe my state of being, I'd have to say I'm ecstatic, like crying and laughing together. Like I've been waiting all of my life for this very afternoon.

Later, much later that evening, he walks me back to my building. Before I can tell him that I don't want him to leave, he says, "Come to my place tomorrow?"

I nod. I know where he lives. We've passed by his building several times over the last month, and each time I thought he'd invite me in.

"It's twenty-seven minutes walking," he says. "And a half... Twenty-seven-and-a-half."

He sounds like he might know the exact number of steps between our two apartments, but I don't ask.

We kiss one more time, or more, I'm not sure, and then he asks for the building key, unlocks the door, hands the key back to me, and blocks the door from closing with his boot, the yellow stitching on black leather. He places his palms one on top of the other over his heart, the palms I've felt on my cheeks and neck the whole day.

"'Parting is such sweet sorrow, that I shall say good night till it be morrow.'"

I enter the building, and he still holds the door open.

"Come as soon as you wake up," he shouts after me in his baritone, probably waking everyone in the building.

I run upstairs without stopping. I'm barely able to keep from squealing aloud. I'm out of breath when my sweet neighbor Sharina comes out of her apartment.

"Hey, Marica, is that you? How's it going?"

"Well, thank you." I try to sound calm as I unlock my apartment door.

"Girl! You look haaappy! I haven't seen you like that." She waves her index finger up-down, up-down, pointing at me. "E-ver." She seems to squeal for me.

Sharina knows that Will and I spend Friday evenings and Saturdays together. She told me once that Will is a good-looking hunk. I had to look it up in the dictionary to find out what *hunk* meant.

I wish to scream back a *Yes!* but I hold it in. I just grin at her.

"You wanna talk? Water, tea, wine… Will Ford." She winks at me. "I'm here."

I laugh, realizing what she must be seeing in my face. "I need to go to bed, but thank you, dear Sharina."

Once I tell her, I imagine she'll say *Hallelujah! I was thinking of getting someone to give you two instructions on dating! None of this walking-*

around-San-Fran thing." She'll be happy for me, I know it.

But I'm not ready to share it with her, or anyone. Yet. It's too fresh. I want to keep it within me in full force. I don't want to dilute it with words.

"Just knock, you know where I am," Sharina tells me, as if she can feel my wish to relive it myself for a moment.

I nod at her, trying to control the grin attempting to wrap around my face.

And then I'm inside, bending over my bed, squealing into my pillow, as quiet on the outside as I can be. *Not over. It's not over.* I spring up and rip my "decision" note from the board above my table, rip it into the smallest shreds my fingers can make, and throw the shreds into the toilet. I flush so hard that the handle gets stuck.

I don't sleep well. It's only when the sun starts coming out that I collapse into rest, and then jolt back into consciousness a few hours later, anxious I might have missed it. This is the first Sunday since I landed in the US that I don't go to church. I forget to go to Mrs. Jane's. I forget it's a Sunday altogether—Will and I don't see each other on Sundays. But the one thing I don't forget is *Come as soon as you wake up.*

I arrive in front of Will's building before nine in the morning. I buzz his interphone and he responds instantly, startling me.

"Fifth floor," he says, without checking that I am the one at the door.

I try to calm my breathing as I go upstairs. His building smells like a sage bush. I see him looking over the banister while I'm still on the first floor. He leans so far out, I hope he's holding hard onto the handrail.

As I come to the fifth floor, he steps back inside his apartment, his eyes calling me in, his voice quiet. The door is open as wide as it will go, and when I stop in front of it, suddenly unsure of all this, he extends his arms and cloaks my sweaty, freezing hands with his own, drawing me inside, discharging my sense of insecurity. He pushes the door closed behind us, and his lips are gliding over mine, opening them, inviting, his palms guiding my face. We speak no words.

The rush of expectation coursing through my body is choking me. I have to make myself slow down to heed his unhurried, deliberate movements. His attempt to study every fragment of my skin with his senses.

I absorb his scent. I learn his breathing. The way his belly twitches when the touch is right. The way his neck vein pulses like it's going to break free of the flesh. The way another vein coils on the side of his forehead, from his hairline to his eyebrow, like an attachment, unknown and unexpected. The way his skin feels under mine, taut over the muscles, silky beneath the leg hair, and so tenuous, so delicate where exposed. The way he lifts his arms up and rumples his hair when I take over, looking at me with trusting eyes, releasing himself to me, all expectation. The way his skin tastes. The way my body responds.

It's nothing I've ever known. This slowness, this giving of myself.

*

I wake up in Will's bed on Monday. It's six in the morning, he is next to me, his head propped up on his palm, looking at me, not half a step away. I'm levitating even before I'm awake. I know he's there. I fear saying anything, changing anything. I fear the bubble will burst.

We sit on his balcony with breakfast Will made for us. Blueberries, pecan halves, and oatmeal in three small red ceramic bowls served on a flat white plate. Only a trail of dark liquid chocolate is missing to make it a breakfast of royals. We're wrapped in one blanket, intertwined with one another. His skin warm on mine.

His old book of sonnets in green binding with gold cursive letters is still open on his table, I see from the balcony. I'd never heard Shakespeare come out of a man like it did yesterday. *O, learn to read what silent love hath writ: To hear with eyes belongs to love's fine wit.* I want more of it. This whole moment, our bodies against one another, the feast we share, the way each blueberry erupts in my mouth releasing its sweetness, the sonnets in his baritone still beating in my mind. *Lo, thus, by day my limbs, by night my mind, For thee and for myself no quiet find.* I want to capture it all unto eternity.

"Go to your place tonight, I'll wait for you there after work, and let's bring everything here. You have a notice to give before the first."

At once, the bubble bursts and a chill goes through me. A spoonful of oatmeal is stuck in my mouth and I cannot swallow it. After no sound comes out of me, Will pulls away a little to look at me. Then he just waits for me to speak.

I take my time, force myself to swallow, calm my body. "I'll keep my place."

He breathes in, two wrinkles forming between his eyebrows. He's quiet, just looking at me, and then he looks away and exhales heavily with an "Of course." He pauses, then looks over my shoulder toward the street. "Of course. It's too quick," he adds, like he's explaining to himself.

Later, I realize why he held back for so long. Over a month. Not the green card, not objections from Belfast, not some strange joy in holding back. But because *it would have been too quick.* For *me.* Just as Katarina said it, *I* needed to be ready.

He pinches his lower lip with his index finger and thumb, thinking, wrinkling his forehead. Looking into the street, his voice barely audible, he says, "How about we talk this week, see where we are?"

"Yes."

He gets up, leaving me with the sense of chill. "I'll make us coffee."

I stay on his balcony while he brews us coffee, double-wrapping myself in the blanket and still freezing. *I need time*, I tell myself. *I just need time to be on my own, to decide.* It was so slow, and now it's all done: living together, marrying, having kids, dying. It *is* too quick.

I sit on his balcony until he invites me in for coffee. I'm still wrapped in the blanket, and he's already dressed in a T-shirt and jeans. We sip our coffee and talk about a movie that just came out, careful not to imply we'll watch it together. I take my clothes to the bathroom, dress myself, and come back out to where he's still sitting at the table, his eyebrows divided by two deep lines reaching the bridge of his nose. I put on my hoodie. He puts on his shoes to walk me out, but I ask him not to. We kiss goodbye—the kiss has no meaning in it, and his hands are not coddling my cheeks and my neck. He stays inside, and I don't hear him close the door when I'm downstairs. But I don't listen for it and don't look up.

I get to my apartment, take a shower, and dress for work. I walk to the office, though I know I'll be late. I don't notice any of the intersections or the mountains. I descend steep California Street hills, unaware of the wind, the air, the sun, the sounds, the magic of memory—all the usual reasons I seek to walk along them.

What is it? I wonder. *Why is it that I cannot be with him? Why is it that I was going to drop it all just yesterday, and now that I know he likes me and we're together, I can't do it?*

Today: Seattle

Aoife

I sit in the attic, suspending the Belfast suitcase above the notebooks box as I think things through. I go between snapping closed the working lock and then unsnapping it back open. I don't want to do this. I don't want to be reminded of what's inside. I don't want to pry.

But maybe this morning's letter is inside. If I read it, maybe I'll know how to bring us back to being a happy family.

I breathe in and decide against it. It's Will's past. I made a mistake when I stayed with him that Saturday morning when the suitcase arrived. I will not make the same mistake again. He'll tell me about the letter, and we'll resolve whatever's inside it together.

I bolt the good lock and fold over both rings. The ring over the broken lock is a little flimsy, but it holds. I push the suitcase over the notebooks box to slide it back into its place. There's little space for maneuvering in the attic box room in general, but especially here where the ceiling sharply slants. My hands are shaking from the weight of the suitcase, and my torso throbs pain from twisting as I repeatedly push at the box.

The suitcase edges rut the ceiling, leaving permanent proof of what I'm doing. But the suitcase still won't slide back. Now that I've pulled it out of place, everything has shifted, so I have to bring the notebooks box closer to me to make more room behind it. I hold onto the suitcase with one hand and try to pull the notebooks box closer with my other hand. Wiggling the suitcase snaps open the good lock.

I relock and re-latch it and try again. I hold onto the suitcase and pull the notebooks box toward me. When the attempt doesn't work for the second time, I decide to take both the box and the suitcase completely out. Then I'll set them in order, like I did two months ago.

I grab for the suitcase handle and pull it forward, but it gets stuck at an angle between the slanting wall and the notebooks box. I jerk it toward me, and just as it's freed from the slope in the ceiling, it slips open, spilling out its contents. Some fall onto my lap, some go into the notebooks box, and some land in the space between the boxes.

Panic takes over me. My hands won't stop shaking, the desire to flee overwhelming me.

Black and white pictures everywhere. The orange sash. The crimson collarette. The flag with a red hand and a *No Surrender* promise. John's shirt. It all spills out.

I breathe in, out, in, out, hearing the wheezing sound of my throat. I rush to put everything back into the suitcase as best as my hands will allow— not bending the pictures, not crumpling the flag and the sashes.

The letter in Will's father's handwriting stares at me from my lap. *For God and Ulster.* A red hand drawn next to it, followed by a greeting: *To my son William, named after the Great William of Orange.*

I refold the letter as calmly as I can and stick it inside the suitcase. The recollection of the deaths, of the bombs in the shrubs, of his warnings. *I told him, William, how many times have I said it, never pass through a shrub, my boy, never step on anything but solid pavement.* Of Will's mother's last bread that she baked with the taste of her tears inside. Of the blame. *My one good boy died for the cause, William, but you just packed up and ran. Weakling that you are, loving poetry like some woman. Not cut out for a fighter, you said. You're a shame to your father, boy. It killed your mother when you left, but you didn't even think it worthy to honor her at her funeral, never came back.*

I pick up the black-and-white family pictures and lay them on top of the letter in the suitcase. Nothing but grief.

In the notebooks box, a fallen envelope is stuck on the side of the notebooks and faces me from the see-through plastic. I shimmy my hand against the paper edges of the notebooks to get to it. A paper cut splits the second knuckle on my index finger as I pull at the envelope. I jerk my hand and the envelope falls right next to me. It's the letter from this morning.

A photograph partly slips out of the envelope. It's in color, not like the rest of the photos that came with the Belfast suitcase. My breathing speeds up, but I don't slide the picture back inside.

Instead, I look at the man and woman in the photo. The man is so much like Will. Smiling. Just like Will from California twenty years ago. I only know it's not Will because the man in the picture has a split chin, resembling the woman standing beside him. And he has a dark mole above his lip, which the woman doesn't have. But those are the only differences between my Will from twenty years ago and this man in the picture.

I'm aware I should put the photograph back inside the envelope, put it back with everything that belongs to the suitcase, lock it, latch it, and set it hidden. Wait for Will to share the letter with me. Any minute, the kids could come up to the attic, and Will could return from the dump. I am where I should not be, prying. I know it, but I continue staring.

The man in the picture is in his twenties with a woman about my age today, maybe a little older. They stand on a lawn in front of a red brick building that looks like an old university, and they are smiling and waving as if at me, the viewer.

The woman is tall and dignified, in a bright flowery dress billowing in the wind. Her big brown eyes sparkle, and her smile is wide with angular jaw and split chin, like life has always demanded for her to be determined.

She's full of color, a contrast to the young man in a long black university gown with a pressed, snow-white shirt underneath. His neck bands are flailing toward the woman. The gown of a judge or a lawyer. There is a gray wig in this young man's waving hand. His eyes, with the eyebrows heavy over them, the smile threatening to overtake his face, the shiny chestnut hair, the height, the composure—it's all Will as I knew him in his twenties. All except for the chin and the beauty mark.

The woman's long brown hair shines as it flies in the wind, following the direction of her bright flowery dress and the young man's snow-white neck bands. His arm is around her shoulders, like he's protecting her, like he's making sure she's there. The dark mole is big in the crease of his smile lines.

I feel invited to join them in their celebration, and I realize my breathing has calmed from seeing Will's father's letter. I'm smiling back at them. There's something familiar about them, a warmth, like I used to feel back home. Like they're family.

I wonder what this picture is doing in the Belfast suitcase. I don't want to put it back with the rest of the pain. I'd like to put the photo into a frame, hang it on a wall. This must be Will's family I've never heard of, but that I'm sure to like when I meet. We have pictures all over the house of Katarina, her boys and husband, Mom, and Simonida's and Petar's kids. It would be joyous to have some of Will's family, too.

I hear someone coming up the stairs and I hope it's Will. I'm not afraid any longer that he'll catch me prying. I want to ask him about these people, so like him. I'd like to tell him to frame this photo, have it displayed alongside my family. I listen for him without turning around, hopeful, but disappointed when no one comes up.

I hold the picture. I don't want to let go of the happiness in it. And then I feel a warning. Something tells me I'll regret what I'm about to do.

I flip the picture over anyway. On its back, a beautiful cursive writing with calligraphy-like curves forming the heads of the R's and the tails of the A's. Penmanship as if learned with a teacher holding a switch for the little palms when the curves were inadequate. The words are written deliberately, like they are meant to adorn the page forever.

To Willbo,
With all our long-belated love!
Forever yours,
Tiárnach and Aoife

In the smaller letters alongside the very bottom edge of the picture, it says, *Barrister.*

Another warning, this time a rush in my belly. I'll regret this.

I nearly rip the envelope as I pull out the pages packed inside.

Monday, 6th of May, 2018
Belfast

Willbo! Our dearest!

It's been a lifetime! I've always known you'd forgive me some day, I only hoped I'd live to hear it.

You need not worry, Willbo, I'm not angry. I'm not sad, either. There were too many things to be angry about, too many, I couldn't live with them all within me. It's been years since I let it all go. I've taken my life as the Good Lord bestowed it upon me—no blame, no sorrow.

It's not all gone, though, I shouldn't lie. I don't expect it ever will be. Sometimes I wake up remembering the moment when you came to tell me, and it's always back as something I already knew. I was prepared, I can't explain how, but I had it in my ears before you said anything. Did I tell you that? I think I remember saying "I know" before your first word. Do you remember the same, or the years have twisted my memory? It's all possible.

I've spent years regretting the words that followed, Willbo. I wish I'd been able to catch myself on, to be there for you. I know what it did to you, too. I'm grateful you forgave me. I forgave everything years ago. I had Tiárnach to help me. He's a big man now, Willbo. He was an invisible seed when you left, and now he's a whole man.

Do you ever remember our beautiful dreams? Sometimes, inside my mind I hear your voices before I wake up. "Our revels now are ended. These our actors, as I foretold you, were all spirits, and are melted into air, into thin air." And I'm "cheerful, sir," I'm cheerful for as long as I can hold on to your voices within me. "All spirits." Do you still have the green tomes with golden cursive? Probably not, I know, it'd be like endlessly pressing a bruise, never letting it heal. You had other things to pack for your New World, I'm sure. But imagine this—the bookshop where we got it is still there on Shankill. Tiárnach loves digging though their volumes. He says it's the best bookshop in the whole of Belfast. Imagine, the very one on Shankill! Belfast is a small town, when you think of it—the past and the present have no peace walls to separate them.

Remember how the two of us dreamt of the baby inside of me? Our brilliant future. A peacemaker. A latch to hold our homeland together. Both of us, despite everything, despite our clans. He was conceived in so much love, Willbo! In so much hope. That's come out of him, I swear to you. He's never been an angry lad, never fired bricks at the peelers, not even when his mates called him a coward, he's never made troubles around your father's people. He's always been a good lad, like he's always known he was born to be the hope and the future. He's in restorative justice now. I think he'd be a pride to his pa, to you. He even has his pa's lips. His spitting image, isn't he?!

I want you to know that I kept my word. I told Tiárnach only when your letter arrived. He's now the only other person, other than you and me, who knows. Mari knows, I've no doubt, but that's on you.

My tale was of a Republican journalist. Married. Queen's had many of them visit, remember, it wasn't suspect. (By the way, Tiárnach had some of John's friends teach him at Queen's. Remember Andrew? He's still there. In a different world, John could've taught Tiárnach. I stopped imagining that world, though.) Dad wanted to kill me when he heard. Lorcán and Cian wanted to kill me. A proper-bred Catholic girl transgressing before marriage with a married man. Imagine if I'd told them the truth! A Paisleyite man's son, the father of an O'Connor baby! They'd have killed us both. For my blinded aunt's sake. For all my Provos. For the Rory O'Connors in all of these veins coursing through us. I hope you understand why I had to name him Tiárnach and raise him Catholic. There were no sidelines, Willbo, you know it. He had to have a side to survive. You were gone, I was all alone, no one else knew. I hope you understand.

All the years that the money was coming, I didn't tell him. He knew it was from America, he knew it was from someone he should love, a relative, but he didn't know it was you. One time, he was only a wee man, he asked if it's from his dad. I said no, he has no dad. I was so sad to tell him that, but he'd never asked again. It took a lot to not tell. It was hard to hear the wee lads shout, when he was six and nine and twelve, how their dads would knock his ballix in, but my Tiárnach could say nothing in return. It hurt, Willbo, it hurt to live. But I kept on telling him to wind his neck in, that he's a craic, that one day things would be better. "All which it inherit, shall dissolve." That's my peace. Amen.

No, I've never married. I had a soulmate once, you know it. It's only been Tiárnach since.

When your letter arrived, we read it together and I told him everything. He listened to me all night about our hopes of going to America all together, of your American granddad and how we'd get the papers because of him, of how we'd rally to help end violence here. To create a whole clan of the in-betweens. He is a full man now, nearly 30. You were barely eighteen when you left. Imagine him now, older than John. How strange that is to think.

When I told him, he asked about your church and we went together. I felt the Good Lord in your West Kirk, Willbo. I did! Tiárnach did, too. I think, in a different world where he'd grown up Protestant, I'd have been equally proud of him. A voice in your service told me so.

He very much wishes to meet you and your family. You look so happy, Willbo, the four of you. Mari is beautiful. She has sadness about her. There's weight in her eyelids, like she's hiding all her dead in them. She's like us, it's in her eyes. And she's so full of love, I see it. You've chosen well, Willbo, I'm happy for you. Thank you for sending your photo, it gave me a sense of what could've been, if only... I was never able to imagine it before, with all that we lived through, but now I finally have that vision. "We know what we are, but know not what we may be." Remember how we recited it? I've felt like Ophelia for more years than I can recall. "And will 'a not come again? And will 'a not come again? No, no... He never will come again."

It's better here now, much better. Not all better, but better. My heart has learned to continue beating when a car slows down next to me, and I don't dive for cover from the bangers and sparklers anymore. But we are a land of pain, still. Every-one I know takes some kind of medication, there's violence, and more people have died by suicide since '98 than have died in the Troubles. There're no jobs for the young ones. The Troubles never ended but are still living within our marrow. I'm glad your lasses know nothing of it. I hope your bones are free, as well.

I did regret having him, yes. For years I did. There were many years when I thought I was a fool for letting myself fall in love with the other side. For thinking the world could be different with an in-between life just because it's a life of love. I was a fool for wanting to bring him into this world. But then, there he was, and there was nothing else but to get on with things and raise him. I was angry at you for years. For making off from here and leaving us behind. The first few cheques that came, I ripped up and promised to never take your help. But then Tiárnach needed food and a home, and I decided to take it. Dad and Mum thought it was the Republican journalist sending the money. You can't imagine the names they called me, but I kept quiet. There's no place in our land for a wee man from the other side, whichever way you look.

We brought flowers to John and your ma last week. Potted rosemary and violets for John, and pansies for your ma. I think you'd be glad to see their headstone. Your father made it in black marble, John's picture on the left, and your ma's on the right. John's is with your namesake's sash, with the red hand above it. (Sorry, I should scratch that out. I've known from the first time I heard of you that you take after the Swan of Avon, not the Orange one. It's that the sash bothered me for Tiárnach's sake, that's all. But he didn't say anything. It's the coming marching season and the shouting tripe all over that always makes me think we'll have to relive it. I couldn't do it again. It's like it's all been for nothing. Sorry, I shouldn't have written any of this, it's too bitter.)

Your ma in the picture is just as you described her, a beautiful woman, gentle. I'd never visited them before last week. I didn't want to have to really believe it, all these years. But I went again yesterday, when we decided that I'd write back to you. I sat with them both. Something told me your ma would've loved Tiárnach. With all that had been, I still believe she would've loved her grandson. I felt she forgave me, too. Did you know that she died on the day Tiárnach was born? I walked by your door with him on his very first wee dander, we just came out of the hospital, and he was like a loaf of bread, a wee, wee lad. I wanted him to know where his pa's home was. I'm sure I still hoped for a miracle, but instead I saw her obituary. I nearly collapsed right in front of your door. I'm glad you named Mariah after her. (Mariah looks so much like Tiárnach when he was little, determined and quiet. Emma looks just like Mari, only without that weight in her eyes. You have a beautiful family, Willbo.)

Alright mucker? Enough sadness and memories. They shouldn't be part and parcel of who we are anymore. All's well. Remember, "We are such stuff as dreams are made on, and our little lives are rounded with a sleep."

Maybe our lives will intersect once again, dearest Willbo. I'm sorry for all you've suffered. I'm grateful you forgave me. I hope Mari and the lasses bring you happiness forever.

We send love from your Belfast.

Forever yours,
Tiárnach and Aoife

P.S. The next letter will be from Tiárnach. Only, you owe us a reply to this letter first.

I hold the letter, keep holding it in front of me, though there is nothing left to read. It feels like time has stopped and I'm between two heartbeats. Will—he left his son behind and came here on his own. The attic space, bound by the rows of boxes, is too narrow for me to take a full breath. I can't stretch my torso to get air in. I can't move. How little we know anybody.

I sit, staring at the curves of the words as if they could join in a different pattern, like in word games. As if they could produce a different meaning. *Remember?* I zoom in on the bubbling cursive flowing like sermons in the Bibles before Gutenberg. *Conceived in so much love.* Like the meaning of life in an artist's hand.

His pa's home. The two letters *p* and *a* are inseparable in the calligrapher's quilt. A foaming ocean wave. The way I wrote the name I had for Dad in one of our second-grade school assignments—*Tayko*, curved in Cyrillic calligraphy, as in a sacred script, way back, when we were all there, when we had a home.

He has no dad.

My sob comes from the image of Dad's sunken eyes the last time I saw him. I feel my body become unstable, shaking with sobs. This man in the picture and I, we have no dads.

But there is a difference, I realize. I did have him while he was alive. Dad carving a shepherd's flute out of a *dren* tree branch, promising he'd teach me how to do it when I turned ten. *These carving knives are too sharp, Mara-my-sparrow, but when you have a stable hand, when you turn ten, I'll teach you how to carve our mountains and home and all of us here, on your own shepherd's flute.* I had *Mara-my-sparrow.* I had a promise. Tiárnach, he'd never even had a promise, not a single memory.

My stomach starts torquing like the magnets in physics lab class long ago, forcing whatever's within my gut to cyclone up. I fear I won't be able to hold it. I straighten up my torso, expand my chest by taking a loud and deep breath through my nose and closing my throat muscle. I think I hear the steps coming up again, but I just feel for a cloth under my fingers, raise it to my mouth and breathe into it. No one comes. The tears stream down my face and I taste blood on my lips. I realize I'm breathing into John's shirt, the stains reactivated into live blood cells on my lips.

I cannot tell if anything audible comes out of me. It's so loud inside my head, I don't know if the sound rings out like my screams had in front of Dad's hospital room, with the nurse in nylon pantyhose guarding his door. My hands shake so hard, I realize I'm crushing the letter in my palm. I keep John's shirt against my mouth and drop the letter. I see it's smudged, the fountain pen ink marks coming off blue on my wet hand. I fear to move the shirt from my mouth, I fear I won't hold inside all that's rolling up from my stomach.

I take deep breaths through my nose and focus on the space around me. It helps. I look at the path, not even two feet wide, between the two front rows of boxes, clear plastic showing all that's inside them. Kids' outgrown clothes, boxes and boxes of their drawings, their notebooks for every class and every grade. All of their toys, from the teethers and musical mobiles that hung on their cribs, to the things they've discarded just a week ago. Everything.

Mariah once said *We'll need to add another room to our house only to store all of the things Mama saves*. I know I should be selective, that we don't need all of it, but I can't make myself. You never know what might be the one thing you're allowed to keep. When you grow up with twelve generations of everything and are left with one sunflower tablecloth hiding in the bottom of a box against the wall, you don't know what to select. What if it's a wrong thing that you're not allowed to keep?

I observe all of it and breathe into the shirt as deeply as I can, following the therapist's advice from long ago. Blood and tears are joined in one taste. My brain is filling with so much oxygen, I need to lean onto the front row of boxes to keep my head up. I just stay put. I hear the air whizzing through my throat, which won't open up like it should. Deep inhale, exhale, deep inhale, exhale. I can't tell for how long.

You'll manage, I finally say to myself. *You've lived through worse, you managed then, you'll manage now. You just need a plan. You know what's important.*

Then the sense of torquing slows.

What I know is that Mariah and Emma won't grow up without their father. They won't live what I have lived. Not if I can help it.

I extend my arm to reach for the box with my sunflowers. To affirm me, to draw strength from the long line of Popovics, from Great-Great-

Grandma whose hands crocheted this tablecloth. All the chips off of the mountain.

I breathe in slowly through the nose, fill in the sides of the ribcage. Blow out though the mouth, count to four as I do it. Hold. Breathe in through the nose again, fill in the sides of the ribcage, slowly. Blow out through the mouth to a count of four. Hold.

When I've forced calm into my body, I focus all my attention on my hands and every move I make. I pick up John's shirt, which I dropped some time ago, where blotches of brighter red are leaking into the old stains. I spread the shirt over the notebooks box to dry for a moment. I wave the letter in the air to dry the wetness from my hands. The smudges are there, but I can do nothing about them. I refold the letter as best as I can and put it back in the envelope with the picture. The envelope bulges on both sides with crumpled paper, but it is what it is. No helping it.

I put all that belongs to the Belfast suitcase inside it. Testaments of death and betrayal. When everything is inside, the shirt and the letter I just read, too, I snap the lock and the latches closed. I pull the notebooks box out in front and slide the suitcase against the wall. I put another box on top of the suitcase, the lid of the box scraping the ceiling, like I stacked them two months ago. Not like I found them today.

I know who moved them. And why.

I put the notebooks box back in front and close the lid. Mariah's painting of a cat-Mona Lisa is staring at me through the plastic. I sit for a few minutes, breathing deeply.

Then I get up.

The urge to throw up is almost all gone. I have managed before. I can do it again. But Mariah and Emma cannot. It is for them that I must live, I must not wish to not be. It is for them that I must make a plan to manage things and go on.

I don't really feel anything that I have a name for. Just emptiness. Like when I realized Dad was dead, there was no home to go back to, and I had to become a new me, the one from Belgrade. To harden my heart and go on.

Then I get up and step into the narrow stairwell. I hold onto the railing, still breathing in and out. I am a mother, and my children's fates will not be stitched together with losses. They will never know what it is to grow up without a family household, without a parent, without a sense of belonging. Whatever it takes.

As I come downstairs, I feel that each step beneath me is more stable than the last. About seven steps up from the landing, my eyes come into a line with the three green tomes on the top shelf of the bookcase. The tomes from the bookstore on Shankill. The one tome among them from which I heard verses the first day we spent together in San Francisco— the *Day of the Sonnets*, he calls it. I don't falter at the memory, I can take it.

By the time I'm three steps above the living room floor, I can let go of the stairwell railing. I am steady. I breathe in deeply once again, hold, let it out, and straighten up. I'll think of a plan when they all go to bed tonight. I'll think it all through, prepare myself. That's all I need. A plan. For now, I'll just go through today. Small steps, no overwhelming big picture.

I'm in the living room, and I hear no arguments from the kids' bedroom. It's all quiet. I come toward their bedroom door and hear William's calm voice inside. When did he return? The cyclone in my stomach reminds me it hasn't completely calmed, but I force another stop on my body. I am in control.

I step inside the kids' room. "Okay, where are we with the box for the attic?" I look only at Emma, feigning lightness.

"Mama! Where have you been all this time? I called you and called you and called you, and Mariah went to Mr. Mike to ask him where you went, but he wasn't there, then Mariah said we'll be fine and I shouldn't cry and then Pa came and told us you were in your box room, but he didn't let us call you down. He said you were busy and you'd come when you're ready and it's been sooo long." Emma jumps up and hugs me for a moment. I'd like her body to stay against me forever. Then she points at the *Happy Birthday* decoration banner above her bed. "Look, Mama, this is what I put up. Like it?"

"It's beautiful, Liubav. I love it." I pat her on the back, and she goes to press her fingers against all the tape pieces, making sure they won't unstick from the wall.

So, you snuck up on me, villain, saw me read your letter. But I don't look at him, despite feeling his eyes on me.

"Are you okay, Mama?" Mariah asks quietly. She has her father's eyes completely. *So much like Tiárnach's when he was little.*

"Of course, Liubav, why wouldn't I be? It's your sister's birthday, and we're celebrating today."

William-the-father-of-my-children is staring at me, but I don't look at him. There is nothing there. A different man, not my Will. Not the one for whom, if the whole world had said he'd done wrong, I'd have stood fast and certain and claimed otherwise against everyone, the whole world if need be, knowing he couldn't have. *Thou viperous worm. Left your child behind. In a war.* And I'd compared him to Dad. Foolish Marica! Dad who knew he was dying and first rushed us to safety before he died. Who always thought of us before himself.

At once, William's face nose-dives into my hair, he smells it and kisses it. "Oh, Mari," he whispers. His whole body is against mine, his arms tightening around me.

For a moment I have an urge to release myself to him, hoping he'll tell me none of it is true. That I got it all wrong, Aoife and Tiárnach are not real, they're someone else's family. It cannot be true. It cannot be that he has a son, that he left his son behind. But his hug breathes of guilt, a plea for forgiveness. It shrieks at me that I'm alone.

A volcano welling up in my throat threatens to choke me once again, and I stand as still as a tree trunk, breathing in and out to prevent it.

The kids come to us and we're all four in a hug. I just wait, I know it will end.

After a moment, he moves away and says in a normal voice, "I told kids I need to fix up the fence in the front yard. It's too wobbly." He says it like a passing remark, like all is well. "I'll try to get it done before the kids start coming, but if not, I'll have to finish it when they're here. Just a hammer, no saws. Won't let it out of my hand, no one will fall over it."

At first, I don't know why he's saying all this, then I remember Nora's mother. He's trying to save me from meeting her. *"Thou double villain!"* Pretending to be my savior.

I wish I could disappear, just walk away, like I walked away from the *fly-on-the-wall* Lexington boyfriends. Just flee. But I know I'll stay put this time. I'll have to take my life as the Good Lord bestowed it upon me, just like Aoife. In another circumstance, I know I'd like her. The mother of my husband's son.

William is staring at me, and his head drops to one side as if the weight on his mind is too much for him to bear. His eyebrows are heavy over his eyes.

But I look at the bridge of his nose and respond calmly, "Please do not start fixing anything now. Do it next week if you want to."

I hear a faint yelp come out of him, like a broken breath, a sob-cry, but I turn to the kids. Conversation with William-their-father completed.

"Okay, is this the box for the attic, then?" I point at the box packed so full, the lid snaps only on one side. The world map puzzle at the top is preventing it from closing.

"Yes, Mama, that's all," Emma says. "We're going to leave the puzzle for next time, but Mariah will give me her world map to show my friends where you and Pa are from." She's looking at Mariah, who's rummaging through the low wall cupboard next to her desk, where she stores her map roll. Then Emma turns to me and adds, her words full of excitement, "Oh, and where Nora's mama is from, too."

William steps forward, ready to put his hands around me again, but I evade him by stepping toward the box to pick it up. I balance the box to make sure the lid won't slide off.

I'll figure it out, as I always have. *No, William Ford, we're no more.* It's all for the kids now, no more of *us*. Just the roles we play, the mother and father of our two children.

How silly I was to think that we, the two of us, were building a home. Starting a family tree.

I make myself think step-by-step: Step one, take the box to the attic; step two, have the kids get some rest. Once those two steps are done, I'll think of steps three and four. Focus on the small things, not everything all at once.

"Oh," Emma remembers, her lips in a pout, "But I think she has no pa. I can't ask her to show where he's from."

I hold straight and stiff as a plank, focusing to prevent a howl. All these kids without fathers.

1995: San Francisco
Love Story Take Three

When I come to the office after spending the night with Will, I barely notice anyone. But that's how it's been for weeks already. I almost never go for walks with Isabella and Lizzy, and when I do, our talks never venture outside of work. I fear accidentally mentioning Will. I'm very alert with every word I say. Lizzy and Isabella feel it, I have no doubt. That's why they give me space. I'm very sorry I can't let them in. If only we knew each other in a different way. I still constantly fear that someone might think my mind is elsewhere and that I'm not working hard enough to deserve the green card sponsorship. I never forget it costs Blazoning to sponsor me.

Eric doesn't come to my cubicle. He barely squeezes out a *Hi* when we see each other in the office. I keep my distance from him, he's not safe, I know it.

Rob is nice again, discreet, doesn't ask me anything, doesn't act like he knows, and I'm grateful for it.

I haven't been to a Barsync since the second time when Will sat with Lizzy. I've become like Dan—do my work and leave. Except I have no family to go home to, and my stay in the US is only a potential. The threat to go back to Belgrade is still its equal. There's always room for it to go wrong, I know, as long as it's not in my hands.

Today, as I sit in my cubicle, I decide to make myself think through things as carefully as I can. This is my future, and I know it.

I get out a piece of paper and a pen, I write down my pros and cons. I write in Serbian, for caution. Putting the reasons on a page is the only way I know to make sound decisions. I did it when I decided on the high school back in Belgrade. I did it when I decided to apply for a college in the US. I did it when I decided on marketing and web design, and on the move to San Francisco. I need reasons and reason confirmations. That's how I decide. No shilly-shallying about it. It's all binary, Yes or No, This or That.

Live with Will, pros: I can barely think of anything other than him. I think he feels the same.

Live with Will, cons: When I need space, I'll have nowhere to go. I'll never be able to just leave. I'll have to wait to find a new place, maybe months. It was pure luck I found my place as quickly as I did, everyone told me so. If I let it go, I'll be stuck with no way out. Mark won't be able to help me twice, I'm sure.

There's a lingering thought I try to ignore—Mom and Dad's story: meant for each other, married, had kids, Dad died. Not reasonable to fear this for my life, I know, but it's there within me, nevertheless.

The paper is next to my computer and I look at it throughout the day. And then I feel a laser beam tear through my mind. *There are extended-stay hotels!* I can always leave to an extended-stay.

I open my English dictionary at random for my daily word guidance, randomly, something I've been doing every day since I bought it back in high school. *Refulgent: brilliant, radiant, resplendent.* I take it as a sign.

Will doesn't call when I come back from work. He doesn't call on Tuesday evening, either. He doesn't call on Wednesday. He calls on Thursday.

"Mari... hi."

"I miss you." It just comes out.

"May I come?"

"Yes."

And he is here in fewer than twenty-five minutes.

When he buzzes, I don't ask who is at the entrance door, I press the interphone buzzer and say, "Third floor," though I think he knows it. I stand inside of the apartment, holding the door wide open. He leaps up the stairs and gets me, one arm around my waist, the other to my back, his palm on my head. He wraps me tight, like I'll try to escape.

"We don't have to," he whispers. I feel his warm breath on my neck, as he bends his head to be closer to mine. "We can just be together like this."

If I were a person who easily cries, I'd be crying now. With a clear knowledge that I long for this, I can't be without it.

Then he straightens his head and looks around, not releasing his hold of me even a bit. "Your place is nicer, anyway. I wouldn't leave it, either."

I have a studio I can walk across in exactly fifteen steps, with a nook for my twin bed, a foldable table, a two-burner camp stove, a mini fridge, and one cupboard for all the pots and pans. But I'm grateful for his comment.

It's not five minutes before we're both shirtless and his fingers are tinkering with my bra, in the front along its edges, in the back around the hook, under the straps, without ever taking his eyes off of mine. It drives me wild the way he tinkers with it, pretending to be taking it off, but making me wait. This playacting never stops turning me senseless in all our years to come.

Late at night, past midnight, he gets up and dresses to leave. I don't want to let him, but I don't say anything. He's keeping it cool, though I can see it's hard on him.

"Do you want to call me when you want to?" he asks, as lightly as he can.

"Sure."

We kiss at the door for a long time, I don't want him to go, he doesn't want to let me out of his arms. And then he leaves.

I start to call him before he gets back to his apartment. When twenty-seven minutes lapse, I panic. *Is he hit by a car, attacked at gunpoint, did he slip and fall?* But then he finally answers, all breathless, like he ran up the stairs when he heard the ring. I ask if he'll come back. He brings his toothbrush, a razor, and a change of clothes for work tomorrow.

*

I move to his one-bedroom the next evening. His building's sage-scented entrance, with its Art Nouveau relief and mosaics, reminds me of Alphonse Mucha's *Ruby* painting, which I saw in my high school art book back in Belgrade. Mystical, lush, floral, Slavic—known, like a place to be.

Will helps me pack and transport everything. It's only my sunflower tablecloth that I take out of the clothes cupboard, fold, and lock in my carry-on bag before he arrives. Everything else, we pack together. As we get into the cab, Will offers to help me with the carry-on bag, to lodge it between us on the back seat. I tell him I can handle it and keep it on my lap.

When we come up to his apartment, he empties a filing cabinet that's been in his closet and points at my carry-on. He taps on the two keys on top of the cabinet in passing, making sure I see them. I put the cabinet keys on the ring with the copy of his apartment keys he gives me. I know he won't open it, locked or not. I know, but I still lock both, my carry-on and the cabinet.

The following day, we start looking for a new apartment for the two of us. Will insists on it. We find out there's nothing with a rent cap left in the city, and we can't find an airy one-bedroom with a pledge to not increase the rent every month. The agent gives us a buzzer and tells us to respond to it as soon as it beeps. "Otherwise, within minutes your home goes to someone else who responds quicker," the agent warns. We look for two weeks and can't find anything.

I like his apartment, though. I tell him I don't mind staying in it. He strips his pictures off the walls and moves to one side all that is his. We repaint it, then he makes us go and find what I want, to arrange it in my way. To make it our place. Neither of us ever calls it *home*. It's *our place*.

We join our finances right away. Will insists on it. I accept to do the budgeting for us, food, rent, utilities. But when he asks that I take over sending his family tithe, it sounds right to say that we should each arrange things for our own family back home. I don't exactly know why I reason against it, but there was something timid or reluctant in his voice, like he felt that he must suggest it, that he doesn't really want to. When I respond, he looks at me like debating an objection, but he doesn't say anything, and I think I see relief in his eyes.

As for his past, it's only the first time I feel his body jerking in the middle of the night, calling for his mother, whimpering, "It's a legging, it's a legging with a leg inside, Mummy," that I wonder what to do. But he doesn't say anything about it in the morning, and I decide that it's not my place to pry.

I don't react to anything. Not when we go to open a joint bank account, and he steps right in front of the bank wall and puts his hands up against it, ready for frisking by the stunned bank guard. Not when, on our first Fourth of July together, a neighbor kid throws a firecracker in front of our apartment building as we're leaving, and Will ducks, pulling me so violently with him behind a couch in the lobby that my shoulder stays sore for days. His face barren of life, he grips onto the couch and me as if preparing for the earth to swerve under us. I don't say anything. To his "I thought it was petrol," I just say, "So did I."

Today: Seattle

Beginning of the End

"'That one may smile, and smile, and be a villain,'" is what I say to William-the-father-of-my-daughters when step two has been achieved and the kids are taking their rest. I struggle to devise a step three, but I move around the living room-kitchen, trying to figure it out. He follows right behind me, like something stuck to the sole of my shoe I strain to scrape off, but that just sticks like a chewed-up piece of gum.

I march around the house being busy, putting things into place, making sure the cake is holding in the fridge, and that the chicken pilaf is in the oven, baking very slowly, to be done just in time for dinner at seven o'clock. For the first time ever, I wish the house were bigger than the two bedrooms and an open kitchen-living room. I wish we hadn't been looking for cozy warmth when we were buying it years ago. I wish the house had space somewhere to hide. I used to feel that the attic was unassailable, but now I know that anyone can spy on you there without being noticed. He'd watched me read his letter.

For the first time ever, I wish I weren't so organized and didn't have it all under control, everything finished the day before yesterday. There would've been another step to take care of now, and I wouldn't be running around the kitchen-living room like a body of a chicken just beheaded, seeking a mission, seeking life severed from it.

But I keep moving as I can. If I pause for a moment, he'll reach for me—he's that close behind. And that, his touch, that's the very last thing I can take.

In the old times, I'd remind him to go shower. He's still in his green shirt, which I understand now. His son is Irish Catholic, and his son's mother is Irish Catholic. He may as well join them and wear green. But if the shirt is worn in solidarity, he should at least change his jeans. He had them on when he was kneeling on the ground, taking down the shed, and going to the dump. But in these new times, I don't care. If he'll greet his youngest child's guests in dirty clothes, so be it. I won't care.

He is quiet, and he doesn't respond to my *Hamlet* quote, so I fill in the silence with more bile. "If you wish to know, that's the wisest quote from your namesake, in my opinion." I speak turned with my back to him, as I pick invisible threads off of a couch pillow. "'That one may smile, and smile, and be a villain,'" I repeat. Then I pause, think again, and almost accidentally turn to him. I stop myself in time and fluff the couch pillow instead. "Or this one, 'The devil hath power to assume a pleasing shape.'"

I know I need to hold the fury inside of me, not exacerbate it, not let him know what I understand of his other family, even if he saw me reading the letter, even if he knows that I know. I must keep it inside, at least for now. Deal with each day in its own right. That's my comfort: Each day is a unit, separate from every other. Every day a new step toward the final one: the end.

There are eight years and four months before Emma goes to college, which is 3,031 days from today. Tomorrow, it will be 3,030 days. After church tomorrow, I'll make a calendar to mark off each day, to honor my motherhood. To have a daily reminder that I'm earning my peace. The peace that's 433 weeks away. Since I've done the math in my head, it stopped being overwhelming. There is a number to it. A finite number. I have a plan now, the separate units of 3,031 days, or 433 weeks. *You can do it, Marica*, I tell myself. I must.

One thing I need to remember, though, is to avoid compounding my mistakes. When I let the wrath out, saying things like I'm saying now,

I need to stop myself and act as if I meant nothing by them. Let him wonder what I know, never let him come clean. Not until we're done raising our kids together. If he does come clean, I'm not sure I'll be able to live with such betrayal out in the open. But splitting up while the kids are young is the one thing I will not do. I will not destroy their lives like mine was destroyed. I am a mother first, and my kids need both of us together. He's a good father to them, whatever he is to Tiárnach. Mariah and Emma will have a father and a mother together until they leave on their own, whatever it takes. Then I'll be free.

But I just can't understand it. I can't understand that I had no idea in the two decades we've been together. That he knew about his son when he quit his job at Blazoning in order for us to be together. That he knew about his son when we sat on the cushions of our balcony in California, and he asked me to marry him, to marry in my church—a Paisleyite Protestant from Northern Ireland's Troubles marrying into Eastern Orthodoxy—no qualms, no questions. That he'd sent them money all these years. A *family tithe*, he called it. And that I'd never sensed a single breath of it. That he abandoned his son in a war, to grow up without a single memory of a father. Treacherous, negligent, cruel. *That one may smile, and smile, and be a villain.*

How could have I been married to such a man for all this time? How could have I imagined we were building a home for our kids? To think that I knew him. To think that he was so much like Dad. So much like Dad.

My throat closes up again, and I need to remind myself to breathe through it. I lean over the invisible lint on the couch pillow, picking at it and trying to prevent angry tears from welling up. Treacherous liar, a betrayer, and silly, naïve Marica.

He still keeps quiet, a foot and a half away from me. I can feel his body close. I don't know how, but I feel the pain his body exudes. It tries to touch me, but I won't let it.

How does Tiárnach imagine his father? At least I *had* Dad. He gave me his pieces of Zhito cake when Mom and Grandma weren't looking. He rushed us away, knowing he was dying, so we wouldn't stay unprotected with all the new families. He didn't want to leave us, the three of us. I had him, even if he died. Tiárnach has had nothing of a father.

I feel the tears on my lips. And then the dreaded thought comes: *How could you rob him of a father for eight more years, Marica?* I hear a moan from within me, and then I still myself and block out the thought. *You have a plan, you can adjust it, you can reconsider it, only not now. Emma's party is the now.* I straighten up stiffly again.

As I step back, I almost fall into him. His arms tighten all around me, his body against my back and his head on mine. All so warm. I want to scream, to wail, to not exist. I want him to tell me this is all wrong. That I've got it all wrong.

But I come back to my senses. I know better.

His grip is strong. I wiggle out of it, though he doesn't let me go easily. His "Mari, please," is the same shocking string of sounds he made when he leaned over my cubicle wall and pleaded for me to go to his last Barsync. But there is no seduction in it anymore. I don't turn around to look at him. I just squeeze out of his hug, step toward the back entrance, see the bucket with water balloons, and remember I must run and get more.

A relief. Step three: Run to the store.

"You need to shower." I point my finger at his shirt and don't look at his face. "The kids are coming in an hour."

I know he's looking at me. I know the pleading eyes, but I won't be tricked into trusting them again. I know he can see the tears on my face, but I don't care.

As I'm closing the front door after grabbing my purse from the entrance bench, his "Please Mari, please, let me…" reaches me.

But I'm outside already and feel the air flowing into my lungs again. It feels like I've been holding my breath the whole afternoon. I breathe in as deeply as my lungs will allow, making myself dizzy. I mentally award myself a medal for not screaming back at him and telling him to go to hell and to never return. A small achievement, worth a celebration. I managed to hold back.

*

I spend a long time at the store, mostly trying to remember what it was that I needed. But I finally remember and come back with two boxes of fifty water balloons each. As I park the car, I realize it's five minutes past four o'clock, and there is another car I don't recognize parked right where we normally park on the street. It's hers, I know it. The churning in my stomach tells me so.

I straighten up as tall as I can and walk up the path toward the house. Right from the street, I can see a woman and a girl. Emma and the girl are already embracing and squealing together on the house side of the fence. William has showered, he has on fresh jeans and a gray shirt. He stands close to Emma and the girl on the house side of the fence. The woman is on the street side.

When William sees me, he calls out, "Mari, this is Emma's new friend, Nora. And her mother. They've just arrived." He's holding Nora's pillow and sleeping bag under his arms.

I come up the curving path, with the two adults I wish I'd never known looking at me. Then my gut censures me: *You have kids with him, you fool.*

The woman is in jeans and a T-shirt, no headscarf as I imagined her wearing. Not at all like the new boys' mothers and sisters back in Kosovo. She looks instead like any of the girls who went to school with me, Serbian or Albanian, but a grown-up version. For a moment, I have difficulty processing what I see. She and I look at each other, and I don't know what to say at first. Then I muster a "Hello" and stop there.

She takes a moment to speak, and when she does, I detect an accent, a light one. She must have emigrated in youth, like I did.

"Thank you for inviting Nora." She pauses, looking like she'd rather be anywhere other than here.

I continue walking up. As I approach, about five feet from her, she moves aside for me to pass by, leaving me a lot more space than I need. I go through the gate to the other side of the fence.

"Nora is new here. We just moved to Seattle three days ago. Emma has been so kind to her." She pauses between each complete sentence, looking like she's forcing herself to continue on.

All my life feels drained from me, it's a struggle to keep standing. Her eyelids have that weight Aoife described—hiding her dead beneath them. Something reminds me of Aunt Fatima and her hands covering her face, her contorted body shaking with inaudible sobs. I feel so empty.

Emma's and Nora's voices rip me from the blankness. Their giggles are loud as they jump together in a hug, the way only kids know how to. William tells them to take the balloon boxes from me and to start filling the balloons with water. I remind myself to breathe.

Nora's mother and I don't look directly at each other, like we're both waiting for a prompt from the other. The gate is open between us, but she's keeping to the street side, and I to the house side.

I finally look at her and say, "She's welcome." And then, "You're welcome."

She looks at me like she's confirming the truth of my words. She wrinkles her face and responds with a voice just above a whisper, "Thank you."

I take a few steps aside and pick up a cornflower pot that William and I filled last night. "A welcome to the neighborhood."

I almost drop the pot as I hand it to her, my hands that unstable. In my peripheral vision I see William turn and walk away slowly toward the house. I think I hear his quiet groan first, before Nora's mother makes a sound of her own. She sighs with her whole torso as she takes the pot from me. I'm sure a *Thank you* comes out, though I don't quite hear it.

We are quiet for a moment.

She speaks first. "When should I come to get her?"

"In the morning, between nine and nine-thirty... If you can."

"I'll be here."

Then Kami runs up, and right behind Kami come Siyona, Sydney, Anna, Ember, and Lisel, shouting in one voice for Emma all the way up the path. All the parents except for Lisa, Anna's mom, wave at me from the street and shout a polyphony of *Thank you*s. We all know the protocol— our kids have been at each other's sleepovers dozens of times.

"Hey Mar!" Lisa comes up to where I am and hugs me.

The kids squeeze through between us, their sleeping bags and pillows nearly knocking over Nora's mother first, then Lisa and me. Nora's mother holds onto the cornflower pot like it's an infant, in the crook of her arm, protected by her other palm.

"Senseless, yet again, huh!" Lisa says, then turns to Nora's mom. "I'm Anna's mom, nice to meet you."

Mothers have roles as personal identifiers.

"Nice to meet you. I'm Nora's mom."

"Oh, the new girl. Nice." She nods and continues right on. "This is one wild family, lemme tell ya. Every year they hold these outrageous parties with a bazillion screaming little creatures, whom they claim to enjoy listening to for endless hours, and I'm just so happy to not be like them." Then she turns around and hugs me again. "My wonderful *loco* friends."

Lisa is a great friend. Our two families have dinners together nearly every week. She and I take walks together when we can. She might be the first of my friends to know that William and I won't stay together—when the time comes, of course. Not in the next few years.

Nora's mother smiles at Lisa and me, then Amalia comes up, bringing Yitzen, Aya, Bridget, Haven, Malia, and Piper.

"Just unloading." She hugs Lisa and me, and nods at Nora's mom. "Bridget's mom."

"Nora's mom."

"Oh, sweet, the new girl! We heard aaall about 'er. So glad she's here." Then she turns to me, makes sure the kids are all gone inside, and then winks with excitement. "Sorry, Darlin', can't stay a minute, have a date to catch." She spins a pirouette and heads back down the path.

Lisa's shout reaches her when she's already on the street. "Oh, that hunk a' yours, tell him to invite Aaron to his match next Saturday, so I can have y'all over."

Amalia nods a *Yes* and shouts back, "Bye y'all."

Lisa looks at Nora's mom. "Red Tent Day. I hope you come."

Nora's mother nods an acknowledgement of the words, not knowing that she's already on Lisa's list of invitees. Lisa is genuine—she includes everyone.

The rest of the girls come in the same pattern, with their parents waving *Thank you* from the street. I've counted fifteen. Two more girls to come.

The kids that are here have already changed into their bathing suits and are throwing water balloons at each other. They are circling the house, squealing loud enough to be heard in Canada.

Lisa smiles and shakes her head left and right. "My dear ridiculous friend, good luck," she says, before she slips to the street side of the fence next to Nora's mother. She points at the kids in the front yard. "Only you can keep this under control, Mar." And then she's stepping down toward the street.

I feel a water balloon splash near my feet.

"Thank you," Nora's mother says, tipping her head in a bow, still holding the cornflower pot like a newborn.

I nod back the same way. "You're welcome."

Then she turns towards the street and leaves, following Lisa down the path.

Not the new boys' kin. No. She's Uncle Bekim and Aunt Fata's kin.

Tomorrow morning, I decide, when she comes to pick up Nora, I'll pack a piece of Zhito cake for her. Grandma would be glad I did.

Then I go back to my focus, Emma's birthday party. I have a role to play.

As soon as I turn, I see that William is back in the front yard, a few steps away from me. I almost walk toward him. I have to stop my senses from smelling his musk and letting myself be drawn to it. It's too much. Too much, all at once, I don't know how I'll manage. *But you must.* I need to rewire this habit of needing him. *You can't rely on him. He's a betrayer. Not like Dad.*

"All well?"

"Yes," I declare, as a termination to our conversation.

He steps toward me, and I prevent the hug just by looking at him. His arms stay suspended halfway between us.

The kids run around to the front yard again, and we're both splashed. In normal times, we'd both get balloons and chase the kids, and each other as well. But not anymore. Those times are gone now.

His words come quietly after an extended sigh. "I know it's irredeemable."

You think? I just look at him in disbelief that there's anything left to be said.

"I know," he continues, with his head bent low, like it's too heavy for his neck.

I look over the fence, away from him, and see the last two girls, Jackie and Ellie, running up the path.

"Thank you, Fords! You're the best!" Jackie's mom, Meredith, shouts as the girls run up and whizz by me with "Hi, Ms. Mari, hi Mr. Will."

"I hope we stay friends after tonight!" Ellie's mom, Gretchen, shouts from the street with a swooping wave.

I laugh as best as I can and wave at both of them, glad no one is coming closer to chat. "It'll be great, no worries!" Then I turn to talk to the girls. "Leave your bags and pillows in the living room. When you're done, change into your bathing suits and join the fun."

Then I turn back to him with eyebrows arched as high as I can arch them, clearly conveying that we won't be talking about this. *Irredeemable, indeed.*

He looks at me, troubled, trying to continue speaking, but I'm going around the house to the other side of the yard, in search of Emma. Not sure why, but she's a moving target anyway. *One step at a time*, I tell myself. I walk inside. Again, not sure why.

He follows me right in. "Please, Mari… please."

"Would you mind! I have our daughter's birthday to celebrate. I don't want to talk about your past. I don't care about it one bit, William!" *Irredeemable.*

He somehow looks shorter. Tall man that he is, he looks like he's lost half a foot of his stature. I move to leave, to search for Emma, but he starts speaking like a text-to-speech paragraph without punctuation, all in one sentence. It's the unknown cadence that stops me.

"I know I left them I should never have left them there we should've come together I know." Then he pauses, like he's fighting the urge to utter what comes next, his voice stumbling over the words. "I couldn't forgive her, Mari. Just couldn't." He stops, swallows, breathes in, then continues, more composed. "John went to her that night. He would've lived, had he not gone to her that night.... to Aoife." His breath now cascades down his throat, his words forced along in the tumbling. "If only she hadn't asked him to come to her that night..." The sound that comes out next is like a yelp in a moment of body tearing. "He would've lived... if only she hadn't asked."

I've never heard this sound from him. Not when the Belfast suitcase arrived. Not when he read the letter from his father. Not when he unfolded John's shirt and held it against his cheek. This is a brand-new sound. I'm seized by it, the meaning of his words not yet reaching me. I just feel them inside, unable to move.

He continues, now with too much punctuation between his sentences, "It's not Tiárnach's fault. I should've been there. For him. I shouldn't have left him. Them." He drops his whole body onto the couch, like all of him is a heavy sack one just cannot bear on one's back any longer. "He could've at least had an uncle."

I stare at him, trying to connect the dots in what he's saying, to add understanding to his tone.

"I was the only man left for him. No one else knew he was John's. Just the three of us. I should've been there for him. For them both. But I didn't have it in me, Mari, I didn't have it in me to forgive."

I don't know when I start to see a little boy in him, doing his utmost to prevent the sobs from coming out. He's curled on the couch like a contortionist trying to take up the smallest space possible. Trying to disappear.

"They lived. We all lived. But he didn't." The pain in his face looks centuries-old. Will looks like he never has in all the years that I've known him. "I couldn't." He pauses. "I just couldn't. He died because he loved her. You shouldn't die because you love someone." His head is in his hands, his elbows on his knees, his torso folded in half.

I don't think. I just walk the few steps to him, stand right between his knees, and he grabs for my waist like he's drowning and I'm a post to help keep his head above water. He lays his head on my belly and the sobs rush out.

I comb my fingers through his hair, the strands feeling silky between my fingers, releasing the scent from the shower and his musk. I do my best not to let my own sounds be heard. But the tears are unstoppable, dripping onto his head and onto my hands, an insistent flow stemming from the days before Dad died.

All the years he's tried telling me, and only now do I begin to understand. Years ago, when we were still in California, before kids, he'd asked if I'd start transferring his *family tithe*. I'd done our family accounting from the day I moved in with him, but I couldn't handle anything involving his past. I'd told him it was his to deal with. *I didn't have it in me.*

I'm aware the kids could come running inside at any moment, but I stay there, my face all wet, Will's sobs slowing.

"I've never gone to see them," he says into my shirt, like I don't know this. "They're all I have left from John."

I comb my fingers through his hair, realizing I'm whispering "Shh," trying to silence all that I've judged him in the past two hours. *Treacherous... cruel...* The words grate at me as I do my best to breathe through my own verdict. *Villain... betrayer.* A black hole of condemnation of what *he's lived through all alone.* A gaping void of love. Of trust.

Will sighs like he's just come out of the deep sea, gasping for air. He looks at me with a face I've never seen before. Not holding it together.

"He was so happy when he found out she was with child. He loved her so much." He wipes at his tears with his palm, his other arm still wrapped tight around my waist. "Their *in-between*. That's what they called the baby, their in-between." He smiles. "We were supposed to leave in two weeks to America, the three of us and the in-between. John enrolled me at a uni, he was going to start teaching, we had airplane tickets, they were going to marry once we arrived." A pause and a sigh again. His face is all wrinkled, eyes sunken with his thick brows over-shadowing them. He's looking past me. "But then they brought him... home... and I left alone."

His head is again on my belly, and I don't know what to do with all this. With this knowledge that I had never been there for him in all this. All these years, he's borne this on his own.

"You'd have forgiven. You'd never have left them, you'd have forgiv-en," he says into my shirt. "Even Nora's mother is welcome here." His head moves away from my belly, cautiously, leaving the cool wetness on my skin underneath the shirt. His eyebrows try to meet when he looks at me. I can see it just slipped out.

My whole body has stiffened up. I look aside.

Will hugs my waist with both his arms again, his head pressing on my belly. I wipe my face, breathe in, and take control of myself.

"The kids could come in," I whisper.

He pushes his head harder against my belly. I feel his tears imprinted in my skin. It's the first time I've ever seen him cry. He kisses my belly button, like he did when the pregnancy tests showed two lines.

I wipe my face again, breathe in, breathe out, take his head into my hands, bend toward him, and kiss him on the lips. I wipe his eyes with my palms. "I wish I were as good as you think I am."

He won't let go of me, his hands tight around my waist, another sob into my belly. "My Mari."

After another moment, I go to the restroom and breathe in and breathe out for four cycles. Then I clean myself up. I go back to the couch where he is still sitting as I left him, tell him to go clean himself up, and then I go outside to meet Emma and her squealing friends. I realize

I've forgotten to make sure that all their sandals are properly tied, that there won't be any bare feet under any circumstances at any time while they are here.

When I go out, ready to line them up for the examination and lecture they undergo every time they come to our house, Emma announces, "No need, Mama. Mariah checked all of our shoes and told us the rules. We know!"

Tonight: Seattle

All the kids are asleep, the last whispers having quieted down about ten minutes ago. Will and I are sitting on the couch we managed to maneuver onto the deck. The table and the armchair from the living room had to come out to the deck as well, to make space for the sleeping bags. We moved the wicker chairs and the deck table to the side and then set the living room table and the armchair across from the couch, just like we have them inside.

The oddity of it strikes me—we are outside on the deck, and the furniture we brought out from the inside mimics the exact order of the living room. The standard, once set, is always followed. I think of getting up and rearranging everything on the deck, of making a new order, just for the sake of change. I think it would feel good to do it. To defy the proverb *Wherever you go, there you are*—always carrying the same patterns within you. But I continue leaning into Will instead, enjoying the fresh air, Will's musk, and his warmth enveloping me like we are one body.

The night is beautiful, the breeze so light it's barely noticeable, the sky clear and starry. I'm sure we'll see shooting stars if we look up long enough. No rain is predicted for this May weekend in Seattle. It's one of the warmest spring days in recorded history, the papers claim.

I remember late-spring nights like this back in Kosovo, when we were all there, the first nights in the season to stay out late. All of us would sit at the table under the canopy of our big linden tree. Grandpa, Uncle Bekim, Dad, and Uncle Sima would play their shepherd's flutes, and the rest of us would open the outdoor singing season with Grandpa and Uncle Bekim's favorite *Zapevala soyka ptica* song. Then we'd sing Grandma's favorite *Ey, u Prizrenu* and Mom's favorite *Duni mi, duni, ladjane,* and Dad's favorite, *Udade se, Jagodo,* and so on and on and on for half the night. Simonida and I would come down from the haystack and join them. Little Abdul would bring a stool from the summer kitchen to squeeze next to Dad, his favorite Uncle Yovan. Ismet, his twin, would try to squeeze in between Simonida and me, and after some grunting, we'd usually let him. The neighbors would come as well. None of us wanted to miss a night like this.

Will and I are both quiet tonight. Our lungs are following the same breathing rhythm. The only other movements are Will's palms on my arms, stroking them up and down. We're facing toward the barren space where the shed used to stand.

Then we see her. The raccoon mother. We hear the shrubs crackling first, then she comes from the side of the garage and tracks toward the dirt square. When she gets to it, she sniffs around the square first, then steps onto it, moving warily over the leftover raked lines intercepted by many kids' footprints. She's slow, looking around, smelling, trying to find, trying to understand. Her home—it's all gone.

Then she sees us. I think my moan surprises her. Will's arms tighten around me, an extended "Shh" coming into my ear.

She looks straight at me, she stares and stares. I hold my breath. *You're no threat anymore,* I read in her eyes. *You've done your worst.* I lower my gaze. I can't look into her eyes. After a while, she turns around and crawls back toward the garage and into the shrubs. She's not rushing to leave.

Will sighs as if the air in his lungs were pushed down Grandma's old washboard. The rhythm of my breathing has changed, too. Our breaths are not aligned anymore.

"How strange they are sometimes… the numbers." Will's voice is a step above a whisper, like I'm hearing the inside of his thoughts. "There were about three thousand people who died in each—on September 11th, in the Troubles, and in the NATO bombing of Yugoslavia." His breath is touching my ear, but it simultaneously feels as if he were speaking from a distance, only to himself. "Each about three thousand." He pauses, thinking. I imagine his face is strained before he sighs. Then his arms tighten around me, as if he just remembered I was there. "But what's strange is how we see them. Never just as people, as someone's kids, brothers, fathers. They're either *theirs* or *ours*, *enemies* or *victims*, never just family that leaves broken souls behind. Shards inside the flesh of those who stay." Another pause. "It's strange how we keep seeing the same numbers."

I look up at the skies. A patchwork of nothingness in between the light flashes. Sometimes, when we go camping in Eastern Washington, we see the whole Milky Way. A place for all of us, a great equalizer where we all belong. I wish we could see it from our backyard tonight.

"I'm not from Belfast." Will's voice is not soft anymore. It's determined, directed at me. A deliberate break from stillness.

I stiffen up, hold my breath.

"I'm from Londonderr..." he stops. Then in an exhale he finishes, "From Derry. I'm from the City of Derry." He takes a deep breath. "That's where I grew up, in Derry, not Belfast." Another pause, his head up toward the skies. "I was born on the day of the Bogside. Aoife's aunt was blinded that day. John was there with Father, with the paratroopers, and white armbands. He was a wee lad, eight years old, but he remembered it." Another sigh that breaks the flow of sound. "My birth in exchange for fourteen deaths."

In all these years, Will has never welcomed celebrations around his birthday. He avoided all well-wishers until Mariah started asking about it. I never felt it was my place to find out why. But I remember one time, back in California, after we just got married and needed a copy of our marriage license for something. The woman helping us had the same accent as Will. She asked for his date of birth, and when he gave it, her pen paused halfway through recording it. She didn't look at us, but I saw her chest rise with a silent gasp.

"That's how I began, straight out of violence. Conceived in the bloodiest year of the Troubles, came to the world on the day of the massacre. Bloody Sunday. My day of birth as Bloody Sunday." Will's head is back down, his voice quieter now. "Not a famous beginning."

I don't think about the question before I ask it. "But your passport says Place of birth, Belfast." Like mine says *Belgrade*.

"Aye. I was born in Belfast. Father sent Ma to my aunt's family a week before my birth. He was preparing, he knew what was coming to Lon... to Derry." Another pause. I realize I've never heard him say the name of his hometown before, either as *Londonderry* or as *Derry*. "We moved to Belfast only when John started at Queen's. I was almost eleven."

I sit still, stiff, and terrified, a feeling of dread coming over me. But I'm not obeying my instinct to stop all this and to flee.

"That booby trap... it was Father's mates who set it in the bushes. Father knew about it, but he'd never accepted that it was the bomb that killed him. It was meant for the Provos, for Catholic lads going home that evening. Where Aoife lived, Divis Flats, it was all Catholic."

He looks up into the skies again and inhales heavily.

"Before he snuck out that night, I told him to wait, just two weeks, two weeks, and we'd all be safe. I felt something. But he said there was nothing in the world that could stop their love. 'It's meant to be,' he whispered. 'Our love is meant to be, Willbo.' And he went." A long pause, a broken-up sigh, and his head down again. "And then he was brought back to us."

His hands glide again down my arms, warm and soothing. I can feel his breathing steadying again as I lean against him. It feels like he's resigned to all that he's saying. My hands are both sweaty and freezing. I feel a cool, lined breeze on my face before I realize it's from the tears. All this pain he held onto alone, without a word, through all these years.

"Father thought he went on a secret mission. He thought it was his kind of missions that kept John quiet. He would never have believed his good boy strayed from him. At the funeral, he said it filled him with pride that he gave his firstborn to the cause. Ma nearly collapsed into the pit after John when he said it."

His body jolts in a shudder before calming again.

"But Father was broken after John died, too. The letter he sent, it's all grief. He lived and died with it. Just grief." Another big sigh. "So many thousands more than just three."

I lift my head to the sky again. It's easier to get a breath that way.

"I wish Ma knew there was Tiárnach. She would've loved him from the seed. Ma would've."

I know Will's smiling from the way his voice sounds. "I heard him recite, 'Now tell me how long you would have her after you have possessed her,' before he left that night. His eyes were glowing like he'd light the planet with them. He was in front of the mirror, and when he caught me watching him, he put his palms to his heart and said to me, 'Forever and a day.' That's what he said, 'Forever and a day.' He smiled, winked at me, and a few minutes later he was gone."

Will's head goes up to the skies again. It must be easier for him to catch a breath that way, as well.

"Nothing could've stopped him. Nothing." His words are slow. "You know what else he said to me? He said, 'When you know someone's for life, you ought to be patient. Patient, most of all. You can't rush love and forever.' Those were his words—'Can't rush love and forever.' It took him a whole year to convince Aoife to go out with him, he told me. But he knew right away she was the one for him, and he was patient." Another deep sigh. "If only that night he'd been patient."

His nose is in my hair, he's kissing my head, his arms tightening around me, like he's afraid I'll fight to break free.

"I was almost eighteen when John told me. The only other person who knew. But he hid it for longer than a year even from me. He told me only when they made the plans, when UC Berkeley accepted us, that he would teach, and I would study. I didn't even know he'd applied for me."

Will's voice stops, then a chuckle comes out like he's about to tell a joke. "You know how I ended up an engineer? He said we had enough people in the family who knew the law—he, Aoife, and naturally, their in-between would know it one day. He said we needed a person who knew technology, that 'You can love literature, Willbo, become a poet if you want to, but you must know technology. That's where the future is.'"

There is a long pause after this. A long, long pause. I'm trying to hear every word that comes after the pause, despite the tears and the ragged breathing they cause.

"I think Ma felt it. She knew John was nothing like Father... But she loved Father so much. With all that he was, she'd never allowed anyone to think him in the wrong. That's what I could never understand. How could she look and not see?"

Then another long pause, and I hear the smile in his voice again. His head moves against me in gentle motions.

"But she would've loved Tiárnach. Despite Father, she would've loved her grandson."

He lifts his arms to the sides of his head and pushes his torso forward, like he's trying to open up his chest. I straighten up thinking I'm too heavy on him, but his hands pull me right back against him.

"Nathan, Rob's older brother—their family was the one who took me in the night I came alone. He was one of the people who'd reviewed John's teaching application and interviewed him on the phone. I saw his name on the letter from Berkeley that John had, and I looked him up when I arrived in San Francisco... I had to tell them why... where John... why

I was alone."

There is another slight jolt before his torso calms again.

"Their parents took me in for the whole first year. That's how Rob and I know each other. I lived with them for a year. Wouldn't let me go, wouldn't let me pay for anything, took me in like a son. They didn't even know John, but they took me in like their son." He sighs again. "Good people. Truly good people, Rob and Nathan's parents."

Last week, when Rob and Stacy visited from San Francisco, it came to me again, like it always does when I see Will and Rob together, how much they look like brothers.

Rob has always known. It's strange to think how you can live with someone for decades, learn how he breathes, know what he's thinking from the way he looks at you and the way he touches you. You can recognize the state before there are any signs, but you won't know the pain inside. *You don't have it in you to face it.*

"Mrs. Jane told me I'll be good to you." Will's tone switched, all lightness now, as if none of what he just said carried any weight. "When I came looking for you at the market that Sunday, she sat me down and ordered me to tell her all about myself. Like a pupil, I had to answer why was I looking for you, what I liked about you, were my intentions honorable." Will chuckles, and I chuckle with him. "That's what she asked me, if my intentions with you were honorable."

Just what Mrs. Jane would do. I can imagine her saying to him, *Now, sit down and tell me all about it. Take your time, love, don't rush through anything.*

"And did I know that you were a nice girl, not the trifling kind, and should I always remember it? I felt like I was in front of the Grand Inquisitor, terrified I'd fail and not be allowed to see you after all. She let me loose only a moment before you showed up." His laugh is short and quiet. "When I was leaving, she said I was a nice boy and I'd be good to you. Only then, she gave me her blessings. She said, 'God bless you two, and your children, and your children's children, and their children's children.'"

Mrs. Jane. I remember how he bowed to her, a deep bow from the waist, with the extended arm and leg. I wish our girls could have known her. She died eight months after Will and I moved in together. Before our wedding. She died of a heart attack, and we only found out two weeks after her funeral.

She died like Dad—just gone, no goodbyes, no hand-holding, no wakes. Alive one day, dead another. I had never asked for her sons' phone numbers. I could've asked any Sunday I spent with her, but I didn't. It didn't occur to me that she could be gone like that. Incredible that I could still take life for granted like that.

By the time we found out, she'd already been buried. We went to her grave many times, and we still do every time we go to California, but that's not the same. I wish I'd been there for her wake.

Will's nose is in my hair again. "She warned me that when we married, life wouldn't always be easy."

He stops, and my stomach hurls another warning bolt at me.

"She told me you won't share your grief with anyone." His voice is tentative, his body without movement.

I try to get through a chopped-up breath.

"That I should never ask about it. That I should wait until you're ready to say it."

My body stiffens, and Will's palms lie motionless on my arms. I look up to the sky. I feel a sigh, heaving a surge of air into my chest. The sky is now so studded with stars, that it's hard to recognize it as a Seattle sky. When Simonida and I spent late summer evenings lounging on the haystack, before they'd make us go back inside, the sky was like this.

Will's hands are warm on my skin, quiet and expectant.

"Mrs. Jane... she smelled like a wildflower valley in spring. Like Grandma did." I don't listen to my tight throat, the warning to stop. I just go on. "The first time I passed by her stall, her tomatoes smelled like Uncle Sima and Aunt Vera's orchard. I almost stole a tomato from her, do you know that?"

Will is quiet.

"I didn't even see her standing there, watching me bend over to smell them, take one, rub it against my shirt, and bite into it. 'You know your tomatoes, Miss,' she said, making me jump back in surprise. She was so much like home."

If I didn't feel the warmth Will's body injects into me, I'd wonder if he was still there. I'm defying the years of silence, and he isn't disrupting it.

My thoughts are not connected, they just come out as they are. I don't know how much he can understand from what I'm saying. But I'm not sure I'm saying it to him.

"There's a box up there, in the attic... with a sunflower tablecloth. The only thing I have left. I wanted to take Grandma's blanket, it was so beautiful and warm, it smelled of her, but it was too big for the suitcase. Dad snuck out with the sunflowers before we left. His last gift to me."

"It's not your fault."

Will's voice, soft and gentle, barely audible, brings up a yelp I can't suppress. An irresistible urge to flee jump-starts my blood, and I must squeeze my palms together over my belly and flex my toes to prevent any movement. I try to box-breathe.

"It was cancer, not blood poisoning. They found out he had it when he was at the hospital. It's not your fault, not from chasing you."

His palms are now on my head and my cheek, trying to turn my face toward him. But I cannot look at him. I'm frozen in this new, entirely unknown state. Everything feels tentative.

He keeps speaking into my ear, but his voice sounds like Morse code he's sending from his mind into mine, soft and persistent, beep-beep-beepbeep-beeeep-beep.

My mind is doing what it can to avoid understanding his words.

"It wasn't from stepping on the nail… It wasn't. It wasn't from chasing you in the field. It was from the mine. Lung cancer. Not blood poisoning. There was nothing you could've done."

I'm frozen against his voice, listening to his words, fighting to not let my body do as it always does—take off.

"In your sleep, you cry out for him. You tell him you're sorry. Sometimes you're happy." The pauses between sentences are slow and insistent, as are his words. "You ask him to teach you to carve a flute. Sometimes you say these things in English."

I taste blood on my lips and make a conscious effort to loosen my jaw.

"Katarina told me. How attached you were to him. How you used to be, you and Simonida."

Simonida, my cousin, a picture of success with a void in her eyes, as if life is a habit she'd gladly shake off if only she could. She was the youngest pediatrician in the history of Yugoslav medicine when she finished her studies. She heals kids' pain, but I fear looking into her eyes for the grief in them. Ironed blouses, pants with perfect creases, frown lines. Nothing to ever reveal the spirit she used to be. I'd never asked her what happened after we left. She'd never asked me how it was when Dad died. We're both *From Belgrade* to everyone. Each other included.

"The way you both used to be. Like Emma."

I become aware of something breaking within me. Like a dam that's resisted a surge for as long as it could, now caving in, swished by a flood, concrete and steel being crushed piece by piece.

I shake in Will's arms, he holds me tight, the whispers of "Shh" are continuous. I don't know for how long or how loud, but it stops at some point. The tears don't, though. Their stream is unstoppable. I am slow, each sentence a novel in itself.

"There was an Albanian family. Grandpa's brother-by-milk, Uncle Bekim, and Aunt Fatima. They had grandsons, Abdul and Ismet. Two years younger than me. I don't know what happened to them. We were supposed to be a family."

"They're in Michigan. Uncle Sima told me."

At first, I don't understand what he's saying. But when the meaning of his words comes to me, it rips open the scar.

"Only the bones are left." I say it more to myself.

I feel Will's breathing speeding up, his heart beating hard against my back. "The bones and, and…" His voice is tearing through the air around us, the fury funneled inside it in a way I'd never heard before.

He doesn't finish, and I'm relieved. It frightens me to hear what else he might know. He breathes in heavily as if his throat has closed in on him, and he shakes his head. The movement of his chest jostles me.

When he continues, he's calmer. "Sometimes I think, Father, as bad things as he did, he'd never profited from any of it. In fact, he lost it all. He believed in a Protestant Northern Ireland, he believed in what he was fighting for, honestly, however wrong he was. And he lost the dearest to him for it."

Sharp shakes run through my body, and I cannot calm them. Will's arms are around me, tight and soothing.

I turn to the side and lean into Will, my face in his neck, his T-shirt collar wet. His breathing is slowing. My back is against the couch and the side of my torso is all tucked into his body. I can't stop the flow down my face. The tears release all that's been inside for thirty-five years. Our two decades of silence together. Our dead, our pains, our losses. Will, myself, home.

We lie quietly for a long time. It could be midnight, maybe later.

When I'm calm again, I whisper to him, "But the kids' bones must never know it. Like Aoife said."

Will's warm arms are trying to enroot my body into his. The kids are asleep, the raccoon mom is with her babies, displaced.

We'll stop pressing the bruise and let it heal. Build a home. Maybe.

"Be it so," Will says. "Amen."

Acknowledgements

Threads and Tethers began as a short story many years ago during one of the two-year Literary Fiction writing programs I attended at the University of Washington. There are many people who have read its short, longer, and novel versions, and I am profoundly grateful to every one of them, whether listed below or not.

Scott Driscoll, my developmental editor, as well as an incredible instructor, writer, and person, taught the classes where *Threads and Tethers* in its many variants was born. He became instrumental in my own evolution as a writer, as well as the development of many other local authors. Some of the best writing advice I have ever heard, and still hold fast onto, came from his classes—write every day, even if only for fifteen minutes; write first thing in the morning, just as you wake up; when inspired by something, write it down in as much atmospheric detail as possible to recapture it when you are ready; and be part of a writing group. I am forever indebted to Scott for all these years of trust that something tangible would come out of my writing. Scott is a gift to any writer!

My writing group came out of Scott's classes about a decade ago. I would not have gone anywhere without these brilliant authors and people: Katherine Kirkpatrick, Elizabeth Sharpe, Rishabh Shukla, David Brewer, Janet O'Leary, Rasa Tautvydas, and Ember Sol. They have been reading this work throughout the years, and their support and knowledge helped shape it into its present form.

Rachel Weaver, another incredible instructor, editor, and author, was the first official developmental editor for *Threads and Tethers*. Her perspicuity in noting what worked, what did not, why, and how to fix it bordered on magical. After her first editing round and my revisions that followed, I began loving my novel. I have always loved my characters, but it was

Rachel's knowledge that made the seams of my novel connect. Rachel's classes, like Scott's, are a privilege to attend.

Milica Golic is a friend whose architectural background blends technology and beauty to represent one and the same, one perfect union. In my mind, her cover design based on Aleksandar Juric's photograph is indistinguishable from that of a book published by a major publishing house. Milica is a person with whom I would choose to do impossible tasks.

My copyeditor, Jin Zeng, has come into my life as my latest life blessing through one of Scott Driscoll's classes. He is detailed and meticulous like no one I have ever met before him. Jin is a dream editor—he points at an issue, explains why it is an issue, and suggests a solution. Line by line. Sometimes, however, as I write the way I write, I listen intently to the ways my characters say what they say in my head, and in some cases I decided to forgo Jin's wise advice. It is not inconceivable that I'll regret not listening to Jin more than to my Marica, Will, and Aoife. We shall see.

Many of my personal friends have read different versions of this story, and all of them gave me very thoughtful suggestions about how to improve it, be it a character, a scene, a chapter, a transition, or the entire novel. I could not have hoped for better friends or better beta readers: Gretchen Fues, Aleksandra Stefanovic, Milan Stefanovic, Tanja Milovanovic, Snezana Radosavljevic, Bjanka Marceta, Terri Green, Craig Magaret, Milica Dozic, and Petra Menz.

There are three particular friends to whom I remain indebted forever: Nikola Rudic, Zoran Glisic, and Zmajko Milosavljevic. Zoran and Nikola read *Threads and Tethers* when it was a very short story with continually changing titles. They followed its progress, always supportive and interested in what came next, and their comments and suggestions left their marks throughout the novel. Zmajko, a friend from Kosovo and Metohija, read my narrative that in some instances spoke to what he and his family have endured and embodied. I cannot imagine what he might have felt while reading Marica's account. His suggestions have been simply invaluable.

My sister, Ljilja Djukanovic, and our parents, Bora and Nada Kevic, forever remain my lifeline. My sister has read this story-turned-novel more times than either of us could recount. She went to San Francisco with me in search of Marica and Will. She loved every version and was ecstatic and inconsolable in the same sections where I was. The world would be so much happier if everyone had a sister such as I have. Our parents asked for more details about Marica and Will before I even defined them in my head. They listened to me think aloud for days and days as I worked out what came next, why, and how. Mom and Dad are grounding forces that always remind my sister and me of where we came from and who we are.

Our whole extended family, all seventy-five of us closest relatives, as we counted back in 1988, have helped make me into who I am today. I left Belgrade right out of high school, but I carried within me parts of them all. I so wish I had an opportunity to show this novel to my grandparents, aunts, great-aunt, and uncles who died years ago. But I am grateful to have had them. My aunt Vida used to say Grandma Popovic's words, that a person dies only when you forget them. What grace it is to have ancestors such as her.

Five other women I so wish I had an opportunity to share my novel with are my mother-in-law, Svetlana Martinovic, my childhood neighbors Slavica and Olga Pajevic, our Seattle community member Sonja Orlovic, and my colleague Meredith Owens Reed. They each had so much life in them, so much wisdom, kindness, and integrity, that I grieve for the world for losing them.

Most of all, I am grateful for my husband and our children. They are my reasons for being— they give meaning to life itself.

Ancestors and Descendants

Mira Martinovic's next novel, *Ancestors and Descendants*, is slated to come out in 2027.

Ancestors and Descendants is another immigrant saga narrated through several time periods, moving from the beginnings of Washington State to today. It tells the story of a Serbian and an Irish family, their deep friendship, their later separation, and their descendants' finding their way to each other five generations later.